THE HOT MONTH

THE

HOT

MONTH

Clifford Hanley

The Riverside Press Cambridge

HOUGHTON MIFFLIN COMPANY BOSTON

1967

To Allan, Maureen, Norman, Joan, A. K.,
Charlie, Archie, Ian, Alastair, Kath, Angus,
Mary, Jimmy, George, Peter, Frank, Bill, Isobel,
Isobel, Jimmy, Jimmy, Douglas, Celly, Mary,
Margaret, Neil, Tom, Nan, Avril, Muriel, Meg,
Iain, Pat, Eoghan, Vickie, Donald, Gordon, Tom
and many others—none of whom appears
in this piece of total fiction.

THE HOT MONTH

ONE

As she passed the front window downstairs, carrying a box of paint, Stacey noticed the children outside, grouped round the rear end of the Land Rover and poking at the luggage to make it fit better. The picture they made seemed suddenly significant. It was charged, she thought, with, er, what's its name . . . significance. She put down the box of paint and pulled from her jacket pocket a scribbling pad, with a short pencil tied to it by a long length of fine twine.

"Children . . . Land Rover," she scribbled, in the bastard mixture that remained from her shorthand lessons. "Significant? Charged with et cetera. Three lives . . . hovering on brink of et cetera." She was irritated at her lack of fluency, but to hell, she thought, you always manage to find something to put in place of the et ceteras. It's part of the agony. She crossed out the last "et cetera" and wrote "agony" in its place. It looked silly. She stared hard at the children as if she might be able to dissolve them into words if she stared hard enough. Nothing happened at all. They went on being human beings.

"She's doing it again," said Sally, out in the street. There was a pasteboard crate in the back of the Land Rover with an old label gummed to it. She reached in and started to pick at the corner of the label with her fingernail. Her brother Harry slapped viciously at her hand and she snarled at him.

"Stop picking at things," he said. "Or I'll chop both your arms off at the elbow."

"She's at a funny age," said Dee. Dee was wearing a white sweater and tight jeans. She looked at her long shadow on the pavement and wondered if she would like to be as tall as the shadow. She moved her feet apart to give her legs separate shadows, and studied the ins and outs of her legs on the pavement. Then she tilted one hip to make the shadow look sexier. Sally landed a stinging whack on her tight rump and said, "Your age is funnier than mine!"

"She was talking about Stacey," Harry interrupted, and stepped solidly between them before Dee could punch her sister. "Go and get the bits of timber." Sally skipped in through the front door, shaking her hand to get rid of the sting. Dee started to rub her buttock, where the pain had just penetrated through her thoughts. Inside, Stacey pushed the notebook and pencil back into her jacket pocket and picked up the box of paint quickly. The truth was that the children were unpromising material. Considering they were related to her, they were disappointingly dull. Harry was the stolid kind of adolescent who worked his way doggedly into middle age without ever feeling agony or ecstasy, and Dee was a vapid child who probably would never know that she was hovering on the brink of anything. She dressed like a boy and bought gramophone records, and that was all there was to Dee. Sally was really a simple brat, off an assembly line of brats. Stacey liked this. She took out the notebook again and scribbled "Brat off assembly line." Sally came into the room, staring at her.

"Can I get you something, Sally?" Stacey asked her, and the child kept on staring and said "No," and went through to the kitchen. Now, Stacey thought, an amateur psychologist might say that the kid had difficulty in communicating. When you got right down to it, she had nothing to communicate. Not to worry, the world was full of other people, seething, passionate, alive people, and there must be plenty of them at Ochie. Ochie. She would change that name, for a start, to something more ringingly Highland. Alt-na-Carracher, something like that, or something beginning with "l" to alliterate with lust . . . or something. She carried the box of paint out to the Land Rover and absent-mindedly handed it to the dull Harry.

In the room upstairs, Nat Boag stood at the window and looked down at the Land Rover. He was wearing the new Italian cardigan and the very slim slacks, and he looked fine. "How did that bitch ever get into this safari?" he asked bitterly. "Her bum's too big."

"Her bum has nothing to do with it," Mary said reasonably. "It's not my fault if you have relations."

"Nag nag nag," he said. "She's your sister-in-law, isn't she? You picked her," he went on, pursuing an interesting thought. "I didn't pick her for a sister, but people can pick their sisters-in-law. It *is* your fault. I should bloody well divorce you and get rid of her."

"You do that. That's what to do. Give me peace from your miserable brats and your relations. I hate you, I loathe you, I despise you."

"Nag nag nag."

"You haven't any gum boots," she said, checking a list. "We'll have to buy you a pair when we get there."

"Gum boots pah!" he said, outraged. "Listen, if it rains, I'm staying in bed. No West Highland fever for this boy," he muttered, still staring down at the Land Rover. "It honestly is too big. Funny, mine isn't. Mine is nice." He patted his hips complacently.

"Emaciated," Mary said.

"Emaciated is my word."

"Skinny."

"Nag nag nag. Skinny? It's athletic. I might just do a nude of myself. From the back."

"Leaving out your paunch?" Out of the corner of her eye she saw him pulling in his stomach and patting it.

"Shut up!" he said. "Nothing you say can change my beautiful bum. Women, nag nag nag, oh God, if I could only get away." He said this in a practiced monotone and unthinkingly started patting the close fit of the new slacks on his hips again. Mary pulled her mind away from them and stood up from the bed. She saw herself as she moved, in a mirror across the bedroom, and didn't look. He turned from the window and she thought he might touch her, but he didn't.

"That's everything," she said. "I'll miss this." She looked at the oversized double bed.

"Women," Nat said. "Only one thing in their minds. The only consolation about this trek is freedom from your toenails. I'll be able to snore in peace."

"Nag nag nag," she said halfheartedly. He went downstairs in front of her. There was a thin spot beginning to show through the hair on his crown, but that was all. He went downstairs flip-flip-flip like a tap dancer and straight out to the Land Rover. Everything would be all right in Ochie. If it wasn't all right in every single direction, at least the fresh air and the rest would be good for everybody, and there would be plenty of work for her to do, nice, satisfying work. By the time she had checked the windows and locked the doors, he was already in the car, in one of the front passenger seats, with Dee beside him in the middle. Harry was closing up the tail gate with help from Sally, and Stacey was standing on the pavement looking remote and thoughtful. Harry and Sally got into the back seat and left the door open for Stacey. Mary climbed into the driving seat. They all waited for Stacey to stop looking thoughtful, and after a few seconds she came to, rather unconvincingly, shook the cobwebs out of her brain and climbed in beside the children.

"Don't try any dicing with death," Nat said, almost before they had moved away. "I don't want this cardigan covered with blood."

"It wouldn't matter," Mary said. "It's not paid for yet."

"Oh, that's fine, that's just fine! Leaving the house shut up for an army of creditors to batter open!"

"He's always like that," Stacey comforted Mary, and Mary smiled indulgently. Stacey couldn't help being helpful. But Nat turned round to his sister and said,

"If you plan to discuss me in the third person you're going home by the first boat. Nobody invited you, you know, you're only a bloody gate-crasher."

Stacey laughed merrily, to Mary's relief, taking this as one of Nat's "character" lines. It was, of course, but it was often difficult to tell how much Nat talked as a character and how much he used his character to say exactly what he was thinking. It was all part of his charm. Damn him.

As she changed into top on a long straight, she shot a glance at him, over Dee's head, and saw him in profile, looking truculent, and injured, and pleased with himself. And beautiful. He caught the movement of her head and turned and winked at her, and she giggled.

"You don't trust me to drive, is that it?" he snarled at once. "I'm not responsible?"

"You said it!"

"Yes," he sighed heavily. "And I'm right. Faster, faster, get it over with."

"Have you ever thought of shutting up, Pop?" Dee asked him sweetly. It was very difficult. All the kids talked like him, of course, at least inside the family. Even she herself used his words, or they both used a common pool of words that he had started. It was a form of semantic incest. Mary half-thought of offering this splendid phrase to Stacey for her notebook, and decided not to bother.

"Precocious insolence" was the phrase that Stacey was turning over in her mind as she looked without much affection at the back of Dee's head. It bothered her, this crudity of language in a girl who should surely be hovering on the brink of et cetera. It was none of her, Stacey's, business, of course, except insofar as all human affairs were her business, as a writer. Still, Dee was irritating, with her juvenile dullness, at an age when she ought to be reaching out tremulously for half-imagined experience. It was impossible to get any raw material out of this lot.

Dee was grateful that her father simply glared at her in hurt reproach and didn't say anything. She wanted to let her mind drift and be free of the noise of the everlasting family and think about Ochie, because she had never seen the village, and she enjoyed creating pictures of it from her mother's descriptions, and then changing them; and peopling the houses with strange unknown villagers. Some of them would have dim rustic teen-age sons who would gape at her, and she would flash past them like the wind without seeming to see.

"Looking forward to Ochie, Harry?" Stacey asked the boy kindly, for she was kindhearted in spite of her professional contempt for her brother's children; and the banal question was the best she could do with this overgrown cabbagey boy.

Harry gave her a polite smile and a nod and a shrug of the shoulders.

If he had jumped in fast and spoken to Magda, perhaps everything would have been all right. Perhaps, in fact, the entire world wouldn't be in ruins. It would have been very pleasant, after all, to have got in fast enough to arrange to spend the holidays with Magda. Away from the University, just the two of them, they could probably have enjoyed being affectionate and perhaps naturally graduated to the other thing too, so that the two things wouldn't be separate. It was the idea of spoiling her that worried him, a fact which he assumed made him a bit old-fashioned and maybe even neurotic.

So he hadn't jumped in fast enough, because he hadn't thought an invitation to a dreary Highland village would be very attractive to Magda; and she was away to that camp in the South of France. And she was only human, he had to admit that — she probably didn't consider the idea of being spoiled, she just enjoyed life, and in all that hot sunshine and with all these people round the place, why wouldn't she get friendly with somebody who would spoil her, if that was the word? Well, it was the word, he decided sadly. He wouldn't be able to think the same of her if it happened. *He* would be spoiled.

Really, the easiest way to stop feeling sad about it was to dislike her. He decided to dislike her, and the decision made him feel slightly better. He thought he might do something despicable himself. He might forget all about any slender ties he had with Magda and pick up any girl who offered herself in Ochie. He couldn't bring himself to decide that he would spoil the girl, whoever she was, but he would be quite reckless about having an affair — no, that phrase was too primeval altogether. He would go to bed with her, without scruple. He had a picture of an unidentified girl sitting in bed and saying, "Are you coming to bed without a scruple?" and he heard himself answering, "I couldn't get one, the chemists are all shut," and his mouth moved in a faint smile.

It must be scorching, all the same, in the South of France. It was hot enough in dreary old Britain, and he was beginning to sweat. He pulled off his jacket and threw it behind the seat, and slid open the window of the Land Rover. Stacey was fanning herself with her notebook, being hypersensitive to everything.

Nat felt the draft of this operation on the back of his neck, and turned round.

"Do you propose to write the Great Novel in that wee book?" he asked his sister. She shook her head with sad contempt for this stupidity.

"I've sent my typewriter ahead," she said, and Nat turned away and looked at his wife.

"J. C.!" he said. "Peace and serenity, eh? Gate-crashing females battering at machines in the night, and looking up noisy dictionaries! Let me out and I can walk home." Mary ignored him and overtook a lorry, and he sulked for a while, and then said thoughtfully, "Mary was saying you have an enormous bottom, Stacey. I was forced to agree with her."

"I was saying nothing of the sort." Mary tried not to giggle, because she was annoyed.

"Don't be daft," said Nat, "nobody could blame you for saying it. Even Stacey must have noticed it, haven't you, Stacey? Where do you think you're going to set up your machine shop at Ochie? It isn't a forty-roomed castle, is it, Mary? It's a tiny slum about the size of an outside privy, isn't it? You'll have to strap your typewriter round your neck and play it along the beach, Stacey. You sit down too much anyway, that's why your bottom is so enormous. It is enormous, I've been watching it."

"Pay no attention to him, Mary," Stacey said, but red in the face. "We're used to his alleged humor."

"The bitch called it my soi-disant humor the last time," Nat muttered. "She must have given up her French period. Ochie is going to be pure hell."

The children sat unembarrassed and paid no attention to the conversation, except that Sally squinted down to see if Stacey was as enormous as Nat had described her.

"We'll stop for lunch at Crianlarich," Mary said, and Nat immediately muttered, "More money thrown to the winds, money money money is all you women ever think about. Lunch at Crianlarich, forsooth."

"Too right," Mary said cheerfully. "Remember five years ago when we could hardly afford sandwiches?"

"We didn't need sandwiches," Nat said, reasonably enough. "We didn't have a car and we weren't going anywhere. Ah, we were poor, but those were happy days."

"Ha, ha," said Mary, delighted by the hope that the sun would keep shining. Ochie was her place, her invention, and she wanted it to be perfect for everybody.

"They were, honestly," Nat said. "I *liked* being evicted, didn't you?"

"Yes, it was lovely." Mary's voice was dreamy. It was lovely to remember it, and be done with it. Everything was lovely, in fact; having a family, and a car and a tiny slum far away on the coast, and Nat prospering, nearly famous. She could have done without Stacey, but life had to have a few difficulties. If Stacey had been her own sister, Mary would have been able to give her a flat No when Stacey invited herself to Ochie. But she was Nat's sister, and Mary was prepared to love everything connected with Nat; and Stacey wasn't really a nuisance, more of a mere bore. She might even dislike Ochie and go home. In any case, everything was going to be fine and it was marvelous to be rich.

It was the children, really, who would suffer more from Stacey's presence, because she bored them so much that they stopped talking when she was there. But if the sun kept shining, they would be out and away from her all the time. It was going to be glorious.

Stacey smiled privately and reached automatically for the pencil on the end of the string before she remembered that she was in a carful of people. She had almost decided that Nat's family might be raw material after all, as long as she just used them as lay figures and put new personalities in them. A bit of artistic exaggeration could do it, in fact. The father, spoiled and unmannerly, *that* was all right; and the mother brisk and efficient and absolutely, but absolutely, vegetable. Efficient housewives almost always *were* vegetable. And of course the kids, sullen and inarticulate. And just a minute, of course, the father was sexually frustrated — maybe that was why he was such a boor. He wasn't anything romantic or creative, like a painter. In fact, she couldn't accept her real-life brother as a convincing painter, no matter how many pictures he sold.

And the kids, of course, sullen and inarticulate, yes, we've got that bit — because what else could they be in this atmosphere, where their parents had no point of contact? They were dull kids, of course, depressingly normal dull kids. But normal kids were the kind who broke out. The more she thought of it, the more Stacey realized that she didn't have to embellish Nat's family all that much to make them good material. It was all there, all right, for somebody with enough perception to see under the surface.

In a flash of discovery, Stacey saw that Dee, with her loose sweater and boy's jeans, was heading inexorably for lesbianism. Not that the jeans meant anything — millions of girls wore them. But this kid wore them all the time, and even her figure was ominously straight up-and-down.

But that would be saved up, probably till the second half
of the book.

Well, if she used lesbianism as the shock discovery for the
girl, she couldn't use homosexuality for the boy. Violence,
violence was better anyway, a kind of Lizzie Borden explosion. She glanced sideways at Harry, who was sitting with
the shine of sweat on his forehead, staring ahead of him with
astonishing blankness, and she grew quite thrilled at this new
discovery. It could be the key scene in the last part of the
book, in a low-ceilinged cottage kitchen, or even an outhouse
with an oil lamp (if the oil lamp got knocked over, she could
have a fire too) and the son and father facing each other
. . . father talking to son in a tone of blistering contempt, son inarticulate, mumbling, but the nostrils flared
and white, yeah, yeah — he would mumble, yeah, yeah, groping for the words he didn't possess, rather Marlon Brando —
fingers groping and finding a pick handle. Maybe a hayfork
would be even better. And then the eyes staring and something going snap, a terrible lunge and bash bash bash, in and
out with the hayfork, while the father fell back and stared
up with an expression of amazement and anger, crash tinkle
the oil lamp, a sheet of yellow flame threw itself across the
loose hay and the boy uttered one long scream of despair,
father's hand clutching at the fork buried in his guts, you
crazy whippersnapper, you . . . gurgle of blood in the throat
as his face was obliterated by a rush of flame. The whole
chapter would write itself.

"Stacey?" Sally had turned to her and was laboriously
thinking out what she wanted to say. Stacey smiled at the
child. The child, of course, skinny and barefoot — Sally
wasn't skinny, but it would be better to have the child skinny
— suddenly bursting from the cottage door, big eyes in thin
face wide with horror, cheeks lit by the flaring light of the
blazing outhouse and mouth opening in a series of short shrill

shrieks. It was a rather filmic conception, that, and *that* wasn't a bad thing either, to write in vivid filmic images. It could help to sell the Hollywood rights.

She was still smiling placidly at Sally, and the little girl narrowed her eyes and said,

"Could you teach me to do the typewriter, if it rains?"

On the point of retorting that her typewriter was not a children's toy, Stacey stopped, resumed her smile, and said, "We'll see." She felt happy and creative and sympathetic.

"This is nice," Nat said, in his empty-headed voice. "Isn't it, children?"

"Yes, Pop, it's nice," they said in chorus, in sickly kiddie-winkie voices. It was nice. The traffic had thinned out and the Land Rover was thundering northwest with high hills on the landscape, and heather and bracken cutting off the pale blue of the sky to the north. The air coming in through the windows was blustery but warm.

"Isn't it nice, Stacey?" Nat said. "To be a happy united family all going on holiday like nice simple ordinary folks? I think it's real nice."

"Yes, it is. Very nice," Stacey said happily. There *was* something nice about a family.

TWO

I⊤ was hot in Ochie. Four dogs who had come out in the morning to look for the hotel bitch had ended up instead strewn along the main street doped with sunshine and gasping feebly. One of them was dreaming, in a series of faint little yup-yups out of the side of its mouth, and the butcher's cat was looking at it out of one eye, from the top of a hot wall. Tom Wishart, the constable, had left off his jacket and rolled up his sleeves, and he was threading his way among the bodies on his bicycle, identifying them and thinking that he might have a word with the owners if he could put it gently enough and not sound objectionable.

Hughie Mackay was sitting on a box in front of the filling station, with a dismantled gearbox laid out on a newspaper. He wiped sweat from his eyes and delicately worked a smooth file over a pinion. Tom Wishart stopped and fanned himself with his cap and said, "Improving the shining hour, Mr. Mackay?" (Was that the title of a song? No, the song was called "This Will Be My Shining Hour," tum-ty tum-ty tum tum.)

"It's a cow," Hughie said curtly. "I'm sweating like a
——'s ——." Tom's ear censored the fruity phrase as it
was uttered, and he smiled determinedly and said, "Aye, a
grand day, grand."

"It's good enough for a fascist lackey wi' nothing better to
do than ride a machine and look superior."

"Aye, it is that," Tom agreed. "Grand weather for singing."

Hughie squinted along the street. Ada Fraser had just
come out of the butcher shop to pull the blind and keep the
sun off the mince. Her skirt was short and her arms were
bare and she was hauled in tight at the waist.

"By God, it would be grand weather for that," Hughie
mused. "She would leap like a leveret in this heat."

"Now, now, Mr. Mackay," Tom complained. "That's not
very nice, a nice young woman like Ada."

"Ach, she's as ripe as a ——'s ——."

"Aye, it's hot, all right." Tom noticed that from the distance the heat haze made Ada's calves shimmer like something under water. "You dirty sod, your mouth's hanging
open," Hughie said, and Tom said, "Aye, a grand day."

"My God, you're a helluva hard man to insult," Hughie
said. "We were better off wi' old McPhater. He was a real
polis. He was as touchy as a ——'s ——."

Tom wished Hughie wouldn't compare everything to a
——'s ——. The thought of a ——'s —— wasn't only
crude, it was upsetting. "Yes," he said, "he was a good man,
they tell me. Well!" He put his foot to the pedal and moved
off slowly, with one eye helplessly fastened on the shimmer-
ing vision of Ada's calves. Hughie looked up and shouted
after him, "And you'll no' get me singing in your bloody
choir either!" Tom waved amiably and wobbled his front
wheel to avoid a prostrate collie mongrel. The light off the

sea was blinding. As he passed the butcher shop he nodded to Ada, remembering to be dignified as well as friendly. She gave him that odd sullen smile of hers, and that opaque stare of hers, directed at his belt buckle, and he tried to stop thinking about ——'s ——. He wondered if she could sing. He hummed the Minstrel Song from *The Mikado* and started pedaling in time to it.

Down at the Tala Hotel, Hughie's brother Geordie was making up his mind to hammer on the side door, and to hell with opening time, and Denis McBain from the hardware shop had come into the yard and was nodding his approval of this decision, when Geordie stayed his hand and listened. From some distance away the still air carried a fervent tenor voice crying, "My catalogue is long through every passion ranging, and to your humours changing." It stopped, and then started again on the same line, this time with more vibrato.

"He's at the bridge," Denis diagnosed, and Geordie blinked and said, "He must be nearer than that."

"No, no, he always stops at the bridge. It's the echo, he's terrible fond of the echo."

"He's sherp," Geordie said angrily. "I'm never done telling him, he takes the high notes sherp. What's the time?"

"Ten minutes short."

Geordie licked his dry teeth and grunted, and Denis tried to comfort him by saying, "Well, at least we don't need to bell the bastard, he lets us know when he's there." Geordie spat on the dusty ground and refused to be comforted. The tenor voice unexpectedly switched to "Trees," and Geordie cast his eyes to heaven and groaned again. He knew he would die of thirst if he had to wait ten minutes for the pub to open legally, and he knew that Tom Wishart would sit at the bridge for half an hour trying out his voice and enjoying the echo. But you could never depend on it, and as long as Andy Anderson could hear the voice in the vicinity, he would never open his door, no matter how ravenous his customers might be.

"Anybody on the boat?" Denis asked, to divert his thoughts.

"Two or three. A load of stuff for Kirk Cottage."

"Oh, that's the new folk," Denis mused. "Were they on the boat?"

"Not them, the silly sods are drivin'."

"Drivin'?"

"Oh, some people know the lot."

"Rather them than me. The cliff road's like a bliddy tightrope," Denis said.

The sun inched its way up, and the hills across the water retreated in a pale haze. Denis took off his tie and put it in his pocket. At three seconds to eleven an old Commer van with one door missing roared up from the direction of the bridge and Hughie Mackay stepped out and strode up to the back door exactly as Andy Anderson opened it from inside. Denis and Geordie looked at each other and shook their heads in admiration. By the time they got into the dark coolness of the bar Andy was already handing a pint across, and Hughie drained two inches of it before he stopped to say hello.

"Some bliddy fools are comin' by road," Denis McBain said, as he drummed his fingers on the bar and itched for the froth building up under the tap.

"Hell mend them," said Hughie.

"The road's no' as bad as that," Andy Anderson said comfortably. He was a man who believed that nothing was ever as bad as that. Geordie Mackay, with a vested interest in the village boat, shook his head with doom in his face, and Hughie sneered at Andy.

"Listen to the mountain goat! Christ, you wouldny catch me on that road without a parachute. Another bit of it fell last month."

"Are you saying that, now!" Andy was politely impressed.

"Ah, hell mend them anyway," Hughie muttered. "Tourists, they're the ruination of the Highlands."

"They'll maybe be rich, and stupid," Denis suggested. "Anyway, say one thing for tourists, they pay cash."

"Ruination," Hughie went on darkly. "First it's the damnt clan chiefs, and then it's the damnt absentee landlords, and then it's the damnt Government, and then it's the damnt tourists, and a parcel of damnt fascists the lot of them."

"You and your clan chiefs," his brother Geordie dismissed him. "You've got clan chiefs on the brain, you've never seen one, they're likely nice enough chaps man to man. I'll have whisky this time, Andy."

"You should not be drinking whisky in weather like this," Hughie told him. "I've told you before, it dehydrates you, it's a drink for ordinary weather. And damn the clan chief that'll ever meet me man to man. A damnt collection of sniveling rogues, the entire boiling of them. They sold out the Highlands to bliddy foreigners like Harper — oh, I know, nice Mister Harper, Mister Harper's all right, he's got you licking his boots for the sake of a wage. A Mackay workin' as a damnt serf to a foreign gin-peddler, it's enough to turn a man in his grave, it's your turn to buy, Denis."

"There's worse than Harper," Andy said placidly, "for all he's an English get. He canny help that."

"The man is a hoor, right enough," said Denis McBain tolerantly, "but I suppose I would be a hoor as well, if I was a millionaire. I would be a right hoor, I expect."

"There should be a law against Ada Fraser in these tight

frocks in this weather," Hughie brooded. "How can a man get his work done wi' that thing catching his eye every minute? Aye, a hoor is right!" he switched back to his main theme. "But you're mixing up cause and effect, Denis, it's because he's a hoor he's a millionaire, it's no' the other way round. Feudalism is the curse of Scotland. We might have a decent road if we got rid of feudal landlords, and people could come to Ochie and bring trade without falling off cliffs and killing themselves every other day."

"But I thought you didn't like tourists," Denis McBain mildly complained.

"They're a damnt sight better than landlords. He doesn't want the tourists, you know, he wants the damnt place kept empty so he can fish and shoot. That's why the road's a damnt death trap. The Devil's Drap. By God, it's well named. I've seen a man drive that road in an Austin Seven and arrive here wi' his hair dead white. Dead white! It's the truth."

"Aye," Andy interrupted. "But that was the old doctor — his hair had been white for twenty years."

"That doesn't invalidate the point," Hughie crushed him. "It was white when he arrived. Yon's not a road, it's the wall of death. And why have we not got a safe road down by the coast?"

"Feudalism," said Denis, because it was expected of him.

"Ach, shut up," said brother Geordie. "We haven't got a coast road because it was torpedoed."

"Aye," Hughie said unwillingly. "I've always wondered who paid them to fire that torpedo."

"It's as well you've got the van working," Geordie said. "There's a load of stuff on the boat for Kirk Cottage."

"Is that the people that are drivin'?" Hughie asked him. "You might as well leave it on the boat, you'll never see them in Ochie. One turn at the steering wheel on the Devil's Drap and bang, you've lost your customers."

Two miles from Ochie, the Boags' Land Rover was bumping along a narrow track and Stacey was clinging to the seat in front of her trying to think up something polite, and patient, but at the same time crushing, about Mary's driving and Nat's navigation. Mary beat her to it.

"Is this really the road?" she asked Nat, for the third time in half an hour.

"This is the road," he said.

"Thin, isn't it?" Sally remarked, not worried.

"If this is the road," Stacey said, "I'm . . ."

"You're a back seat driver with a big bum," Nat told her. "This is the A.A. map and I warned you, it's a dotted line. That means an unsatisfactory road, but it's a road. And it's unsatisfactory," he added.

Stacey closed her eyes and gritted her teeth to stop them from banging together. To one side, reddish moorland fell away toward the hazy sea. A rocky hill rose steeply on the other. They rounded a bend of the hill and Mary stamped on the brake. The narrow track ahead now had a rocky hill rising steeply on one side, and on the other side, the same rocky hill falling vertically into a fifty-foot chasm. Nat looked at it with bright interest.

"Will I take the wheel?" he asked. Mary looked at him undecided, and then shook her head and started up again. She crawled in bottom gear, suspecting that this was excessively cautious but not caring. The road wasn't as bad as it looked from a distance; not quite as bad. It was wider than it looked when the Land Rover was actually on it, but it was still wide enough for only the Land Rover and a few feet to spare, and it twisted endlessly round the cliff. Her right foot was poised ready to leap to the brake pedal. Stacey opened her eyes once, squeaked and closed them again. Sally, in an effort to soothe her aunt, started to sing "Oh why are we waiting —" but Nat lifted a finger and said "Sh!" and she stopped, to Mary's relief.

And after all, it wasn't so bad, as long as you took it slowly. If it was a road, it must be drivable, and it was important not to give up if you wanted to be a complete driver. Nat had told her that, and she had said the same thing to herself. She became almost content, gripping the wheel tight and inching round the curves at two miles an hour. Then she did stamp on the brake again. Across two winding curves, the nose of a little van appeared from behind the cliff wall. Thinking carefully and slowly, she shifted to neutral and pulled the handbrake hard and waited. Nat glanced across at her, but she didn't meet his eye.

The truck moved out of sight again, and then into sight again. It moved round the open bend and stopped five yards away. A hand came out of the driver's window, palm forward, and motioned them back.

"What cheek!" Mary said. "They're used to the road. They don't expect me to reverse on this." Nat already had his hand out and was motioning the van back.

"Stand your ground," he said calmly. "We're bigger than him."

There was a shout from the van, and Nat stuck his head out of the wide window. A middle-aged man in the van poked his head half-out and shouted, "I can't reverse!"

Mary looked at Nat, stupefied.

"I'll reverse the bastard," Nat said. "Come on, Harry, we'll shove him over the edge."

Harry laughed, but didn't move, and Nat got out of the Land Rover on the upward side. Mary was going to shout to him not to shove the van over the edge, but she stopped in time as he walked round the front of the Land Rover, to the edge of the cliff, and opened her door.

"Everybody over one place," he said gaily. "Fangio rides again."

Mary and Dee slid across the seat, and Nat swung himself aboard and grabbed the gear lever. He held the door open and leaned out of the cab, and the Land Rover started moving back along the cliff road, faster than it had come. Mary glanced at the speedometer. It read nine m.p.h. The speed didn't disturb her; she merely thought that Nat was a swine because he was too good at things like driving. Stacey was whimpering gently in the back seat.

When they were clear of the chasm, Nat bumped the Rover straight on to the moorland and the little van shot past them and away.

"He didn't even wave!" Mary cried in vexation.

"The wee rat's too ashamed," Nat said. "He would like to be able to drive like your husband and it churns him up." He drove the Rover back onto the road and Mary waited, tensed.

"You take the wheel?" he asked, and she relaxed and shook her head. Nat flung the car forward at a devil-may-care seven miles an hour. They cleared the cliff road and he stopped at the top of a steep hill. Ochie was beneath them.

"A whole view," Dee intoned, in exactly her father's voice.

Mary tried not to look at anybody, in case anybody should fail to love it. It was only a range of hilly fields with scattered cottages, a road along the seafront and a straggle of houses. And a burn, she remembered. She scanned the road and found the burn, in a deep gully with a narrow bridge over it.

"Where's the house?" Sally demanded, and Mary shook her head.

"You can't see it from here."

"Probably burned to the ground," Nat said coldly.

"— or devoured by driver ants," Harry suggested.

"Or bulldozed by the villainous railroad men," said Dee.

"The sea's fuzzy," Sally complained.

"So you like it," Mary said.

"You're a good kid, kid, a good kid," said Nat, banged into gear and shot down the hill. Then he added, "But there was a thing down there below the road that ought to have been another road, I could see it out of my ear. How come we had to do the ibex bit over the mountains, huh?"

"It's not a whole road," Mary said happily. "It was blown up."

"Egad, a nest of Bolshevik terrorists, that's what you've got us into." He swung right and pulled up beside the Tala Hotel and swung himself out. Mary followed him and he raised his eyebrows at her. She threw her arms round him and said, "You drive not badly, for a bad driver."

Nat patted her and started to shrug his shoulders, and Harry, Dee and Sally all shouted,

"Shucks, twarnt nuthn!"

The noise startled Stacey, who hadn't quite caught the words, and she glowered at them. A stocky man with greasy hands and greasy overalls came out of the hotel and looked at Nat.

"Yes, my good fellow?" Nat said.

"You'll do, you'll do," said the stocky man, and held out one of his greasy hands.

"You're damn right," Nat said, and took his hand.

A genuine countryman, thought Stacey. The simple human warmth, loyal peasant, er, yeoman stock . . .

"I'm Hughie Mackay," the greasy man said, and Nat said, "I would never have believed it!"

Salt of the earth, thought Stacey . . . no passion or intellect or anything, not a main character, but, um, simple humble people, sons of the soil, let the great big world keep turning, naught shall make us rue . . .

"I'm Stacey Boag," she said to Hughie Mackay. He held out his hand.

Jesus, he thought. Keep your eye on this one.

THREE

THE HISTORY of Ochie is possibly one of the dullest tales of the Scottish Highlands. Up to 1700, there are no records of the place whatever, and the scholar can only surmise that the Ochians kept themselves to themselves, or weren't there at all. If you try to trace its beginnings on ancient maps, Ochie is the place where the cartographers started to fill in with phrases like "Here be Dragons"; and it isn't too easy to decide why anybody decided to make it a place at all.

According to legend, which is nearly always a direct lie in these parts, the peninsula of Ochard was bitterly contested by the Mackays, the Campbells (who contested everything on the west coast of Scotland), the McNeills and the McLeans, and several other tribal groups of Pictish descent and no business acumen. There are other peripheral legends of wild men from Ireland who came, or were washed ashore, or sprang out of the heather, and fought with everybody in sight to establish a foothold. It lies ten, or maybe twenty or thirty, miles south of Oban, and it had never been of much use to anybody until somebody announced the Highland Clearances. The difficulty about Ochard was that there was practically nobody to clear, and no clan chieftain had noticed the miserable location before. But as soon as it was put about that there was money to be made in getting rid of the crofter-farmers and bringing in sheep, a far-out descendant of the McOchs of Argyll hurried to tell the English Government that he was the landlord of the district, and got several grants for road-building and improvements, which he spent on drink in Paris. When he died, cheerfully, at the age of 42, his teen-age son invited a number of Northern English sheep farmers to populate the arid land as his tenants. In no time at all the sheep, and their owners, died of various diseases produced by the relentless west wind and the loneliness, and the area was converted into a deer and grouse shoot, after correspondence between the heir Angus McOch and his lawyer in Edinburgh.

The McOch himself visited the district twice, the second time to make sure he had seen right the first time. The boy had been raised by one of his father's mistresses in Paris, and couldn't understand the notion of a piece of the world without street lamps and brothels; and on his second sight of it, he sold it to another laird by the name of the West Pacific Trading Company. There it rotted for half a century, and during this time, human beings dropped in or sprouted from the peat, and created the village of Ochie by accident. There were periods during which the West Pacific Trading Company forgot that it owned the land, and these are sometimes recalled by ancient Ochians as the golden age of Ochie.

In the early part of the twentieth century, however, following Queen Victoria's public relations campaign for the Highlands, the West Pacific Trading Company realized it had a valuable commodity on its hands, and dispatched over some years a series of ambitious clerks to bring the district into full production of dividends. Very little was heard of any of them again, and in 1909 the company put out a dishonest prospectus by which it managed to avoid bankruptcy and some ugly legal inquiries into its affairs by suckering the property onto a Peruvian entrepreneur who had swindled the Romanoffs and become respectable. The price paid was £4,000. The area involved was eighteen thousand acres, including the embryonic village of Ochie.

The Peruvian, who had the interesting names of Jesus Murphy Fernandez, changed his name (all this is perfectly true) to Jesus Murphy Fernandez McOch, and made a serious attempt to learn Gaelic, wear the kilt, and raise a private army among the peasantry. He died of a broken heart during a journey across America, two hours before a platoon of Pinkerton detectives overtook his special train with eight warrants for fraud, and with guns blazing. The train driver and three guests of the laird died of multiple bullet wounds.

After protracted legal proceedings, the estate came into the possession of Jacques Harper, an honest English publican who had notions of setting up a secret distillery in the Scottish Highlands and avoiding the excise duty on spirits. The Great War supervened, and Mr. Harper went into textiles instead, thus failing either to become a criminal or acquire a peerage.

In 1937 it passed to his son, Arnold Harper, who had been brought up in the textile, then the Army Surplus Clothing, industries, and had latterly bought a gin distillery and prospered. Arnold was a hard, realistic businessman, who went crazy with joy on becoming a genuine Highland laird and spent every leisure moment of his life thereafter hating the Duke of Argyll and the Earl of Elgin and trying to find out how they had got their titles while he hadn't.

The name of the place is also obscure. A retired schoolmaster of the district wrote a brochure in 1932 in which he suggested that Ochie is a corruption, or a contraction, or both, of Haakonsford, because, he claimed, this was the place where the Norwegian king disembarked and had his boats hauled overland in order to catch the Scots by surprise at the Battle of Largs (1293). As most of the Vikings were killed at Largs, nobody can deny this story, and King Haakon doesn't mention it in any language understood in the district.

The eighteen thousand acres constitute a peninsula, the isthmus of which is a thin piece of land, called Tarbetochie, very high on one side and very low and flat on the other. On the high side, there is a very old road, originally tramped out by migrating red deer and later leveled by drovers, along the winding side of the saddleback mountain labeled on the maps as Ben Tarbetochie (900 feet) and known locally as Tarbie. On the narrow coastal plain of the isthmus, a low road was put under construction by the Government as a siphon for the unemployed of Glasgow and Clydebank in 1937, but the construction, which had been planned by a surveyor in London without a contour map, ran up against the steep gulley known as the Devil's Drap, and the plan didn't specify the forty-foot bridge needed to bring the road into the village of Ochie.

The unemployed, who lived in a tented camp and were paid subsistence, included several ingenious engineers with a sense of humor, who carried on at the obstacle with a ram-shackle assembly of boulders and tree trunks to form a primitive bridge along which a brave man might walk, if slightly drunk. The history of this noble piece of civil engineering is continued by Nat Boag, who spent the second day of his stay in Ochie stretched out on an expensive steel-framed deck chair behind Kirk Cottage, a chair ordered through the Postal Bargains page of the *Scottish Daily Mail*.

"Some creative bastard cut off the village with a torpedo," he mused, and groped round the raw earth beside him for the whisky and soda that Sally had put there ten minutes earlier. "The only way to use that tape measure is to drive tiny stakes into the ground and loop the tape round them."

Mary, in jeans and a blouse top, carried on carefully measuring the ground and comparing it with a photostat of a chart that had come from the lawyer when she bought the cottage.

"You would be better at this than me," she said, not complaining too much. "You have the eye."

"I've got the only deck chair as well," said Nat. "But so help me God, have you ever heard of anybody blowing up a road with a torpedo? I like that blouse."

"You're not getting it," she said. "What was that about torpedoes?" She looked round hopefully in case somebody had left a pile of tiny stakes in the overgrown garden. What Nat had said was true; the only sensible way to measure the ground was with stakes.

"They've got a lot of real ugly faces in this place," Nat went on. "I met an old bag with snakes growing out of her head. She's buried two husbands. That's her job, burying husbands."

"What color are the snakes?" Mary found a broken length of cane and forced it into the fibrous earth.

"She isn't letting anybody know. She wears a cloth cap night and day. No, it's the mortal truth, somebody blew up the bridge with a torpedo. There used to be a bridge on the coast road and some loony torpedoed it."

Mary had walked out of his line of vision as he lay back and squinted through half-closed eyes. It really was very hot. The neglected trees and rank shrubs round the little garden blocked any breath of wind, and as he lay unmoving he could feel the fresh sip of whisky rising to his forehead and appearing in tiny drops of sweat. He wiped them off and tasted his fingers experimentally, and then took another sip from the glass.

"I got the whole story from Hughie Mackay," he went on sleepily. "It was back in 1943 when the Navy was trying out fiendish new weapons up here, having no doubt discovered that the cutlass and the belaying pin were failing in the struggle against the U-boat menace . . . though it was touch and go for a while . . . By Gad, they were stirring times . . ."

Mary carried on doggedly taking measurements. She was determined to mark the boundaries of her tiny estate before she started work on reclaiming the abandoned garden, and she was happy to let Nat drone on while she worked. He was already talking half in "character" but there would be some actual facts buried in whatever he said. He had spent the previous evening getting acquainted with the peasantry, as he had described it, in the pub; and it was true that people talked to Nat. Total strangers were always unloading their secrets on him, especially in pubs, and the mixture of gossip and fantasy he acquired was always useful if she wanted to get to know all about Ochie in the shortest possible time.

"Ah, they don't make men like that today," he said darkly. "Dammit, it's the truth I'm telling you. Somebody let off a torpedo and it homed straight on the bridge and threw it all over Argyll. Geordie Mackay says it was a natural mistake because the Royal Navy was overrun with amateurs and Englishmen at the time. Denis McBain, on the other hand, has always insisted it wasn't the Royal Navy at all. It was a torpedo from a Japanese submarine manned by special suicide squads."

"Japanese?" Mary hadn't meant to betray interest, but the question came out automatically.

"Clever people. Look at these cameras and transistor radios. They could have been making a desperate bid to get

Ochie to sue for a separate peace . . ." Nat pondered this line of thought and decided he was too hot to elaborate on it. "Anyway, Hughie Mackay is the only one who's on the ball. He says the Navy was bribed by the brutal Harper to cut off the village and keep the peasantry in a state of primitive isolation and ignorance. He's a good kid, that Hughie. He's got an old plow, he says he can fix on the Land Rover to demolish this steaming malarial swamp."

Mary refused to comment on any of this, and Nat started playing a game of throwing the empty glass in the air with his eyes shut and keeping them shut till the last possible moment before he caught it coming down.

"You don't believe it," he accused her. "You don't think a pillar of society like Harper could stoop to such dastardy because he's your landlord. But Hughie Mackay's got evidence, I tell you. He's seen Harper wearing knickerbockers. A man who can wear knickerbockers is capable of any bestiality. You never thought of that when you dragged us to this fetid backwater to slave under a brutal oppressor like Harper. Hughie Mackay says Harper is your feudal superior."

"He isn't."

"Women don't understand these things, Hughie Mackay says. You bought the cottage with the money I sweated in the salt-mines to earn, but it means nothing. You're only a vassal. Harper is the overlord of the whole jungle." Nat turned his head to stare narrowly at Mary. "He can probably claim the droit de seigneur."

"Hughie Mackay's cuckoo."

"Just try saying that when Harper arrives on his piebald hunter to work his will on you, while he sends me out to the marshes to keep the frogs quiet all night. Hughie Mackay says the day of the revolution can't be far away."

"Hughie Mackay is for the birds." The confusing thing about talking to Nat was that he already had a whole collection of people's names that meant nothing to her, and he discussed them as if he had known them for years. "Harper isn't my feudal superior. This bit of land belongs to the Church of Scotland."

Nat absorbed this setback rather petulantly, and then brightened up.

"You would rather have a po-faced parson claiming his insolent rights! We'll see about that. I can still wield a broadsword, even if my hands have gone soft from easy living." He threw the glass in the air, cocked a forefinger at it and shouted "Pow!" The glass fell on his left kneecap and he yelped.

"I haven't noticed anybody hurrying to claim any rights round here," Mary said, on her hands and knees under a bramble bush. Nat contemplated her back view appreciatively and said,

"No, it would be hard to be an insolent aristocrat in a two-foot bunk bed. That was very cunning of you, I compliment you, madam."

He closed his eyes and pondered. Mary turned to look at him, shrugged, and went back to feeding the inch-tape round the far side of the bush. But the subject wouldn't leave her mind in the soft dreamy heat.

"That's something that suddenly worries me about these aristocrats jumping into bed with peasant girls," she said, her voice half-muffled as she stooped. "Their spurs must have made an awful mess of the sheets."

"I was going to say that," Nat complained. "Hello there, David, man!" he added in a shout. A thin man with a heavy black moustache was hurrying in a shuffle walk along the little side road beneath the garden, just visible through the rank vegetation. He jerked at the sound and looked round puzzled, then waved his hand timidly and shuffled quickly on.

"That's Davie Fitzgerald," Nat muttered. "It's his wife that has the headful of snakes."

"How do you *discover* these things?" Mary asked him, and Nat looked complacent and said, "People love me, they tell me their troubles."

He was reaching far out to the side to pick up the empty glass, and in a burst of what might have been irritation, or affection, or anything else, Mary tipped over the deck chair. Nat rolled over on the spiky grass and looked up at her and said, "This is going to be a difficult month, I can tell already. Bunk beds, for God's sake!"

Davie Fitzgerald's wife didn't have a headful of snakes. Her hair had been going thin for years and she wore a cotton cap over it permanently to prevent herself from noticing. She owned the Tarbie Private Hotel, and a vigorous bank-book, and Davie Fitzgerald. This didn't worry Davie very much, or at least, it was well down on the priority list of his worries. He was more disturbed at the prospect of losing his owner, because everybody assured him that the indestructi-ble Maggie was going to die any day. Maggie herself was a lot more exact than that. Every morning when he took her tea in, she told him menacingly that she would see most of July out, but never another August. And then she ticked the new day off on her bedside calendar, to make him feel guilty.

As he shuffled down the road past Kirk Cottage, he won-dered how much of July she meant. It would be handy if the funeral came along while the weather was still dry, but it would be like Maggie to arrange it for the rainiest day in the year, to spite everybody.

Anyway, that wasn't the worst worry. Davie had always been haunted by the ghosts of Maggie's two previous husbands, and he could feel them closing in on him now. He twitched a lot.

At first, Maggie's illness had come as a partial release. He had to leave the house some time each day, and now Maggie didn't have the concentration to check the times of his movements, and he was suddenly able to hurtle into the Tala and pose as a human being every day with a forbidden glass in his hand. The regulars at the Tala had rallied round to make his life of sin more efficient. Geordie Mackay had put him on to vodka so that Maggie would never smell the dread liquor odor on his breath, and sometimes Hughie Mackay would run him back to the house in his van, thus giving him ten extra minutes of reckless gaiety and corruption at the bar.

But hidden forces threatened him. In fact, at this moment, as he shuffled at high speed toward the Tala, a figure stepped abruptly from a garden gate and stood in his path. He kept shuffling. It was Sadie Pringle. He had known it would be Sadie Pringle, but he thought he might have foxed her by taking the long way round, past Kirk Cottage.

She didn't try to stop him. She just stood and looked at him and did her Harbinger of Doom act, with her lips clamped shut and her eyes slitted, and a terrible warning in her face. Davie twitched some more and shuffled past her, almost weeping with fear and resentment. Big Dod Pringle had been Maggie's first husband, and Sadie was Dod's sister. She had never spoken to Davie in his life, but these past few weeks, she had developed the habit of springing out of bushes and holes in the ground and *looking* at him. The third time it had happened, he had tried to stammer some soothing words to her, but her lips had stayed clamped. Now he simply avoided her terrible eye and shuffled faster. If he had been wearing his teeth, he would have looked like a cornered rat.

Apart from Sadie, there was always the sickening prospect of running into the Jackson twins, sour and silent potato farmers whose older brother Charlie had been Maggie's second husband. It was true that the Jackson twins never said much to anybody, except possibly God — they muttered a good deal in church, as if making private arrangements for the harvest and suchlike — but Davie found that when they said nothing to him, it was a particularly baleful nothing, as if they had got something specially disagreeable arranged with God for Davie's benefit. He rarely met them without feeling that one or both of his arms were going to fall off, or his flesh be consumed by locusts. "I'm innocent!" he sometimes wanted to scream. "It's not my fault Maggie married me!" because he knew their silent hatred must be connected with Dod Pringle, and Charlie Jackson, and Maggie. And honestly, it wasn't his fault. Maggie always got her own way, and when she decided to marry somebody, that man was as good as married.

He was as good as buried too. Dod Pringle and Charlie Jackson had been strong, fit specimens, and neither of them had lasted more than five years. On that time-scale, he himself, Davie, would be about due for the undertaker in six months if Maggie herself hadn't had two attacks and gone to bed to die. But surely that wasn't his fault either. He hadn't asked her to have an attack. He would have been easier in his mind if he had had one, just like Dod and Charlie.

Anybody in Ochie could have told Davie he was making a lot out of nothing, if he had had the courage to tell anybody what was going on in his mind. But Davie didn't mention any of his nightmare fears about Sadie and the Jacksons, because he assumed he must be guilty of something if they made him feel guilty, and he didn't want anybody else to know what he was guilty of. He cut in his booster rocket as he shuffled past the accusing figure of Sadie and swung into the main street in little spurts of dust and sweat, and when he found himself facing another figure, the more amiable figure of Ada Fraser outside the butcher's shop, he was too exhausted to twitch, but kept on going, powered by fear and guilt and a lust for a quick double vodka.

"I've got your order ready, Mr. Pringle," Ada called after him. She had called him Mr. Pringle, but he fought down his superstitious shiver at this, because she always called him Mr. Pringle. It was too much trouble for Ada to keep learning new names for Maggie's husbands.

"After, after," he muttered, waving a hand to make her disappear.

"You're not very friendly, Mr. Pringle," Ada said, and made her coy gesture of jerking her pelvis forward so that her thighs stood out hard against the seams of her skirt. Davie thought they looked quite nice, but he had no time for that kind of thought. That was the kind of thought that had got him married to Maggie, and landed him in his present hell. He saw the dark open door of the Tala ahead of him, and he plunged toward it counting his grocery money and sucking his moustache.

"Welcome to the merry band!" a woman's voice shouted out of the gloom, and Davie had a tertiary attack of the twitches. But even as his eyes were adjusting themselves, Andy Anderson was reaching across the bar and putting a glass of colorless fluid in his hand, and Davie knocked half of it back and felt ready to brace himself. The woman who had shouted had her hand out toward him, and he shook it limply. She was a biggish, frightening lassie in a red-and-white-striped dress, and he wished she would go away, but she persisted in being there. It upset him to meet surprising people, especially in the Tala bar, because he had got used to the quiet helpful company of the regulars.

"What's your name?" she demanded. "I'm Stacey Boag — not that it matters."

"Fitzgerald," he said humbly.

"I like you, Fitz," she said. "Have another." There was a faint generalized sound of masculine protest at the bar, but the woman thumped her fist on the counter and turned to Hughie Mackay.

"Am I not entitled?" she said. "Do you not believe in the equality of women?" Her voice was loud and gay, and then it dropped to a coy murmur. "Or do you feel your masculine stronghold is being undermined?" She laughed in two hammer blows.

"Oh, I wouldn't know that," Hughie was saying. "I've never met the woman yet that I was the equal of, and that's the truth."

"O-oh!" The woman lowered her lashes at Hughie and Hughie stared thoughtfully back at her, and then she turned her lashes on Davie. Davie looked into his glass and drank it. Stoddart, the schoolteacher, was there too, and Davie didn't enjoy Stoddart's company. He concentrated on the sweet warmth that the vodka was sending through his chest, and heard Stoddart saying, "That's very kind of you, Miss Boag. Make mine a whisky this time, Andy."

"Eh, mm, I never noticed anybody offering *you* a drink," Hughie Mackay said amiably to Stoddart, but the woman turned gaily and said, "I did. Fill 'em up, bartender. When I drink, everybody drinks, ha ha." The two hammer blows bounced on Davie's skull again. Andy was pouring drinks for everybody.

"No, I mean it," the woman said. "Nobody in the cities

has any *conception* how much sheer *life* there is in a village like Ochie. Oh, tourists, yes, but they never get under the *surface*. The . . . the *inwardness*. The flavor! Life! That's the writer's job — distilling the flavor."

"Oh, there's been a bit of distilling here," Andy Anderson said. "That was Dod Pringle's uncle, oh, away back before the war. You mind of him, Davie." Davie shook his head violently. "Never got a smell of him, they had men through the heather wi' microscopes for a month, but never a sniff. It was poisonous stuff, poisonous."

"That's the kind of thing!" Stacey's voice was loud and vibrant, and Davie thought he couldn't stand another minute of it. "The secret life, the . . . oh, you can feel it throbbing. That's where life is, in the hamlets, the . . . the hills . . . where people are *real*. Do you not agree, Mr. Stoddart?"

Hughie Mackay was whistling silently, and Denis McBain was gazing at Stacey with glazed eyes. Such a thing had never been heard in the back bar at the Tala.

"Oh, it's a quiet wee place, Ochie," Stoddart said primly. "Good, God-fearing people. That's the attraction of it, nothing much ever happens here."

"Ach, now!" Stacey's accent nearly turned Highland, "I can feel the vibrations, Mr. Stoddart. It's going to be a very fruitful month for me, I assure you!" Even to her own ears, her voice sounded louder than necessary and Stacey wondered if she had been drinking too much. It was childish to show off like this, to boast about being a novelist. She would have been better to play it quiet, be unobtrusive, the silent watching eye, the vibrating antenna. But what the hell, she was getting to know people, she was getting under the surface.

"Well!" Stoddart said. "It's very nice to have a writer among us. Em . . ." Stacey was instantly on guard for the question she knew must be coming; but she was ready for it

— a laugh, a wave of the hand, *I don't publish under my own name, no — I enjoy the privacy of a pseudonym, perhaps I'll tell you when I know you better* . . . Why not? she thought. She could pick out some ordinary novelist with a dozen published books and say that was her pseudonym. It would be a harmless deception. No, no. There was such a thing as the integrity of the artist. She would simply say that she didn't publish under her own name. That was the God's honest truth, at least so far.

But the crisis didn't come. As Stoddart felt for words, Hughie Mackay cut in smoothly.

"Aye, it's your turn, Mr. Stoddart, I think."

Stoddart stammered, and Davie Fitzgerald, with new resolution in his veins, said, "No, they're on me, the same again, Andy."

Hughie glared at him. You could trust Davie always to muck everything up. This was the best chance in three years to force Stoddart to buy a round of drinks, and Davie had ruined it. Stoddart's confusion had already turned to a smirk, and he was muttering, "Eh, yes, it was whisky," to Andy Anderson. By Hughie's calculations, that was three whiskies and a half-pint Stoddart had had for eleven pence, and before the round was finished it would be time for Stoddart's instant vanishing trick.

"Cheers, Fitz," Stacey said, trying to moderate her volume. "Here's to a fruitful month."

"Aye, well," Hughie said, abandoning his disappointment over Stoddart, "we'll have the Town Regatta. And the fete. And if the polis can blackmail enough people we'll have an operatic entertainment in the tin hut . . ."

"And the laird's coming," Stoddart interrupted. Hughie looked at him sourly.

"Aye, the feudal superior cometh in his glory to nod to his vassals."

"Marvelous!" Stacey clapped her hands.

"And the fireworks, they're not bad," Denis McBain said, coming out of his stupor.

"Yes, the birthday fireworks." Stoddart nodded in a judicial fashion. "It should be an interesting month for you, Miss Boag."

"And the f— " Davie Fitzgerald choked on the letter, and blushed, and Hughie Mackay immediately said, "Yes, we've mentioned the fireworks, Davie."

"Aha!" Stacey's nose sharpened to a spear. "You're hiding something from me. Fitz! You're blushing!"

"Ach, he never stops thinking about the free beer," Hughie cried. It would never do to let this nosy bird know that Davie was expecting a funeral. "Oh, it'll be a grand month, very eventful."

Stacey's mind was now made up. Throughout her career as a novelist, she had been determined on one thing: that her novels would be utterly realistic and fresh and contemporary. She had started with one modeled on the style of Howard Fast, because she realized that he had discovered what was her true style. Her next had been inspired by reading *Borstal Boy*, where she found at last the approach to the language and people that had been lying dormant in her own talent. Her third had been written in a frenzy, in only fifteen months, after the publication of *Saturday Night and Sunday Morning*, when she admitted her own, unacknowledged need to write simply about simple, squalid, working-class people. Now she knew that these failures had been nothing more than essays in search of a style, and the more she thought of Ochie and the turbulent life bubbling under its surface, the more she realized that she had finally come home, to Peyton Place.

But with a touch of Françoise Sagan, she decided, because the last thing she was going to do was to imitate any single author. Her own style would have its own subtle but unmistakable mixture . . . *With her first novel Miss Boag leaps into the ranks of the masters of our century . . . style subtle but unmistakable . . . unforgettable characters striding out of the page* . . . Yippee.

By the shingly beach below the Tala Hotel stood a concrete plateau that had once led to a pier, when sizable steamers actually called at Ochie in the 1920's. On this, Harry Boag was sitting on an old cast-iron bollard, pretending to look at a mob of young people dragging sailing dinghies down the beach and into the water. Sally was helping to carry one of them, and would undoubtedly sail away in it, because it would never occur to Sally not to ask bluntly for a sail. Dee, who would wait till she was asked and then probably refuse with a ravishing smile, was standing on the shingle skimming flat stones across the water.

There was another bollard on the concrete plateau, and on it there sat a girl of dreamlike beauty, with soft dark hair and a transparent complexion, and great dark eyes that seemed to be gazing rather into her own spirit than out to sea. A quiet girl, utterly self-contained, whose lips appeared to fall naturally into a grave smile. Harry had splendid eyesight, and even from twenty feet he could see some tiny beads of perspiration on her upper lip. They were delicious.

"Not much wind," he said, after trying and discarding several phrases in his mind. The girl didn't pay any attention. It was very annoying. If he repeated the remark more loudly, it would seem as if he were trying to strike up an acquaintance. But if he didn't say something, he wouldn't strike up an acquaintance at all. He looked all round the bay for some seconds.

"Don't you sail?" he said, very loudly. The girl turned her head toward him and smiled shyly and said,

"No."

"Neither do I," Harry said.

"Oh."

"No."

And that was a perfectly good beginning, he figured. Nothing they ever said to each other from then on could possibly be as banal as what they had just said. He planted his feet on the concrete and stood up lazily and started to stroll toward her bollard. Then a man in a dark suit came out of the Tala Hotel and shouted,

"Linda! Time to be off home!"

And Linda got up from her bollard and ran up to the road without looking back. Linda. Sweet name. Harry jumped elegantly down from the concrete onto the shingle and picked up a flat stone. There was no reason why it shouldn't be an eventful month.

FOUR

THE HARPERS arrived in Ochie by sea, in a 120-foot twin-
screw diesel yacht with white topsides and an imitation buff
funnel, which would spend the next few weeks at anchor off
the derelict pier as an annex to the Big House. The uncomplicated members of the Ochie community regarded it with
pride and envy and speculated on what life could be like on
so opulent a scale. Hughie Mackay was not one of the uncomplicated members. He was, however, one of the few lo-
cals who had been on board, to overhaul one of the diesels,
and he reported that the boat had eight bathrooms, all with
platinum taps which ran with Blue Water Gin instead of water, and that it carried five tons of gold bullion as internal
ballast against the day when the laird would have to flee for
refuge in a banana republic when the workers, or the Fraud
Squad, rose against him.

The summer arrival of the laird always brought out the
worst in Hughie. When Harper walked past the garage, as
he was bound to do sometime, and made democratic gestures
of friendship, Hughie was very particular to have ready a

right hand impregnated with heavy oil and iron filings, and he had an ostentatious technique of wiping the *back* of his hand on his overalls before offering it for a firm handshake. He called his technique the Reign of Terror, because his manner was so calculated that there could be no doubt that he was bullying the laird, but every insult carried a thick layer of sycophancy that couldn't be questioned. Even more deadly than the greasy handshake was his invariable question, "And how's the wife and kid, then . . . Squire?"

Every word of this sentence grated on the laird, and yet it would have destroyed his dignity to object to it. He sometimes tried to restore his self-esteem by retailing the remark to his wife, as an example of the unconscious humor of the simple rustic folk; but Joyce, his American wife, didn't think it was funny, and privately, neither did the laird. He was well aware that only servants and employees and tenants had wives and kids. Lairds had Mrs. Harper and the Young Master, or Your Good Lady and Master Winston. Hughie Mackay was one of the crosses Arnold Harper had to bear, and he bore it sullenly while he waited for a chance to pull Hughie's feet from under him.

Mary Boag had no interest at all in the laird or his family, except to hope that Nat would never run into any of them. Though he talked a good deal of how good Ochie was for a painter, he had never got round to painting anything since they arrived. He spent most of his time sitting in the pub, or in the garage, talking nonsense with Hughie Mackay and exchanging plans for bloody revolution. Mary liked Hughie, but she wished he lived in some other village where Nat would never have met him. She was careful not to suggest to Nat that he might like to start painting as he had planned. She tidied the big stone outhouse that went with the cottage and cleaned the windows on the north side, and said nothing.

"Mañana, mañana," Nat would say, watching her carrying old clothes-wringers and dank, germinating mattresses out of the outhouse for a bonfire. "I'm suffering from the famous West Coast Rot."

"You brought the rot with you," she said automatically. "I don't mind, as long as you're enjoying the rest."

"So you say." He assumed a whining tone. "You're mad because your money machine's switched off, that's all I am in this family, feed flake-white in at one end and wait for the groceries to pour out at the other."

"Another word out you and you'll *sleep* in the outhouse," she said, making it sound like a part of the dialogue. He shrugged without reacting.

But if the West Coast Rot prevented him from painting, it seemed to mellow his response to people too. When he persuaded her to stop laboring and walk to the village for shopping and a drink, they ran into the kind of situation that had always wearied and worried her, and nothing bad happened after all.

It was in the newspaper shop, a long low wooden building cluttered with postcards and paperbacks and faded souvenirs on printed cards, and a prissy man whom she now knew as Martin Stoddart, the schoolmaster, was already there, idly reading a *Daily Express* to see if it was worth buying. He glanced at them with a smirk and turned to Jenny McNeill, behind the counter. She was fat and had bad feet, and spent most of the day sitting on a stool with her bosom resting on the newspapers and her eyes glinting eagerly for any dark secrets the village could yield.

"You didn't know we had *two* celebrities in the village, Mrs. McNeill," Stoddart said coyly, and Mary could have slapped him from simple dislike. She smiled charmingly.

"Oh yes," Stoddart went on, "Mr. Boag is *the* Mr. Boag. *Nathaniel* Boag."

"Uhuh?" Jenny McNeill was delighted and still baffled. She blinked several times at Nat and tried to suck his secret out of him.

"The eminent dabbler in oils," Stoddart said. Mary waited for him to be cut to shreds, and for once, she thought it was a good idea.

"Oh, are you at the refinery, Mr. Boag?" Jenny McNeill asked eagerly, and Nat immediately began to nod in reply, but Stoddart had emitted a giggle of delight and was at it again.

"That's not what Mr. Boag would call a very complimentary remark," he smirked. "He'll think you've never heard of the Royal Academy."

"And why should you?" Nat asked airily. "It's a load of inflated muck."

Jenny was already shaping an enormous "Oh" of respect, and Stoddart added,

"*Quite* the budding Rembrandt!" Mary held her breath; but to her relief and annoyance, Nat assumed a hideous expression of humility and said,

"Ah, that's an exaggeration, chum. Tintoretto, maybe, and a wee touch of the Riveras." His use of the word "chum" was the only hint of his loathing. Jenny McNeill was patting her heap of straggly hair and grimacing dreadfully.

"Maybe you'll do a snap of me," she said, and Nat turned his full thousand-candle-power smile on her. Mary had never seen it fail on middle-aged women; or on anybody.

"My skill is too feeble for your beauty, Miss," he said, and Jenny McNeill collapsed in sniggers. Stoddart followed them out of the shop, the kind of man who will go on prodding a tiger till he gets his money's worth. He fell into step beside them.

"There's a lot of very artistic views round Ochie," he told Nat. "Yes, very artistic."

"I never look at landscapes." Nat had abandoned his sweet courtesy, but Stoddart didn't detect any change in him.

"We had an art *teacher* here last year," he announced. "He said Ochie was an artist's paradise."

"Did he paint by numbers?"

"He was a qualified *teacher*."

"*There's* something like a landscape," Nat said in a faraway tone, and looked ahead at where Ada Fraser was bending forward to peer at something in the butcher shop window. Stoddart giggled uneasily.

"Not exactly what you'd call . . . fine art," he said. But Nat wasn't listening. As they reached the butcher shop, he said abruptly to Ada,

"I'll paint you. Come up to Kirk Cottage tomorrow."

Ada raised her opaque grey eyes to him and after a pause for thought, jerked her shoulders and said,

"Hm, you fancy yourself! Oh! Is this your husband, Mrs. Boag?" Mary was smiling and nodding to her, suppressing a giggle as she watched Stoddart out of the corner of her eye.

"Well. I don't mind if you don't." Ade pulled her stomach in and stuck her chest out. She smoothed the tight, tight skirt on her thighs, as Mary walked into the shop. Then, after a moment's hesitation, Ada threw back her long hair and waltzed into the shop. Nat lit a cigarette like Noel Coward and breathed smoke through his nose.

"Em. Don't know if that's very wise, Mr. Boag," Stoddart twittered. "It's not a big city, Ochie . . . you know, that kind of thing."

"What kind of thing?" Nat asked innocently. Stoddart funked the question, and said,

"Frankly, I may not be an artist, but that is not my taste. She's not very . . . *edifying*, is she?"

"She's got a rump like a Clydesdale!" Nat smacked his lips and suddenly started off toward the Tala. Stoddart jumped to walk beside him, and gave a little skip to get into proper step. Nat immediately skipped to get out of step. Stoddart, his mind whirling, struggled to regain the sophistication of an educated man.

"Of course, it's different with artists," he said breathlessly. "It's purely a matter of composition, there's no, er, you know, unsophisticated people get a lot of wrong ideas about . . . that kind of thing. It's simply another . . . job of painting . . ."

"A lassie's skin is more fun than a landscape," Nat said mercilessly. "Well, for Christ's sake, who would want to stroke a landscape?"

"I don't find that in good taste," Stoddart declared, and then, anxious not to quarrel openly, added, "What I mean, as a friend, it's the kind of thing that people in a place like this would misunderstand." He had never got over his Army service and he kept skipping to get back into step, but Nat remorselessly skipped to spoil it. Nat came to a halt, to let Mary catch up on them, and Stoddart stumbled in the middle of a skip.

"Come right out into the open, man," Mary heard Nat say, as she hurried up behind them. "Is there some old religious custom I might be offending? In heaven's name, man, what terrible mystery are you hinting at?"

Mary deduced at once that Nat was breaking out again, and adopting a character that Stoddart would never understand. She smiled brightly and said that the steaks for dinner were beautiful, and Stoddart turned to her in patent relief. Nat had turned to the sea, and was whistling under his breath, and after a few moments, Stoddart remarked gallantly,

"I suppose you'll have modeled for Mr. Boag quite often, Mrs. Boag."

"Oh, yes, in all sorts of ways," Mary assured him, taking

the initiative from Nat: and Stoddart smirked and nodded his entire misunderstanding. And as they still stood there, he asked hopefully, "Were you going into the bar?"

"That's very gracious and hospitable of you, Mr. Stoddart," Nat said. Stoddart's face was working painfully as Nat took his arm and forced him at a quick trot through the side door of the Tala. But by the time they were at the bar, Mary already had her purse open in her hand and a pound on the counter. Enough was enough.

Mary had no difficulty in reconstructing most of the dialogue between Nat and Stoddart. They had been on about sex, that was sure. It was impossible for the two men not to be on about sex after the furtive way Stoddart had been running his eyes up Ada Fraser's legs, with a sneer of disapproval that Mary found distasteful. And she was glad that Nat had obviously been tormenting Stoddart. Even now she could feel his lowered eyes glancing across her bosom and she could hear him wondering exactly what sorts of ways she had modeled. But she had a faint, a very faint, twinge of pity for him. In the heat of the sun it must be hard for him not to be thinking about things he disapproved of.

As they disappeared into the Tala, they were observed by Winston Harper, the laird's son. It was Mary who had caught his eye. Winston was a tall, elegant boy of twenty, with yellow hair that was much admired and a beautiful lightweight silk suit. His hormones were just as restless as Stoddart's. In fact, Winston was sure that unless something happened to him in a day or two, he would explode all over the peninsula. A common peasant might well have looked at Winston and recognized him as the golden child of fortune who had the lot. From inside Winston's lightweight silk suit, life was actually frightful.

It was a problem of translating sound theory into practice,

and Winston's theory was perfectly delicious. He had arrived at the age of twenty in the fixed belief that lower-class women had no conception of chastity, and all that a man had to do was indicate to one of them that he was ready. Winston was hideously ready.

Winston had acquired his theory partly from living a sickly and sheltered childhood, but it had been consolidated by one horrifying encounter with a nymphomaniac cross-eyed cook when he was fifteen, and later by the teaching of his friend Tony Hammer, who knew everything about women. In an effort to bring the boy out of his shell, Tony had spent months in assuring him that all girls of the lower orders were dying for it. Tony had scores of case histories to prove his point, and both he and Winston had overlooked the fact that they included debutantes as well. In fact, all they proved was that Tony was good at it because he worked so hard at it. Never mind that, Winston accepted the theory as a law of nature. What bothered him was that he couldn't picture himself using the simple, barbaric approach that Tony told him was the goods. He knew he wanted it, and he knew the girls were dying to offer it, but he couldn't think of the right form of words in which to open the discussion.

But surely the difficulty would solve itself in Ochie; because any women in Ochie, apart from his father's guests, would not only be lower class, they would be primitive peasants with it, who spoke a Neanderthal patois and slept with their cattle. This thought did worry him a little, but he was almost ready to take the smell of cattle, just as long as he got started.

So he had a swift concentrated survey of Mary as she went into the Tala with Nat and Stoddart. She was a bit old for him, but not bad, not bad, not even too primitive-looking. He had heard that older women were actually more enthusiastic, and that was something he had to confirm for himself some time. But in the meantime, this particular bit was surrounded by male peasants, and he didn't want any unpleasantness. He mooched along the seafront, noting that there was a high incidence of females in the scatter of sailing dinghies out on the water. The situation was perfect, all systems go, ready for blast-off, and if he could once blast off, and get the knack, he was set for a month that would make Tony Hammer goggle.

There was a sad-looking piece on the beach, walking with hands behind her back and idly kicking stones. She was wearing a short summer dress and she looked quite suitable, but there was also a thick-shouldered oaf mooching along behind her, also kicking stones and probably waiting to jump on her, so she would have to be postponed. Then he saw another specimen, skinny but definitely female, in jeans and a T-shirt. She was sitting on a bollard with her ankles crossed, doing nothing and obviously free and available.

Now it came to the starting point, Winston was infuriated to find his heart banging about in the chest and his wrists prickling; not at all the proper masterful condition as prescribed by Tony. He was panic-stricken in case his voice might tremble or break, and ruin the whole show, and he almost gave up and went home to the Big House. But dammit, a start had to be made some time, and he tried to look like Tony and adopt Tony's head-back posture of command.

"You!" he shouted.

The skinny piece looked round at once. It worked.

"You!" he shouted. That's all. He didn't beckon or move or anything. A little confidence trickled into him. The skinny piece uncrossed her ankles and got off the bollard and walked toward him. She was actually not bad at all. He would be able to describe this one to Tony without having to fake it up. She had short hair and a wide mouth with thin lips. A bit of the devil in her, he thought. She stopped three yards from him and stared at him, definitely interested.

"I'll take you for a walk," he said curtly. His voice didn't tremble too much. What will I do, he reflected, if she starts screaming her head off right now at this moment? But she looked at him and her eyes opened wide.

"Will you?" she said.

"I don't mind."

"Honest?"

"No. Come on."

"You *are* kind," the girl said. It was all *true*. Tony had been right from the beginning, and this was how it was bound to happen — not a gradual warming up, but a sudden decision, in one moment, and the thing was finally done.

"We'll go this way." Winston turned and started walking. He tried not to look to see if she was coming. She wasn't coming. He stopped and turned round.

"Hurry up," he said. The girl moved a few paces toward him and said,

"Are you honestly going to take me for a walk?"

"Why not?" He was carefully offhand and brusque.

"It's too great an honor, sir," she said. Winston's heart rose. Everything was splendid.

"That's all right," he said. "Come on."

He turned, and this time she skipped forward and walked beside him. They walked for a minute without saying anything. It didn't seem necessary to say anything else now that the matter was clinched. Anyway, what could one say to girls like this? There couldn't be much in the way of communication.

He didn't have to think out the route. That was already entirely established in his mind. He glanced at the girl, who was walking with her eyes ahead, smiling to herself. Hot little bitch, he thought, she can't wait. She turned her face to him with an expression he couldn't exactly define. It was probably what people called a simper.

"What's your name?" he demanded.

"Dee. Sir."

"Quite pretty. That your first name?"

"Yes, sir."

"Good."

He turned off the road onto a faint track through the scrubby gorse and she fell in behind him. Two hundred yards farther on, he left the track and sprang up the steeply rising bank.

"Oh sir, you are agile!" the girl said. Winston shrugged his shoulders and held out a hand to help her up. She bounced up beside him. Soon they were forty feet above the path, on a little plateau that dipped sharply. It couldn't be overlooked from any place in Ochie except the top of Tarbie, and there were clumps of bush on that side. The two of them stood and gasped lightly from the climb.

"Are you enjoying it?" Winston asked, on a sudden impulse to be kindly.

"If I had dreamed it, it couldn't be any better," the girl said earnestly.

"Right," he said, returning to the curt manner. It wouldn't do to get too sentimental about it. "This place'll do."

"What for?"

"I think we understand each other," Winston said. "If you like to sit down . . ."

The girl sat down, and looked up at him expectantly. Winston loosened his jacket and dropped it on the peaty grass, and knelt beside her. Ought he to kiss her? Or was that perhaps irrelevant, or bad protocol in a business of this kind? He decided against it. He placed a hand on her chest and pushed her back on to the grass, quite gently.

"What are you doing?" the girl said.

"I think that's obvious."

"You'll never get that zipp loosened with one hand," she said.

"All right." He was irritated and sulky. "You loosen it."

"No. Actually, no."

"Now don't be coy. I can't tolerate coy women." He had straightened up, and the girl lay back again. She uttered a peal of laughter as she stared up into his eyes. He had a horrid thought that having got this far, he might still be balked by a hysterical girlish whim. He threw himself on top of her. She gripped his shirt and arched her body and he rose buoyantly and flew sideways into a clump of gorse, with something unpleasant and squashy in the middle of it. He rolled onto his hands and knees and snarled.

"You need a sharp lesson!"

The girl had leaped to her feet and picked up his jacket. She waved it in front of her body.

"Toro! Toro!"

He lunged at her legs and found himself covered in his jacket and flat on his face as she yelled "Olé, olé!" By the time he got his head clear of the jacket and stood up, she had vanished. He looked round wildly and saw her sitting crosslegged on a rock outcrop eight feet above him. Winston eyed the face of the rock and tensed his muscles. Then he looked up again at the girl. She was smiling again, and moving her right hand up and down experimentally in a karate chop, not looking at him.

There was no sense in it any more. Of all things, he had picked some kind of mental defective, and the really awful thing was that as she sat up there chop-chopping, she looked quite delicious. And she had smelled nice too, rather soapy and clean. He made a manful effort to curl his lip and swung round to walk away in cold dignity and fell over the lip of the plateau and rolled down the gorse onto the path below. He picked himself up and knew that there must be some utterly foul remark he could make. But nothing foul enough came to mind. He took his jacket in one hand and strode back down the path. The girl shouted after him.

"What a shocking mess you've made of your trousers!"

There could be no law and order in Scotland until the aborigines were wiped out to the last man.

FIVE

HUGHIE MACKAY thought Nat was insane to expose himself deliberately to the presence of Maggie Fitzgerald. Even the genial Denis McBain, who tolerated everybody, thought it was making life needlessly horrible.

"She'll suck your blood out through a wee hole in the side of your neck," Hughie warned Nat. "The woman is a vampire as well as being a rampant capitalist. By God, though," he added in admiration, "there is a real expert at the exploitation of the masses, if you like. She's made a fortune without soiling her hands except to run two good men into the cemetery. I always said they should have postmortemed Dod Pringle and Charlie Jackson to find the wee punctures in their necks. Is it not the truth, Denis?"

"She's a hard woman right enough," Denis agreed. "She has a good head for money."

"Do you mean there's a slot across the top?" Nat asked with bright interest.

"A pair of horns is more like it," Hughie said darkly. "I'm telling you the truth, when they bury her they would be better to put a stake through her heart while they're about it."

"She sounds pretty sexy," Nat said.

"Ach, she would eat a man up like a praying manatee," Hughie cried. "If you want to paint anything you would be better painting a nice Highland cattle like everybody else, I believe there's a big demand in America for Highland cattle. Look at poor Davie Fitzgerald, there's hardly a pint of blood left in him."

"No, thanks," said Nat.

"Ach, there's not much wrong wi' Davie if he would only stop the twitching," Denis said tolerantly. "He'll be fine after the funeral."

"If I was you," Hughie Mackay said, "I would wait for the funeral and then make a death mask of her, as long as you don't get your hand caught in her mouth."

"It's people like you that are the ruination of the Highlands," Nat said contemptuously, borrowing Hughie's own insult. "If you're afraid of an old woman, how could you ever destroy the landlords?"

Hughie looked complacent and furtive at this, and Denis McBain looked at him and shook his head.

"It's all nothing but talk," Denis said to Nat. "He's always on about Harper, but there's not that much wrong wi' the man, and if we didn't have him we might have worse."

"Oh, I've got a wee bang or two ready for the laird." Hughie's face was smug and secret. "Do you like a good salmon?"

"My God, you haveny got more dynamite!" Denis was interested at once, and Nat was goggle-eyed.

"If I've picked up a few bits of candle here and there it's nobody's business," he said. "But I think the Long Pool could do with a wee bit of a detonation now the laird is in residence."

"You're a silly sod," Nat said. "You could get all the salmon you like while he's away."

"Ah, the hoor is entitled to a sporting chance," Hughie said. "When he's away I use the rod like any decent man. When he's here I fancy something a wee bit brutal."

"You'll get five years," Nat said.

"It's better than having your blood taken out of a hole in your neck," Hughie said. "I'm telling you, that woman's got hypodermal needles for teeth, like bloody great stomach-pumps they are. Come away and blow up the hoor's salmon and never mind her."

But apart from warning Hughie not to play with dynamite in his absence, Nat dismissed the invitation and went ahead with his reckless plan to visit Maggie Fitzgerald. He had postponed his painting of Ada Fraser, partly to keep the schoolteacher, Stoddart, in suspense and partly because, when Ada arrived to be painted, the big outhouse was still cluttered with rubbish, and Ada had spent the afternoon helping Mary and Harry to clear it out instead of posing for a picture. Nat had regarded this desertion with some resentment, but after watching the operation for half an hour he had decided that Ada was playing hard to get, and also taking the chance of rubbing herself against Harry while they carried broken chairs about; and in a fit of generosity he had decided that she would be easier to pose once she had had her fill of Harry.

Davie Fitzgerald showed him up to the room on the top floor of the Tarbie Private Hotel, in a state of bafflement that anybody should voluntarily visit his wife. He hung back in the corridor and let Nat knock on the bedroom door, and then vanished downstairs, twitching, as soon as Maggie's voice barked from inside.

Maggie was stretched out on an old-fashioned sofa, in a

woolen dressing gown and cotton cap. The sofa was jammed into the big bay window which overlooked most of the village street and the beach. Beside her was a table with several bottles of dark red medicine.

"You'll have to see Mr. Fitzgerald," she said at once, her eyes closed. "I am preparing to meet my Maker."

"What, with half a case of port?" Nat remarked, picking up one of the bottles and sniffing it.

"As the crackling of thorns under a pot," Maggie intoned, "so is the laughter of a fool."

"How is it going, then, Maggie?" Nat asked. He sat in a hard chair beside the sofa and studied her face closely. It was pale and sunk, but the jaw was firmly closed. Maggie opened her eyes and focused on him.

"Though you speak with the tongues of men and of angels, and have not charity, you are become as sounding brass."

"Saint Paul?"

"The great apostle," she agreed, aggressively.

"I think he was a dirty old goat, myself, but have it your own way."

"You're ungodly, like the rest of them. Ochie is the great beast with four heads. Who's that?"

She had turned her head to the window. He stood up and saw a dark-haired girl in the distance, walking along the shingle and kicking stones. "I can't see any distance," Maggie complained. "The Lord has taken my sight."

"Oh well, He giveth and He taketh away. That's show business." Nat had taken a pad from his pocket and was making quick strokes on it. "It's a girl. Sweet wee thing."

"Proud in the flesh," Maggie muttered. "All flesh is grass and the goodliness thereof is as the flower of the field. What are you doing with that pencil?"

"I'm making a quick sketch," Nat said. "Is it all fixed? Are you all set to die whether anybody likes it or not?"

"Graven images," Maggie complained. "Why do you want to draw me? My hair used to come down to my waist. All is vanity."

"If a woman have long hair it is a glory to her," Nat said, surprising himself. "I like you the way you are, so shut up and sit still."

"You don't care if I live or die. Nobody cares. The widow looks for comfort and findeth none."

"What do you want me to do about it?" Nat asked her brutally. "Dying is your idea."

"I'll die in the Lord's good time. Will you draw me with hair down to my waist?"

"Do you want to look like an old tart?" Nat asked. "Nobody told me you had this religious kick."

"It was as black as a raven," she said complacently. "I've always lived by the word of the Lord. Who's that?"

Nat looked out of the window again and saw a fair-haired youth on the shingle.

"It's a bloke trailing after the girl. You should get yourself a pair of glasses and enjoy life."

"Corruption," she said sadly.

"Mm, it makes the world go round," Nat muttered. "Would you like me to do you in oils?"

"I can't afford any money."

"Never mind, I'll get the money from Davie after the funeral," Nat said. "When have you fixed it for?"

"He'll waste it on riotous living. He's a weak vessel, a woman should have strength to lean on. They're all weak, weak men, I've been afflicted with weak men all my life."

"Sh."

She flicked her eyes to the sketching hand and sat still with her eyes staring straight ahead.

"Hughie Mackay says you eat up men like a praying manatee," Nat remarked idly. "Too bad I never met you when your hair was down to your waist."

A pale smile moved her lips.

"Hughie Mackay's a jealous wee nyaff. He never forgave me for taking Dod Pringle instead of him. They all wanted me, in the flower of their lust."

"And yours."

"You're an evil man, you have no compassion for the old and afflicted."

"Do you want compassion? You're talking too much."

She closed her eyes again and pursed her lips and relaxed, and stayed silent for five or ten minutes. Then she started muttering quietly to herself.

"What will he do when my strong right hand is gone? Ach, he's a silly wee man, I should have left him alone. He put me in mind of somebody, that's why I took him, but everything is different, time passes, there's no bad in him except he's weak. Women are strongest; but above all things truth beareth away the victory." She fell silent again, and after a minute, Nat said,

"He's a nice wee man. You should be grateful."

She opened her eyes and smiled at him.

"I don't like motor cars. I always wanted a funeral with black horses. Dod was a good man. He was as strong as a bull. No hair on his chest, as bare as a girl. He always wanted hair on his chest, the poor man. He was as heavy as a big white dog."

"You're a dirty old woman."

"No compassion for the old and the afflicted. You're evil, it is forbidden to make graven images of anything that is on the earth."

"I'll do an extra one with hair down to your waist."

She smiled again and sat back with her eyes closed. When

she opened them, Nat was putting the pad in his pocket and standing up.

"Aye, go," she said. "Nobody left to pity an old dying woman."

"Too true."

"You don't have to come back, I can make my peace alone."

"Have it your own way. Will you still be here on Tuesday?"

"If God spares me."

"I'll chance it."

"How long does an oil picture take?"

"It depends on the Lord."

She pursed her lips at him, and then grinned, and he waved to her casually and left.

Down at the burn bridge, Tom Wishart had just had a nasty jolt. His bike was abandoned on the roadside and he was standing with one foot on the low parapet trying out the opening bars of "Old Man River" two tones lower than he could usually manage it, when he discovered that a strange woman in a violent orange dress was sitting on the other parapet staring at him and listening. It wasn't only the singing that made him embarrassed. He had unknotted his tie and loosened his collar, and was therefore grossly improperly dressed. But when he broke off, startled, the woman actually clapped her hands

"Bravo!" she shouted. "A place where people sing for joy. Let the people sing!"

He scrambled to fasten his collar and knot his tie.

"It's a half-tone too low for me, really," he babbled. "I'm more of a tenor, ha ha. Not that I agree with singing on duty in the normal way."

"Nonsense, people should respond spontaneously to nature, I mean the Life Force, the deep well of . . . sensual vitality . . . I don't express it too well."

"Oh, yes, Ma'am?"

"I'm Stacey Boag. The novelist."

"Yes, I've heard of you," Tom said respectfully. "I'm Constable Wishart." In embarrassment, he took hold of the bicycle and prepared to escape, but she started to walk beside him and he was trapped.

"Tell me everything about crime in Ochie," she commanded. "You can speak freely, I'm terribly discreet."

"I don't know about crime, Ma'am . . ."

"Come now, you can't get out of it like that, I want to know *everything.* I know a lot about human nature, and in a quiet little place like this, that's where the strangest things happen . . . family feuds and scandals and . . . so on."

"Ah, there's not much like that round here, Ma'am," Tom said uncomfortably, wondering if the woman had heard something about the punch-up between the Jackson twins. But she looked up at him coyly and said,

"Is that because we have such a strong arm of the law in Ochie? I suppose you keep them terrified."

"Well, no, Ma'am." Tom had found a favorite topic. "The way I look at it in a place like Ochie, is, we all have to live together, and the job of a constable is to *prevent* trouble. In fact, he's what you might call a welfare officer, solving problems before they happen, like."

"And what kind of problems?" she pressed, swinging along gaily with hips swaying. "That's the point."

"To make you understand," Tom continued doggedly, "oh, there's plenty of constables ready to jump on anybody to make an arrest, but what my idea is, is — Advice rather than Arrest; Prevention rather than Prosecution; Counsel rather than Conviction." Tom spoke ringingly and waited to see the effect. The woman laid her hand on his bare arm excitedly and said,

"I'll write that down as soon as I get home! Do you know that you are a genuine character? A real-life character? Most people are so pallid, you kow, that's what's wrong with big cities — people are all imitations."

Tom's front wheel wobbled, and rather than be thrown, he nimbly dismounted and walked the bicycle with the woman still gripping his arm. She was eating him with her eyes, and it worried him and flattered him simultaneously. He expanded his chest. Not caring to look straight at her, he thought nevertheless that she wasn't at all a bad-looking woman. Not pretty and not very young, but very well built and healthy. A fine figure of a woman, he thought.

"Do you, er, sing?" he asked wildly.

"Oh, now and then. In my bath," she added with a blatant change of tone. He didn't respond to it, but he decided she must be as hot as a ——'s ——.

"The reason I asked, I'm organizing a light operatic society," he said, and coughed. "There's enough talent in the village to put on *The Mikado*."

"Marvelous! But I'm only a visitor."

"Aye," Tom said sadly, "a lot of the talent is only transient. But you could memorize a short part. Maybe I could hear you singing sometime."

Stacey gave him one of her long meaningful looks and cooed, "Is that a simple invitation or are there hidden meanings between the lines?" She wasn't quite sure whether she meant to be languorous and sensuous, or whether she was unconsciously writing-in the part of a tempestuous diva in the book . . . a Chatterley idyll with a simple young demigod

constable . . . maybe not a constable, she could change it
to a . . . a customs officer? Did they have customs officers
in villages like Ochie? When she surfaced, Tom Wishart
was blushing wildly and smirking, and definitely apprehensive. But all he said was,

"I would think a lady with your chest development would
have good volume — I hope you don't mind me talking like
that, it's only the technical language we use in the singing
game."

"Mind! My dear beautiful man, I'm deeply flattered!"
She swung her chest development a couple of times with a
new interest in it, and Tom shot his eyes upward and over
her head and tried not to see it. The weather really was un-
usually warm, and a patch of sweat was springing out on his
forearm under the firm grip of her hand. He was thankful
when Stacey suddenly loosed her grip and turned to screech
at Hughie Mackay, standing in the forecourt of the garage
and lifting a worn tire from the heap beside the pumps.

"Mister Mackay, the craftsman philosopher!"

Hughie hefted the tire on one arm and waved the other
arm, and without a farewell, Stacey strode over to him. Tom
muttered, "Well . . . " and swung his leg across the saddle
and pedaled briskly into the distance, dizzy with visions of
private rehearsals and sudden assaults and great swinging
chest developments bearing down on him.

Hughie Mackay had no very urgent business with the worn
tire. He had been whiling away a lazy few minutes by
emerging from the darkness of the garage in the mild ex-
pectation of having a look at Ada Fraser's legs, only to remember that the butcher shop was closed for the afternoon.
He remembered hearing, in fact, that Ada was up at Kirk
Cottage being painted, and was pondering the puzzle that
Nat Boag was visiting Maggie Fitzgerald instead of taking
Ada's clothes off in his outhouse and manipulating her into

an artistic posture. These reflections didn't drive him mad
with desire, they merely formed a pleasant mumbling background to his pleasure in the warm sun and reminded him
that he wasn't yet senile, since such things could please him.

When Stacey swooped on him, Ada vanished from his
mind, pop. Stacey by no means had the physical distribu-
tion of Ada, but her sheer quantity was overpowering.

"I was just going to brew up," he said, his eyes filled with
the undulating blaze of orange she was wearing.

"Gorgeous, gorgeous, I've been *promising* myself a visit
to your holy of holies and a nice long chat among all the
gaskets and . . . tires and things." He found himself moving backward into the garage on an ocean roller of bright
orange. The tire dropped and rolled unwanted back to its
heap. Inside, he was going to start apologizing for the mess
in the cool dark shed when Stacey tripped on a lump in the
concrete floor. He jerked to catch her and she fell into his
arms.

"My hands are oiled to hell," he said foolishly. She
gripped his shoulders and they stood frozen for fully a second. Her pneumatic body closed against him and he had
the waxy fruity taste of pale lipstick as she kissed him with
all the strength he would have expected. When she broke
away, she appeared to have two mouths, one made of lipstick
and the other, overlapping it obliquely, made of black
grease.

"Don't," she raised a palm, "don't say you're sorry, I accept it as a friendly greeting, my God, if a man isn't made of
flesh and blood he wouldn't be much of a man!"

"No, no, you've got the truth of it there." Hughie eyed
her, with his hands still half raised where they had left her
waist. Another one for luck? But she had loosed a merry
clanging laugh and was turning vaguely away.

"Just show me everything, and I'll brew up the tea," she

cried. He wondered how she was going to explain the two sharply etched handprints on the orange dress.

"I'll get a tissue or something to wipe your mouth," he said. "What a shame, a dirty beggar like me spoiling you."

"You're a thoughtful man, I knew you were the moment I first saw you," Stacey murmured. She closed her eyes and pouted her lips to be wiped clean.

"By God," Hughie muttered to himself, scratching around on his workbench for the packet of tissues, "it's gey warm for July and that's the God's truth."

SIX

THE STODDARTS were a close-knit old-fashioned family, husband, wife and daughter, with no pretensions and a proper sense of rectitude and responsibility. When Martin Stoddart heard of some of the strange escapades of sons and daughters of other teachers in his school in Glasgow, he was grateful that he had built for himself a household in which there was no nonsense. As a husband and father he was firm, but kindly, and he sacrificed many indulgences that he might have enjoyed to provide a good home for his womenfolk. He mentioned this from time to time in case they should overlook it.

Lunch was potatoes and mince, and a steamed pudding. His wife, Isa, put his plate before him and hovered apprehensively until he picked up his knife and fork.

"I met our fancy new neighbor from Kirk Cottage," Martin remarked. The atmosphere at the table relaxed when he started talking again, and Isa nodded enthusiastically at such interesting news.

"Is he nice?" she asked.

"Is he nice?" Martin mimicked. "The word 'nice' means exact, I've told you a thousand times. It does not mean pleasant or agreeable. Is he nice! It's hopeless. He's all right, I suppose. A bit full of himself for my liking."

"He must be well-off, a painter like that," Isa dared to offer. Linda sat and ate, occasionally glancing calmly at one parent or the other and saying nothing.

"Oh, people will pay for anything nowadays," Martin pronounced. "Except education." Isa nodded agreement at this regular truth, and said with instinctive cunning,

"It must be nice for him to meet somebody educated to talk to."

"Aye, there's not many about here," Martin agreed, overlooking the word in a spirit of kindly forgiveness. "I suppose it's a good thing for the village having two professional men in the place. He's got a funny manner. But he's quite an interesting man. I was able to point out some interesting views to him. This mince is quite nice."

"His wife's a . . . a pleasant-looking woman," Isa said.

"She's all right, I suppose." Martin's mind flickered over Mary Boag's bosom and her impression of cheerful relaxation and he added, "She's no chicken, of course. I saw her going into the public bar at the Tala."

"Tck tck," Isa clicked. "But people don't seem to worry about this these days, I expect it's all right in moderation."

"It might be all right for some people, but that's one so-called modern freedom I don't approve of. And don't ever let me catch you," he waggled his forefinger at Linda, "going in for that sort of so-called freedom."

"No, Daddy."

After lunch, Martin settled in the big chair that had been his father's, and put his feet up, to read his paper. Isa and Linda tiptoed about in the big kitchen, washing dishes si-

lently as he allowed his eyes to close, just for a few moments'
rest. After the dishes were washed, he could hear the sounds
of some massive domestic operation beginning. Such
sounds usually soothed him but he couldn't relax as he usually did. His mind kept flicking back to Mary Boag, and
the tidy profile he had studied . . . had accidentally noticed . . . at the bar of the Tala . . . And from there his
thoughts moved in spite of himself to Ada Fraser, a trollop
he fervently despised. His lips pursed as he thought of her
. . . and her tight, tight skirt and the straining buttons of
her blouse. Suddenly there was a long thin hand at the buttons. It was Nat Boag's hand. Martin had a confused impression of an artist's studio reeking of incense and dark red velvet cushions; and the hand meticulously unbuttoning that
painfully stretched blouse and then . . . and then, um . . .
No, too fast. The film went back to the beginning and the
hand started again on the blouse buttons.

"For heaven's sake!" he cried. "What's all the noise
about? Banging and splashing at this time of day!" He
opened his eyes to see Isa's frightened face, flushed and
damp, and her hair dropping over her brow.

"I'm sorry, Martin, I'm washing blankets! I thought you
were sleeping." Linda was at the tub, with her arms buried
in steaming water.

"Sleeping? Sleeping? I never sleep during the day. As
if anybody could sleep in this racket!" As his wife watched
anxiously, he sprang out of the armchair and tightened his
shoelaces and stamped out of the kitchen and into the open
air. A walk, to digest his food. As he went out by the gate,
the splashing and banging in the kitchen broke out unin-
hibited.

He didn't want to think about Ada Fraser, or Nathaniel
Boag. It was none of his business.

It was mere chance that he found himself walking along the Long Pool road, above the village, instead of the seafront where he usually exercised his legs. To get back onto the coast road he would have to walk down the String Road past Kirk Cottage, he realized.

Voices could be heard indistinctly from the garden. Martin stopped to re-tie one of his shoelaces. First he stooped in the roadway. Then he discovered it would be more comfortable to stand up and prop his foot against the retaining wall.

It was difficult to define what voices they were. They seemed to come from the far side of the garden, near the house or the outhouse. But there was a laughing quality about the conversation that could be detected even without hearing the words. It sounded not so much like a conversation as a series of cheerful shouts from people who were doing something physical, the kind of shouts people might make if they were playing tennis, which of course they weren't. Yes, there was the masculine voice, probably Boag's. And a low voice that must be Mrs. Boag's. The slamming of a door.

Then, quite clearly, he heard the throaty coarse laughter of Ada Fraser, breathless and a trifle hysterical.

To his horror, because he abhorred perverted imaginings, he found that he was picturing an entirely new and horrid situation in which both Boag and his wife were implicated in the stripping of Ada Fraser, that in some bizarre and hideous way they enjoyed this disgusting business communally and took an equal delight in the slow exposure of those revolting thighs, while Ada turned her face first to one and then the other, and laughed in a hysteria of depravity.

It was too much to bear. He crept back up the hill where a gap in the retaining wall opened onto the steep path up to the garden. Step by step he moved up the path, peering through the screen of shrubbery and settling his face into a cheerful smile with which to greet anybody who might burst out on him.

A gap through the bushes gave him a sudden view of the garden, half overgrown and half dug up. In the middle of it was a pile of broken wood and old mattresses. Mary Boag was leaning over it sprinkling something on it from a can. She was dressed in shorts and the top half of a bathing suit, and that at least was quite improper, for a woman of her age with a grown-up family. He had not been entirely wrong in believing that the Boags were loose in their habits. Into the narrow view through the bushes came Harry Boag, carrying one end of a wooden-framed bedspring, and after him, carrying the other end, came Ada Fraser, staggering on the uneven ground and giggling like an idiot. She was fully clothed, if the clothes Ada wore could ever be called full.

Somehow this innocent picture of useful industry brought back his irritation more strongly than ever. There was something silly and irresponsible about the way they laughed, and about the blatant exposure of Mary Boag's legs and torso in full view of her own son. It was as if they were laughing at him, and at decent sober behavior — and it was very interesting that they had never invited *him* to Kirk Cottage, where he could have told them that if they were making a bonfire, they were going about it the wrong way entirely.

Torn between the urge to burst in on them and take command of the operation, and contempt for their silliness, he finally crept back down the path and strode down the String Road, shaking his head at the folly of human beings.

He was in time, as he reached the seafront, to see a flash of dazzling orange at Hughie Mackay's garage. On focusing, he translated this as Boag's sister, the so-called novelist. But that was unfair, to transfer his disapproval of the family to her. She was far too noisy and aggressive for a woman, but she was still a handsome figure and she had shown a nice respect for his qualifications as a literary man; and besides, he had the impression that she too didn't really approve of her brother very much. From the distance, through the shimmer of the haze from the hot roadway, he saw her waving to Hughie Mackay and striding off in the other direction.

It might be pleasant to have conversation and company on his walk. He lingered till Hughie Mackay vanished again into the garage, and then set off briskly in pursuit of Stacey.

His motive was simply to pass the time of day, and perhaps talk about the art of the novel. But as he overhauled the vigorous striding figure, his eyes widened. Yes, it was true. He came closer and could be in no doubt that the vivid orange of her dress was marred at the back by two clear black handprints, just on the waist.

Well! It was none of his business if Hughie Mackay had no thought for his wife and marriage vows. But mphm, he thought to himself with slow satisfaction, he had had his instincts about this Stacey Boag. To put it simply, man-mad. Woman, thy name is frailty, he reflected in genial tolerance.

He was two yards from her and overtaking fast, when she stopped and wheeled round and caught him with the private smile on his face.

"Eh, eh!" he babbled. "Warm day, very clement."

"Are you following me?" she hectored him.

"Following? Following? Em, walking, walking, you know . . ." And she needn't look virtuous and hoity-toity either, with that evidence plastered all over her.

"I don't like being followed." Her face was much pinker than usual, and her hands went to her waist, of course, to cover the oily imprints there. His friendly smile invited her to stop kidding, and his eyes went to her waist where even from the front he could see the ends of the two oily smudges. He waved a hand suavely and kept smiling.

"I thought you might like some company on your constitutional," he said.

In all honesty, Martin hadn't gone so far as to think that he too might lay his hands on those oily smudges and press that big firm body against his own. In the bright light of day, in his native village, such a performance would have seemed insane and undignified. He was simply stimulated by the knowledge of a hot-blooded woman who might *like* such a performance, whose warmth was flattering to his masculinity, however unthinkable it might be that anything should come of it. All in all, he merely wanted to enjoy Stacey's feminine companionship.

The hordes of outraged morality, she was thinking, rather enjoying it . . . their faces were distorted with hate and envy as they crowded round the gate . . . one brave spirit found the courage to throw a stone, tinkling of glass, the sound they made was like an angry river . . . no, a swarm of hornets. Did hornets swarm? — swarm of wasps, then, *We know you're in there* . . . the door flew open to reveal a pale figure, her eyes cold and her mouth a red gash in the white blur of her face . . . *What do you want?* Or, *Scum! What do you want?* The ringleader's shifty, bestial eyes couldn't meet her steady gaze . . .

"Huh!" she snapped.

"Eh?"

Stacey came to and curled her lip at Martin Stoddart.

"Did you? Did you really?" She was still standing on the front porch outfacing the lynch mob, and her voice was hard with contempt. "I prefer to walk alone, thank you!" Her eyes swept up and down him, and she almost turned away, then remembered the marks on the back of her dress.

"Oh." Martin stood confused as she glared at him, and then he succeeded in shrugging his shoulders, but he couldn't keep the edge of resentment out of his voice. "Just as you please!" He turned and walked stiffly away. Hell, Stacey thought, he was only trying to be friendly, what have I got to feel guilty about? But it was too late to call him back. She turned and walked on, and was instantly on the front porch again, this time with blood trickling down her cheek from the jagged stone that some heroic member of the mob had thrown. She threw out her chest development and breathed in deeply through her nose in readiness for a blistering line of dialogue.

Isa Stoddart was more than usually bedraggled. She was craning up to the clothesline in the little garden behind the house, fastening the last of five blankets. Her husband came through the side gate and savagely brushed the blanket aside and it flopped wetly against his face.

"Oh, you're back, Daddy," Isa twittered. "I don't know how these blankets get so heavy, it's the water, it's funny how heavy they get when they're full of water, you wouldn't think water could be so heavy."

"Don't bother me with your blankets!" he shouted. "Blankets! And there'll be no dancing for you either, girl. Linda! Where are you?"

Isa ducked under the flopping blanket and pushed her damp hair back.

"I just told her to away and get some fresh air," she said. "She's been helping me all morning, it's not right, a young girl, you're only young once, I said to her, so just away and enjoy yourself, I can manage the rest, it's only right. Oh dearie me, my back, it's a judgment on me, oh dear."

"Oh, she's away, is she?" Martin stood fuming at the kitchen door. "Well, she'll go to no dance tonight, that girl's getting altogether too much freedom and I'm putting my foot down."

"Oh!" Isa thought of something that terrified her.

"What the matter now?"

"She's away with Retta Mackay and she's having tea there and going straight to the dance, Daddy. She thought you said she could go."

"Oh, is she? Is she indeed? We will just see about that!" And as he said it, he knew that he would never go to Geordie Mackay's house and drag Linda home. He could never expose his family shame to a foul-mouthed drunkard like Geordie Mackay. He was a man utterly defeated.

As Isa started to sidle past him into the kitchen, his iron self-control snapped and he swung his hand at the plump rump under the damp overall. She stopped aghast and stared at him.

"Daddy!"

His eyes were glittering at her. She felt quite frightened, and excited.

"It was an accident," he barked.

"Oh, I know, Daddy." She put a hand on his arm, and he gripped it with his other hand. His fingers were kneading her forearm and he was looking past her, at nothing.

"Will I make a cup of tea?" she whispered. "Just for the two of us?"

"Eh? All right, all right."

She backed into the kitchen and he followed her. She kept her eyes on him as she went to the sink and filled the kettle.

"How anybody can wear a flannelette nightgown in this weather," he gritted, "I cannot understand. I'm sick looking at it. Sick sick sick!"

"Yes, Daddy."

It must be the heat, she realized, he's been walking in the sun without a hat. It certainly gave her a funny shiver to look at him, she felt quite heavy and faint.

SEVEN

NAT KNEW AT A GLANCE that a torrid scene had occurred between Stacey and Hughie Mackay. There was only one pair of hands in the village with that degree of black dirt permanently coating them, and when Stacey came into the garden, she turned right round, making sure nobody was there to see her. Nat was sitting on the roof of the outhouse, and with an evil sense of joy he realized that this made him invisible. He thought for a moment of imitating the voice of God and destroying her, but he resisted the temptation in the hope that he might think of something even better. Stacey never thought of looking up. She bolted into the cottage. Oh well, Nat thought, I created the human race with horny passions, I can't complain if they feel like a feel in the hot weather. Mary came out of the outhouse with a bucket of water in one hand, and in an unusual burst of restraint, Nat didn't mention his delicious discovery.

"Don't fall!" she shouted up to him.

"What are you dripping at?" he yelled back, "I can fly, can't I?"

"Just don't fall before I get some new insurance!"

"Bitch," he said. "From up here your legs are only eight inches long, know that? How the hell did I ever marry a penguin?" He reflected idly as she moved away that she looked pretty good for a penguin; also that the heat didn't seem to have driven her mad with lust like Stacey. Considering the narrow shape of the bunk beds, it was probably just as well.

The bonfire in the middle of the garden was still smoldering. Pale blue smoke climbed straight up in a thin line into the hazy blue sky. They had found a comatose lizard in the undergrowth, and Sally had it in a shoe box in the house, trying to win its confidence with bread and jam. Ada Fraser had taken Harry and Dee away to show them the easy route up Ben Tarbie, and Nat figured that Harry would have to stick close to his sister if he didn't want to be raped out of hand.

The outhouse was practically cleared of rubbish, and Mary was systematically flooding the earthen floor because she had discovered stone flags beneath, and it was going to make quite a useful studio. "Grasping slave-masters," Nat muttered, "I'll die before I yield." They had uncovered a crude stone fireplace, and he was sitting astride the roof to cement an old chimney pot into the chimney stack. He thought that if he could overcharge enough, he might give up painting and specialize in cementing chimney pots.

Mary had just come out of the cottage with a fresh bucket of water when Nat froze into his bird-dog pose. A fat man in green knickerbockers had marched up the path from the road and through the screen of vegetation, and was surveying the place with close interest.

"Hello," Mary said. "Warm, isn't it?" She shouldn't, Nat thought, be so damn friendly to nosy-parker landlords and suchlike riffraff. Clearly the intruder was the infamous Harper, hard at work squeezing the lifeblood out of the village and grinding the poor under his jackboots.

"Working hard, then?" Harper's voice surprised Nat. From the fat face and fat body he had expected some North-of-England accent, plain-bloont-man, no roobish. But the tone was Southern and lightly touched with Cockney. "You're new, aren't you?" he demanded.

"Yes." Mary's friendliness cooled to politeness. "Did you want something?"

"No, no. I like to keep an eye on what's going on. You're tidying the place. Not before time."

"Yes, it's badly neglected." Mary couldn't maintain a cold formality for more than a few seconds. "I'm reclaiming the cowshed, or whatever it was."

"Oh?" the fat man became sharp and suspicious. "You can't change the use of it, you know? You know? Not unless you get permission? You know?" His voice had a sharp little automatic lift at the end of each sentence, and everything sounded like a question.

"Permission?" Mary was now drawing herself up to a pose of cold dignity, slightly bent to one side with the bucket of water.

"That's what I said, you know? Permission? You know?"

Nat went into his Ozark character.

"This yere's a little ole rifle," he said, "pointin' straight at yoh haid, so git off'n mah land, shucks, gee willikins!"

The fat man jumped at the sound from heaven, and Mary spoiled the effect by giggling hysterically. Harper finally saw Nat on the outhouse roof, but the sun was in his eyes, and he backed away a step.

"Ah gave yuh fair wawnin'," Nat said. He swung a leg over the roof ridge, ran lightly down the slates in rubber-soled shoes, and leaped off the edge into the garden. Mary screamed. Nat straightened up, still holding a trowel in one hand.

"One, two, three," he said. "Bang. Doan' take on so," he added. Mary was clinging to his arm and giggling. "Yoh' shamin' me befoh strangers."

Now that it was obvious there were no rifles about Harper carried straight on.

"You have to get permission? You know? It's a change in the feu contract?" As Mary was about to speak, Nat pressed her arm for silence.

"We must give the man food and drink," he said, dropping the Ozark routine. "He must be tired and confused. It's a law of this house," he assured Harper earnestly, "no poor traveler is ever turned away."

There were cans of beer and glasses stacked in the shade under the deck chair, and Nat deftly ripped open a can and filled a glass which he offered to Harper solemnly. Harper took it with a knowing smile.

"You can't soft-soap me, you know?" He allowed Nat to take him by the arm and usher him into the deck chair. Nat poured beer for Mary and himself.

"We don't see many strangers in these parts," Nat said. "What's your problem?" Mary wanted to warn him that this fat man looked too hard to play games with, but he was enjoying it too much.

"Problem?" The fat man laughed and tried to relax in the deck chair, which was so low that he had to twist his neck to look up at Nat. "I've got no problems, you know? You've got the problems — you know?"

"Your tale interests me strangely," Nat said. He was lolling elegantly against the cottage windowsill. "Do you always drink beer at this time of day?"

"That," Harper pointed at the outhouse, "that's a cow-shed, you know? It's not a house? Some people think they can turn anything into a house, but it's not on, you know? You have to get permission, apply for a change in the contract? That's your problem."

"Woe and lackaday! I'll go this very afternoon and ask somebody for permission."

The fat man smiled happily.

"You won't get it, you know? You won't get it?"

"Oh, surely, if I ask nicely," Nat cried. "I'll speak to the landlord myself."

"You're speaking to him. You know?"

"My God, Sir! You're not . . ." Nat put his hand to his brow.

"I am!"

". . . the Moderator of the General Assembly of the Church of Scotland!"

"Eh?"

"You look different in your photographs."

"What are you talking about?"

Nat turned stern.

"Are you or are you not the Moderator of the General Assembly of the Church of Scotland? Come on, don't quibble."

Harper appealed to Mary.

"Is he daft? You know? I'm your landlord. I'm Arnold Harper. This is my land."

"No, no, no." Mary shook her head sadly. "This is glebe land. It belongs to the Church of Scotland."

"I don't believe it, you know?"

"Do you mean to say," said Nat, "that I've been plying you with liquor and you aren't even a parson?"

"Are you sure?" Harper's smile had vanished. "Let me see your feu contract, you know?"

"Get stuffed," Nat said.

"What did you say?"

"Please, Nat. It's a natural mistake."

"I don't make many mistakes, you know?"

"It's the heat, and that thick tweed. A lot of people go off with the cafard in suits like that," Nat said kindly. "Oh, this is Mrs. Boag, the eminent Mrs. Boag. It's her land you're sitting on."

Harper wrestled with the sad discovery that he wasn't everybody's feudal lord. This cut him off from human contact for some seconds. Then he stared at Nat.

"You're Boag, the painter johnny? I've heard about you."

"Life is full of these shocks," Nat said. Mary gave him up, and took the bucket of water into the outhouse. Harper persuaded himself into friendliness.

"I can take a joke, you know? I suppose you types always carry on different from other people? I knew you didn't have a rifle, you know? Quite amusing, that."

"Tell me, Arnold," Nat came off the windowsill and squatted on a broken box. "How is the feudal landlord trade, eh? Have you evicted any good peasants lately?"

"Ha ha! More like them evicting me, you know?"

"By Gad, it sounds like a desperate life. Have another beer."

When Mary emerged from the door of the outhouse, sweeping a river of mud out into the garden, she wasn't too surprised to find Nat and the fat man talking like old friends, or at least, talking and looking like old friends. Most men, even tough fat men, managed to swallow Nat's open insults as the natural exuberance of an eccentric. She didn't like Harper. From inside the cottage she could hear furious unrhythmic typing. Stacey must have found some kind of inspiration during her afternoon walk. Sally would be sitting in the kitchen, with her shoe-box full of lizard on her knees, staring at the typewriter and longing for a chance to batter the keys.

Harper paused in the middle of a monologue, in his odd nasal voice with the jump at the end of every sentence, and Nat, serious and respectful, suddenly leaned forward and said,

"I don't know, you know? You keep asking me if I know, but I don't."

Harper looked puzzled, and then said,

"Oh! That's a mannerism, you know? Eh?" and went straight on. "They think it's all beer and skittles, you know? But I have to think of my children and grandchildren, eh? There's no money in it, you know? No real cash. Some of these houses, you know? only pay a few pounds a year. And they grudge it, you know?"

"Disgusting."

"Well, naturally, you know? say that outhouse, for instance, somebody wants to make it into an extra room — it's plain business, if the landlord's going to agree to the property being mucked about like that, it's a new contract, you know? Naturally he's going to shove the rent up?"

"No, I don't know," Nat said, and poured more beer into Harper's glass. "You're rotten with money, you know? You don't need any more. It's very unedifying, watching a man like you screwing lolly out of the poor hicks in Ochie. You should be bloody ashamed of yourself, you know?"

"Ha ha ha!" It was obvious that Harper knew he was talking to a court jester. "Poor hicks. Take the shirt off your back, you know? They don't know they're living?"

"You're quite right." Nat nodded in sympathy. "They're an ungrateful shower. Why the hell don't you do something about that coast road? Was it you that torpedoed it?"

"Ha ha ha, that's good. Eh? No, no, eh? That's County

Council work. Well, it's not, you know? But who's going to pay for it, eh? They don't appreciate finance. Eh?"

"By God, you're a real wit, Arnold. It's men like you that made the British what they are today," Nat was saying, and Mary disappeared into the cottage to make coffee. Making coffee was one way of dissuading Nat from working his way through all the beer in the house, and she resented the sight of beer being fed to the fat, complacent laird, who must have millions and didn't need to sponge off the new-rich Boags. But when she came out with coffee on a tray, Harper was gone, and she slipped swiftly into the deck chair before Nat could take it.

"Bastard," he said happily.

"Me?"

"Oh, you too. But that Harper is a sweet bastard, I must screw him up."

"Gad gad gad," Mary said. "I'm telling you, Nat Boag, I'll lock you in the cellar if I hear you talking like that."

"Do you like him?"

"No. I don't know." She poured herself a cup of coffee. "Just leave him alone. I thought you were going to paint like a demon."

"One thing I will say, he had the good taste to stare at your abdomen all the time."

"He didn't."

"He did, and why the hell not? It's all right, kid, you've got a good abdomen, you know?"

"You don't stare at it."

"All right, I'll stare at it."

"Well."

"Well, I'm staring, Goddammit. Hughie Mackay is right, we ought to stage a popular uprising. I'll ask Hughie to build a tumbrel tomorrow. Christ, I know, we'll import a boatload of Chinese coolies and rebuild the road, that would fix his wagon. We could do it in dead of night with muffled shovels."

"What *for?*" She could almost believe that he would find a boatload of Chinese coolies.

"Repopulate the Highlands, Hughie Mackay says. It's the only way to defeat the fascist beast landlords. Weight of numbers. That fat sod hopes everybody in Ochie is aiming to die off and leave room for grouse."

"You're not staring any more."

"Dammit, woman, I'm not a voyeur. Anyway, that sex bit isn't practical in your house. I can't climb in the dark, can I? He's really a fan of mine, Arnold. He thinks he might let me paint his wife."

"Green?"

"That is my joke, and you know it. Do you think I could twist a thousand guineas out of him? *That* would kill him."

"He would probably expect you to pay *him*. I'm glad you told him to get stuffed. He looks stuffed already, though."

"I didn't actually tell him to get stuffed, I played it foxy so that we can get a free dinner out of him. These rich sods always like to suck up to celebrities like me."

"You're disgusting," she said equably. He stood up and stretched himself. Most people would say he was too skinny, but I like his bones, she thought, and irritably wished that he would stare at her abdomen again, or pat it, or do something. She cursed the inspiration that had led her to buy bunk beds, very space-saving, very useless. He seemed so cheerful about it, and so self-sufficient, that her interest in him shamed her, after half a lifetime of marriage. I'm exaggerating everything, she reminded herself, maybe it's only the heat of the sun.

"Back to man's work," Nat said. He picked up the trowel from the ground and stuck it in his hip pocket. He bent his knees and jumped up to catch onto the guttering on the low eaves of the outhouse, to swing himself up onto the roof. A three-foot length of guttering came away in his hands and he fell back into the earth still gripping it. Mary sat up and clapped her hands.

"Again, again!" she shouted. She was surprised by her delight. He lay on his back with the piece of guttering held above his head and muttered Bitch bitch bitch. Joyously she laughed.

The heat of the day wore on into an evening that was only slightly cooler. The lads of the village left jackets and ties at home when they set out for the village hall, most of them using the Tala as a staging post. In the public bar, the old cronies had resumed the argument about which other year had been sunny in July. There was almost a feeling of resentment at the unbroken spell of hot weather. It upset the predictable nature of the natural universe.

Hughie Mackay insisted that there had been a month of sunshine in July, 1952, but his brother Geordie claimed that that was the year when the ferryboat had been blown up onto the main road by the summer gales. Andy Anderson couldn't remember real sunshine since 1940, when he had been promoted corporal in the Argyll and Sutherland Highlanders and mentioned in dispatches for his skill in making custard on a field kitchen.

The lads of the village, together with a crowd of aliens from the Youth Hostel, jammed the lounge bar and desperately drank pints of beer and poured with sweat. The lassies of the village wilted wearily in the village hall hoping the Tala would close early or run out of liquor so that the dance could start before it was time to go home.

It was after nine o'clock when Geordie Mackay swung into the hall, steaming, and opened the upright piano. He was greeted with apathetic cheers, and he turned and bowed owlishly to the knots of lassies and the few teetotal lads. His twelve-year-old son Jamie followed him and unwrapped an assembly of drums. Without warning Geordie leaned over the keyboard and threw himself into a medley of "California," "My Love She's But a Lassie Yet," and "Silver Threads Among the Gold." It was the age-old tradition of the Ochie dances; no announcements and no quarter. Geordie could play nearly anything, in the key of C, and mostly in the same tempo. Sally Boag instantly dragged her brother Harry out onto the floor and danced.

There had been the usual noisy battle before anybody would consent to be seen in her company in public, but Sally was accustomed to the noisy battles and she won them. Harry gave in easily, usually. He didn't even object to dancing with her. As they whirled, Harry kept turning so that he could look toward the door. She was there, talking to a very fat, discontented girl in the wrong dress. Or rather, the fat discontented girl was talking, and Linda was listening placidly and nodding from time to time. It might be that she was silent because she was dim, of course. But he would soon find out.

Dee was sitting on a wooden bench, doing her Scarlet O'Hara glitter. Harry wanted to advise her to turn it off until there were more of the lads there to see it, but it was a waste of energy to advise Dee. She sat and looked dangerous, in an unaccustomed dress instead of jeans. Harry saw a boy approaching her and muttering, saw Dee look him up and down with infinite weary distaste, and then stand up and consent to make him miserable by dancing with him.

At least her idiot posture of contempt seemed to get results, and it was time he got some results himself. He fended Sally off when the dance finished, and edged toward the girls by the door. There was a roll of drums, and he started forward. The fat girl, watching him out of the back of her head, turned at once and walked into his arms and swung him savagely into a kind of waltz.

"Nice night," he said wildly.

"Hm, I suppose so," she agreed, clearly resenting it.

"Do you come here often?"

"When I feel like it." This girl was obviously stung to the quick by any witty sallies. But when he stopped trying, she glared at him and asked,

"You gone dumb or something?"

"Uhuh, a bit."

"Hm!"

How was it that girls like Linda always, but absolutely always, managed to get teamed up with vampire bats?

"My name's Harry Boag," he said after further whirls, and the fat girl said,

"Huh! That must be nice for you." There was something almost akin to humor buried under her suspicion of mankind. "I'm Retta Mackay, if it's any of your business."

"That must be fun."

"Very funny."

It was all right dancing with the fat girl, because she was a convenient way of getting to Linda, but he was disappointed to find that the lads were beginning to filter into the hall; and although they grouped in masculine knots and ignored the girls, they were liable to rush Linda before he could grab her. In fact, unless they were insane they were bound to rush Linda. One of them, a black-haired swaggerer whom he knew to be Archie McBain from the hardware shop, was in fact hovering beside her, very poised, very arrogant and very husky in tight trousers and a thick white sweater.

Harry decided it was time he became a man of bold single-minded decision. When he led Retta back to the milling crowd by the door, he braced himself to approach Linda at once. In the confusion he thought she briefly smiled to him, but Retta crossed in front of him and grabbed Archie Mc-Bain familiarly and blotted out his approach. As he shuffled and feinted to get round them, his arm was seized in a death grip by Ada Fraser, who had appeared from nowhere.

"I don't mind, if you don't," she said. It was frightening, how she managed to be banal and sinister at the same time. Geordie Mackay was rattling a long chord on the piano in C major.

"You're not slow, are you?" Harry's disappointment was mellowed by the fact that at least one girl, two in fact, had now positively rushed him.

"In this place? You canny afford to be slow," Ada said, filling the words with strange murky undertones. Even before the music started he was aware of her breasts pressing lightly against him like exploring fingers. People started doing some kind of twist, or bird, or dog, or whatever it was they were calling it in Ochie. She released her hold of him and swiveled herself from the hips. It was the kind of dancing that made him feel foolish and conspicuous, but he shook his shoulders obediently and bent his knees. Ada's eyes were half-closed, but the open halves were concentrated around his navel. He was surprised to find that she danced with rigorous control and the minimum of movement. It was dangerously fascinating to watch. He tried not to think about her, but to think about Linda. Then he thought he shouldn't even be thinking of Linda, but of Magda. Then he decided that since Magda was in the South of France he might as well think of Linda; and that since Linda was dancing with somebody else he might as well carry on looking at Ada and make life simple. She lifted her eyes for a moment and stared into his, with her face blank and heavy and frightening. Then she dropped her eyes again to his navel and jerked her hips.

By the time he succeeded in dancing with Linda, the little floor was crammed with bodies and noise and heat. He held his right arm round her rigid, barely touching her but fending off other people. He was delighted with her air of quiet coolness and the cool dry feel of her palm.

"I like your hair," he said. She flicked her eyes into his face and away again and muttered, "Thank you very much." This was great. Harry had a system of judging girls by their responses to a compliment. If they said thank you, they were absolutely alpha plus. The two of them shuffled on the spot, dodging elbows and feet.

"I've seen you at the beach," the girl murmured. Somebody crashed into his back, and they were squeezed together, and he started to apologize and the girl shook her head to say that no apology was necessary. Suddenly they both said together,

"We're here for the month."

And then both said,

"So are we."

Harry laughed, and the girl laughed, rather shyly.

"Can I see you home?" he asked her without any further fencing. She started to shake her head again.

"I'm with a girl friend," she said, trapped and worried.

"I'll see her home too."

"I don't think I could."

"What, has your father got a shotgun?" he asked wittily, and realized it wasn't very witty when she blushed and looked away. It was a dire and desperate way of getting to know anybody, trying to make social chitchat in the middle of a thundering stampede of Highlanders and English youth-hostelers spattering sweat over everything.

"Can I see you tomorrow?" he demanded, and the girl said doubtfully, "I suppose so."

"Hot, isn't it?"

"Yes, it's lovely." How sweet she was, to think it was lovely and not complain about it.

"I'm going out for some air," he said masterfully. "Come on." It worked. She started to shake her head, but she didn't resist when he pulled her though the crowd by the hand and out of the open door. It was still inconveniently bright and sunny outside. In the South of France, at least darkness came down at a reasonable hour.

"My name's Harry," he said.

"I know."

"That's very clever of you." This sounded too juvenile, too smart-alecky. "Well, everybody knows everybody in a place like this."

"Yes."

She really was sweet, with her quietness and her gentleness, but he wished she would be fiery and adoring as well as quiet. She hadn't tried to take her hand away from his, and he squeezed it. There was no answering squeeze.

"Do you have to go home with your girl friend?"

She nodded.

"I don't mind taking you both home," he insisted, and again she began to shake her head. Retta Mackay, the fat girl, emerged from the doorway.

"Are you supposed to be dancin' or lookin' at the moon?" she demanded, and Linda looked round guiltily and said, "I'm just coming."

"In a minute," Harry said masterfully, waving Retta away, but she didn't disappear.

"I know your type," she said. "Come on, Linda, I've been standin' in there like a fool." Petulant and possessive. As Harry kept his hold of Linda's hand, Retta flounced back through the doorway. Linda started to move after her.

"She doesn't own you!" Harry protested.

"It's not fair to leave her all alone." Linda was soft and easily dominated, but it seemed that Retta had got in first to dominate her, and he knew he was beaten. "I'm sorry," she said, but it was hard to tell why she was sorry, or whether she was merely being polite. He slouched into the hall behind her, detesting fat Retta. Ada Fraser put a hand under his elbow and propelled him into the horrifying exertion of an eightsome reel. Watching Ada's blank, purposeful face, he was miserably confused about his own feelings. He suspected that his passion for Linda was selfish, that he wanted to get closer to her because he would then be able to picture himself with this deliciously pretty girl adoring him, and picture Magda there too, somewhere, seeing them together and realizing that he, Harry, was marvelous and desired by beautiful women.

But even without that complication, he felt sullen and hostile toward fat Retta, yes, the eternal vampire who always turned up in the company of some gorgeous girl so that she could get a share of the boys, or swallow up the gorgeous girl and keep the boys away, to spite them for not being crazy about her. Sally was dancing in the same ring, with a plump life-of-the-party hosteler with a loud English voice and a buffoon style of making the dance a big gag, quaint-Scotch-folklore-nonsense.

It was growing dark when Geordie Mackay ended the dance by slamming down the lid of the piano and making for the door with fast unsteady steps, pulling a whisky bottle from the jacket pocket and waving people aside. Already groups of people were collecting outside, to the music of merry shouts and falling bottles. Harry lingered among them, unwilling to leave.

In a disgusted revelation, as he stood in the shadow of the corrugated iron building, he saw the arrogant Archie

McBain irresistibly taking the arms of Linda and fat Retta and marching them off into the moonlight. Retta sounded protesting and delighted. Harry looked round for Dee and Sally, and carefully put on his cheerful uncaring face. Dee, the man-hater, was amazingly clinging to the arm of a tall youth with red hair and ogling him sweetly. He heard her saying, "It's so *kind* of you, I love company on the way home." The red-haired youth laughed in lecherous understanding, and Dee went on, "Sally! Sally, where are you? Take Eric's other arm." The three set off along the coast road. Eric's shoulders had sagged and he had stopped laughing.

Harry gave them time to disappear, and shrugged his shoulders and started to follow them. As he made his way among the knots on the road, he found his way blocked by Ada Fraser and a tall young man with blond hair. The young man had his hand on her shoulder and was laughing a braying laugh. Ada twisted out of his hold and said, in a strange affected voice,

"Ow, there you are at lawst, Harry, Ai had nearly given you up. Olive oil, well, Mr. Harper!" She grabbed Harry by the arm.

"Here," the young man said. "Just a moment, I'm speaking to you!"

"I'm afraid we have a previous engagement, bad luck," Ada said in wild gaiety. She forced Harry into a brisk trot.

"One moment. Damn!" the young man shouted after them, but she waved her free hand foolishly and kept on going.

"Popular," Harry gasped. "You've got them all, haven't you?"

"Huh! That one? Does he fancy hisself? Thinks you're easy because you work in a butcher's shop. He can get in the queue."

She slowed down to a rapid march.

"Is that one of *the* Harpers?" Harry asked curiously.

"Think they own you, that lot. No, thank you."

"I don't blame him for trying," Harry said with glum gallantry.

"Huh. That type's got one idea, they don't think a girl's got any self-respect."

Winston Harper, bulging with anger, had started to stride in pursuit and reassert his authority, but as he stared at Harry's thick shoulders he recognized that life was excessively troublesome. He stared furiously around as the knots of dancers dispersed and loped away in all directions, leaving him with the moon and his fury. He was not going to put up with much more of this.

Ada, who rarely uttered more than a short sentence at a time, surprised Harry by gabbling as they walked along the road in the moonlight.

"Men, honestly, the way they carry on, only one idea, you would think they could think about something else for a change, they think you're going to jump at them if they whistle, girls aren't like that, a girl has to be able to take care of herself or God help her, the way they carry on do they never think about anything else?"

"What else is there to think about?" Harry asked, trying to be roguish.

"I don't like that kind of talk," she said coldly.

"Sorry."

"Granted."

She was still holding his arm close to her side, and as they walked, her hip now and then bumped softly against him. They arrived at a narrow lane overgrown with thorn hedges.

"I live up here," Ada said.

"Oh. Well, goodnight." As there was a silence, he added, "Or do you want me to walk you up the lane?"

"I don't care one way or the other. It's dark, but . . ."

"Okay."

It was, densely dark. He stumbled on a stone, and Ada, with a little squeal, seemed to be trying to support him, but succeeded in sending him headlong beside a tree. He sat up to feel her kneeling beside him.

"It gets awful dark up this lane," she said, conversationally. "It's all right in the daytime but nighttime? It gets that dark you canny see before your eyes. Are you all right?" She had sat beside him.

"Yes, quite comfy."

"I've fell often, at the same place, but you get to know it better if you live here." Her hand was across his shoulders, and he tentatively put an arm across her body and gripped her at the waist.

"You've got a nice cuddly waist, Ada," he said.

"I told you I don't like that kind of talk," she said. He took his hand away at once, and would have got up, but her hand was heavy and firm on his shoulders, and to his wonderment, she pressed herself against his arm.

"It's murder in winter, believe me," she remarked. "People that come here in the summer, they've got no clue what it's like in winter, of course it's quieter, there's not much work, but the weather! Sometimes the boat canny get across for three or four days." As she spoke, her other hand had slipped inside the open neck of his shirt and was patiently massaging the soft flesh under his arm.

"Mind you, it's murder in that shop in this weather," she went on. "The meat! I would chuck half of it out. It's murder. There's not many flies about now, mind you." She had, yes, she had quite positively, undone two of his shirt buttons. In a dream, Harry heard himself saying, "I don't suppose there'll be any dances in the winter," while at the same

time he resumed his grip on her waist and squeezed it luxuriously in his fingers. She moved closer to him.

"You don't get the customers," she agreed. "Mind, that
youth hostel crowd's a funny lot, you don't know where you
are with that crowd. I suppose some of them are all right, I
just don't like the way they talk, some of them, you have to
put them in their place, I like a boy that's got good manners,
the manners of some of them you would wonder how they
got brought up, the least they could do is show some respect."
The hair on the back of his neck was prickling, and he con-
tracted his stomach muscles as he realized that her hand was
trying to slide down his chest past his waistband.

"I don't suppose they mean any harm," he said, struggling
for casual conversation to cover the fact that he was trying to
unfasten the top of her skirt and doing it rather clumsily
with one hand. She pulled her own hand out from inside his
shirt, and through the pounding in his ears, he heard her in
the distance saying, "Well, it shows the way they're brought
up, I don't think they get the education like us, what is it
you're learning at the university?" The hand she had freed
now descended on his own, and he thought she was prizing
his exploring fingers away, but she forced his hand down her
side to where he discovered he was touching a big button.
Without troubling to conceal his clumsiness, he undid it.
Ada removed her own hand at once and laid it on his
diaphragm, which she started to churn slowly.

"Eh, it's an Arts honors course," he said inanely, as his
hand moved farther down and found another big button. In
the gap that had opened in her skirt he felt an unadorned
area of warm smooth Fraser. "Actually," he said, "I should
be doing a lot of reading down here, but it's hard to concentrate in this weather."

"Oh, Arts? You coming out for a painter like your Dad?

I don't think I would like that, painting all day, I don't know how people can have the patience, I quite like nice pictures, mind you, but artists must be a funny lot, it's a funny way to make a living." There was the sharp rasping sound of a zipp fastener moving and he felt two damp fingers on his abdomen.

"No, Arts isn't the same thing as an art course," he said, with a squeaking break in his voice, and wrenched the last button open. Ada slid downward and the thighs freed from the constriction of the tight skirt stretched comfortably. He had a terror that he would run out of meaningless chatter.

"I'm specializing in modern languages," he burbled. The median area, he thought, that part of the thigh is called the median area. He coughed and said, "I haven't made up my mind what I'll do with them, if I do get through."

"It would give me a headache, all that reading, I don't know how people can do it for years and years, it's bad enough working in a butcher's shop." He jerked as her hand suddenly closed tight. "Still, it's a living," she said breathily. "If you live in a place like this, what can you do? There's not that many jobs you can get." Experimentally, he closed his hand on the soft flesh so tightly that it must have hurt. "Well, it's life," she said, "you could be worse off, at least it's steady work, people have got to eat."

"Yes." He knew that his conversation had dried up for-ever. He moved his hand violently and her body clenched in his grip. "That's right," he said lamely. He was sure the veins must be standing out like snakes on his forehead. He couldn't, he felt sure, he, couldn't, say, an, other, word, word, word.

"I expect a lot of people at the university come out for teachers," she said, and her other hand moved down his back and almost hoisted him off the ground. "Kids all day long, I don't know how they can stand it." He wouldn't have to say another word, word, word, he decided. Ada had invented the talking system and she had it licked. She was pulling him bodily as she might have pulled a bull by the ring in its nose, and he had the impression that she was talking earnestly about the terrible difficulties of transport between Ochie and the big towns like Oban. He let the words dribble past his head, and after a momentary thought of Magda, he stopped thinking and listening. He thought he might kiss her, but a kiss might disturb the train of her conversation. He kissed her ear, and then her jugular vein as she gripped him with brutal hands and moved him and said, "Even the road, that's murder if you're driving a car, you wouldny get me in a car on that road for a hundred pounds, mind you the boat's no' much better especially when Geordie's had a drink, you would think — " she stopped talking. A few moments, or minutes, later, she said, "You would think a man would keep off the drink when he was driving a boat, he's a terrible man that Geordie Mackay."

"He's a grim pianist as well," Harry said. He sat up. "I like this weather, though."

"Aye, it's really quite nice. Here, it's time I was away home, you'll be getting your books for being late."

"No, it's all right . . . Thanks for the dance."

"Don't mention it, I'm sure." She was standing up brushing her skirt with a casual hand.

"Well, goodnight."

"Olive oil!" She vanished up the darkness of the path. Harry walked down to the roadway. He muttered, "Aye, it's quite nice working in a butcher's shop, mind you I don't think much of the tourists but what the hell archy it's a living on the other hand the transport system is a national disgrace pow pow *pow*." He shook his head from time to time as he floated along the road.

*

Martin Stoddart sat in his cottage kitchen, reading a library book, while his wife Isa knitted on the other side of the fireplace. She kept a furtive and apprehensive eye on him. There was sure to be a barney when Linda got home, but if she had the sense to bring Retta Mackay home with her, that would save a lot of trouble. Martin stared at the page of his book, breathing tightly and preparing to crush the weakness and vicious sensuality of the female race, and wondering how he could somehow make this work on Stacey Boag.

At Kirk Cottage, Stacey was at the table by the window, ostentatiously closing her ears and correcting pages of typescript with a green ball-point. Sally was crouching by the empty grate offering a chocolate biscuit to a sickly-looking lizard in a shoe-box. Mary was pouring tea at the table for Nat and Dee and this nervous young Eric individual. Nat was eyeing him earnestly and saying,

"I take it for granted your intentions are honorable, because you're obviously a gentleman by breeding and because the alternative would be too terrible and gory to contemplate."

Dee raised her eyes to the ceiling and muttered "Oh God!"

"Eh?" Eric said. He knew it had been a mistake to get himself persuaded to come into this house. Now he was wondering if it had been not merely a mistake, but an act of suicide.

"I don't intend to go into distasteful details," Nat said. "Hey, do you like these chocolate biscuits? They're yummy." Behind him, Mary shook her head indulgently. Eric took a chocolate biscuit and tried not to look at Dee. She fascinated and terrified him. The perspiration that had cooled on his shirt was warming up again.

"Hellish hot weather," Nat said kindly, and Dee smiled a secret smile.

EIGHT

THE POSTCARD didn't make any requests or leave any loopholes. It simply said, "Only just this minute found out you not at home, been looking forward to good old reunion after all these years, can we arrive Tuesday? Yr Affec. Cousin Louise and family." Mary read it three times with a sick feeling of disaster.

"It's a damn long trip for a paddle in the sea," Nat said. "But your family are all a bit unbalanced, aren't they? Is she the one they keep chained to a ring in the cellar?" He was in the outhouse, stripped to the waist. He had torn an old chest of drawers to pieces and he was screwing the pieces together, quite skillfully, to make a workbench. She reckoned that if he finished this in one operation it would be fine. If he interrupted the work it would never be finished, and he would probably never put a brush to canvas either. She knew now what he meant about the dreaded West Coast Rot. In the relaxing air, and especially in the hot sunshine, it took a massive effort of will to do anything useful at all.

"I wish I thought they were only coming for a paddle in

the sea," she said bleakly. "They would have to leave home
the night before to catch the morning ferryboat. If they get
the afternoon boat they're stuck here for the night at least."

"So?" He still had the childish habit of sticking out his
tongue to one side when he was concentrating, and it was
stuck out now while he gripped a hand drill and bored
through the old mahogany. "We'll have to put another gal-
lon of water in the stew, I suppose. We've got plenty of
blankets, haven't we?"

"Oh, Nat!" She sat down miserably on a creaky wooden
chair. "I thought you would get peace and quiet here.
That's why I wanted the cottage."

"In Ochie?" He hooted. "Christ, it's like a three-ring
circus. We'll never notice a dozen extra bodies."

"But who wants to be cluttered with relatives? I might
have known it. Buy a cottage and you're a sitting duck. You
don't know Louise."

"Every leedle breeze seems to weesper Louise," he
crooned, and then tried to be reasonable. "You never complain about *my* relatives. God knows we've got them oozing
out of the floorboards most of the time. Bastards. You can
kick Stacey out to make room for Louise. Is she seductive?"

"There's nothing wrong with Stacey."

"Nothing that a swift kick in the fat behind wouldn't
cure," he agreed. "There, there, try not to worry, little one,
your relations can arrive in herds if they like. It's about time
your family sickened me for a change."

"We'll have to use the air beds," she said vaguely. It was
obvious that Nat wasn't going to worry about the approaching catastrophe of Louise and family, and he was really trying to reassure her. But she discovered that she was sincere
in saying she didn't object to Stacey. With all her nonsense,
Stacey kept out of the way most of the time, combing the vil-

lage and making up fairy stories; and when she was around the cottage, she didn't hesitate to wash dishes and shift furniture and generally pitch in. And it was also impossible to offend her, she was too confident of her own superiority. It wouldn't be the least bit impossible to offend Cousin Louise.

In the kitchen, Harry was inefficiently nailing a scrap of chicken wire on top of an apple box, to make a luxury home for the ailing lizard, and Sally was crouching at his feet with a handful of nails in one hand and the animal in the other. Stacey was standing at the sink dressed in ill-advised slacks and brassiere, washing her hair. She had no delicate feelings about going about the house half-naked, and the kids ignored her, and that was fine with Mary. Cousin Louise would probably have an embolism at such a sight.

"The water's as hard as . . . as hard as flint," Stacey said cheerfully. "Flint? As hard as . . ."

"Charity," Sally suggested, and Stacey shook her head in weary disgust.

"My cousin's arriving tomorrow," Mary said, holding out the postcard. "And Family." Stacey was wrapping a towel round her head, and she immediately looked shattered and rejected.

"Do you want me to move down to the boardinghouse?"

"No, no, no! But everybody's going to have to squeeze."

"I don't mind moving if you like." Stacey minded so obviously that she looked like a monstrously overgrown beaten puppy, and Mary answered with a touch of irritation.

"I don't want you to move and that's final."

"Nobody's getting my bed," Sally said quickly, and Harry said, "Oh yes, they are, and you'll sleep on the stone floor with the rats gnawing you all night."

"I would hit them with the poker, crunch crunch crunch!"

"You will sleep where you are told to sleep," Mary told

her, and Sally, about to fight for her rights, detected a steely note and shut up and looked hurt, which was just dandy, Mary thought. Cousin Louise hadn't even arrived yet, and already she was undergoing a personality change.

"I'm jack-easy," Stacey said, "I can sleep on a razor blade." Sally laughed merrily and terrified the lizard.

"You're far too big for a razor blade," she yelled. Harry thumped her on the top of the head to silence her.

"We'll arrange something." Mary sighed. It was, it must be, fifteen years since she had seen Cousin Louise, but she was sure she had Louise's sudden reappearance completely analyzed. It would never have happened if Louise hadn't become aware that Nat had arrived in the money, and the notoriety, exhibitions in London and paragraphs in the newspapers. Why else could Louise have possibly emerged from the past? And the cottage, of course. There *was* something about the cottage at the coast that drove people frantic with chumminess.

"Is Cousin Louise my cousin?" Sally asked, trailing after her as she climbed upstairs to the attic bedroom, and tickling the lizard's belly to make it happy, and Mary answered absentmindedly, "No, your aunt. No, your second cousin. I'm not sure."

"Who begat her?" Sally was in the middle of a passion for the Old Testament.

"Your grandfather. No, your great-uncle. Shut up and go away."

"And with that, she exited pursued by bear," Sally muttered. "Nag nag nag."

Mary found that she was hearing this well-worn litany with the ears of Cousin Louise, and pursing her lips in imitation prim horror.

She suddenly thought of black lacing shoes. She had

buried the thought of black lacing shoes in her unconscious for years, but with the reappearance of Louise, they jumped up to make her cringe. That was a laugh, after so many years, that she could still cringe.

In memory, the black lacing shoes appeared as great thick-soled industrial boots, though of course they couldn't have been as awful as that. But they had been awful enough.

She hadn't wanted to go to the dance at all. Well, she had wanted to go to the dance. She had been desperate to go to the dance, crackling with excitement and joy about it. It had been her first real dance, not a children's party but a sophisticated affair, only Sunday School teachers and members of the church choir and no rackety children; and a genuine live quartet, piano, drums, violin and trumpet. That was really living. She even had a startling adult dress, almost with bare shoulders — it had belonged to one of her older sisters, and her mother had taken it in to fit Mary's sixteen-year-old thinness. It was dark blue and she thought it was marvelous, so close-fitting that it had to have a fastener running down the back right to her tail.

But there were no sisters' shoes to fit her feet. She simply had big feet. Louise hadn't. Louise had tiny sweet little feet, which Mary had suspected obscurely at the time were probably the result of being rich. Louise was an only child, and Uncle Brian was a clerk with the County Council, and Louise had everything: bikes and tennis rackets and clothes and a holiday on the Continent. Mary's father was regrettably fertile, and had produced a sprawling household of brothers and sisters, and everything was spread thinly among them, including thick shoes. There was just no question of anybody getting an entire pair of extra shoes for a dance.

The beautiful blue dress had dwindled particularly into tattiness as soon as it saw the glittering new white dress on

Louise, and the black lacing shoes had expanded by six inches as soon as they saw the tiny silver dancing pumps on Louise. Louise sparkled and soared like a bright little bird, and Mary sagged like an underfed cow. It was Louise's shining hour. Mary had felt at the time that there ought to be room for her own shining hour too, without shortening Louise's triumph. Louise had actually been very sweet about it. She had looked quickly at the now enormous black lacing shoes that covered the entire dance floor, and giggled, "It'll take a lot of dances to wear *them* out." And then, nearly immediately, she had touched Mary's arm confidingly and said, "Honestly, Mary, they're very sensible, and nobody'll notice them, boys never notice anything, honestly. Is that a new dress? It's nice."

It was impossible to explain all this to Nat, and she didn't see why Nat should have to hear dreary old childhood stories. But it was odd that while she had moved away from all that, and had gathered confidence and quietness by living in cheerful poverty with Nat, and then reveled in the new prosperity, she was sure that Louise would look at her once and make her feel that she was wearing miners' boots; or at least that she *ought* to be wearing miners' boots. No matter how grown-up she was now, Louise had the hole in her armor. She might be able to put millionaire landlords and kings and queens in their place, but with Louise she would feel like an impostor. She muttered Nat's favorite, old-fashioned, absolutely horrid swear word several times over, and wished she had the moral fiber to use it in front of Louise. It might even make Louise disappear.

Anyway, there were practical things to be done. The cottage which had looked so generously big was shrinking before her eyes at the prospect of new waves of invaders, and not only that, she was seeing it again through Louise's eyes and noticing for the first time how mean and dilapidated it was. It didn't amount to anything except a kitchen on the ground floor, and a toilet and a couple of cupboards: and an attic the same size as the kitchen, but divided into two rooms by a wooden partition, and the staircase up to the attic was more of an open ladder, steep and lethal. In fact, Louise would probably break both legs the first time she came down it, and would have to stay for months.

There was just no possibility of cramming everybody into it, especially if the shadowy Louise family turned out to be three, or four, or eight. She now realized why she was even sicker than a mere crowd of visitors could justify. However the beds were arranged, it stuck out a mile that she and Nat would have to split up, give up their tiny master bedroom and allocate themselves to one-sex dormitories. A fine damned second honeymoon. She was in the little bedroom, staring at the new bunk beds that had seemed so practical and space-saving, and she glowered at them and kicked them and paralyzed one of her small toes. For all the space they saved, she might as well have bought a decent double bed and taken her chances of an accidental seduction; but it was too late to think of that now and she was not, she swore she was not, going to mention it to Nat. He seemed perfectly happy, damn him, and she would wait till *he* suggested it, damn him, and if he didn't, damn him and damn him.

There was another pair of bunks in the second bedroom, for the girls, and a second-hand divan where Stacey had been sleeping. There was nothing much to be done about that arrangement. Harry slept in the put-u-up couch in the kitchen. Why hadn't she taken that over for herself and Nat? Too late again. It would probably do for the horde of Louise's children, and there were still the two air beds. They would have to go in the studio. She fingered the old dingy pine of the partition wall and wondered if it would be possible to strip the centuries of varnish from it and make it bright and Swedish. Somewhere outside, Nat had started to sing "Ah Sweet Mystery of Life" in a true but saw-edged tenor. Damn him, she thought, and laughed out loud.

He was in the garden, still stripped to the waist and earnestly inflating one of the air beds. His skin was turning effortlessly brown without peeling and the soft hairs on the back of his neck were bleached white.

"I shall spend the night at my club," he said, in his cold dignified husband character, and waved his hand toward the ramshackle outhouse.

"Is there room for two?" she asked, carefully flippant. Harry walked out of the house behind her and asked,

"Have you ever tried sleeping on one of these things? It takes a desperate man, I'm telling you." She shrugged and said,

"There's room for two on your couch."

"True, true," Harry agreed, "if they've got tin spines. There's a crossbar that gets you right across the kidneys."

"Dammit, it's the making of you," Nat told him. "Gad, man, at your age I was sleeping under a newspaper on the upper slopes of Kanchenjunga with bamboo shoots growing up through my backside in the night. From scenes like these auld Scotia's grandeur springs." Mary idly considered the idea of a crossbar digging into her kidneys and abandoned the thought of the put-u-up.

"I would love to knock out these panes in the kitchen window," she said, "and put in one big pane. They're a damn nuisance."

"I'll do it tomorrow," Nat said at once.

"You'll show me how to do it and I'll do it," she said firmly. "You'll get in there and paint and keep me rich."

"Nag nag nag."

She had already decided that she would sleep on the other air bed, in the outhouse, with Nat; and to hell with everybody else. And the outhouse would be soundproof against the cottage itself, which the little bedroom never could be.

"Will I go down and meet your cousin at the boat?" Harry asked, polite rather than eager, and Sally darted out of the cottage and shouted, "Me too!" Sally was crazy about new people, she always wanted to get in among them in the hope that they would turn out to be gods or film stars or something. Mary realized she hadn't seen Dee all morning, and wondered if Dee was off with that vulnerable Eric boy, tormenting him to death. She ignored the children and looked in at the outhouse. Now that the stone floor was uncovered, it looked almost better than the cottage itself. Apart from a few heaps of wood shavings, it was tidy and homelike. Nat, damn him, had got over the West Coast Rot long enough to finish the workbench, put up two easels, and scatter the packing cases about with bits of cloth over them. One of the infuriating things about him was that he was good at things, driving, carpentry, plastering, when he ought to have been a helpless artist with no useful skills apart from his art. When she turned round, Hughie Mackay had appeared silently in the garden and was sitting on the stubble watching Nat and clearly wondering if some beer would materialize from the air bed. Sally had thrown herself face down on the other air bed, still uninflated, and Harry was lounging against a bit of wall, looking at his feet. She knew what he was doing, he was trying to look long-legged and lithe and refusing to recognize that he was all right as he was, solid and tidy. She wanted to tell him this, but it would be too much like an intrusion into his private thoughts.

"The hoor's at it again," Hughie Mackay said, when no

beer appeared. "Oh — ts ts, language, sorry." Sally turned her head toward him eagerly.

"I didn't know there was a hoor in the village," she said. "What are they like? Are they like the great hoor of Babylon?"

"Belt up," Nat told her. "He means a hoor of wood and a drawer of water. What is it this time, eh, Hughie? The swine."

"He means Gadarene swine," Harry added automatically, and Mary groaned. They were all spoiled, totally ruined. She went meekly into the cottage to find some beer. As she entered the kitchen, Stacey leaped away from the window and sat down at the little table and immediately started to clatter her typewriter.

"The blood-sucking fascist hyena's got his teeth in the new village hall," Hughie was saying. "Oh, beer! I usually don't bother at this time of day but oh well . . . It's the bitter age-old story of exploitation and oppression, the hoor, I'll fix the Long Pool for him, by God I will."

"Ah, you're a desperate man, Hughie," Nat said equably. "You'll drive the infidel out of the Highlands yet, if you have to sicken him with a speech or two first."

"Ah, it's all very well to scoff, Nat." Hughie downed half of his beer in a gulp. The froth lingered decoratively on the hint of stubble round his mouth. "But think of the impoverished peasantry trying to build a new village hall with its own poor wee hands, and the pig says he'll raise the rent the very minute they nail on the roof."

"Dastardly."

"Well, I wouldn't use such strong language myself, but it is, it's a right dastard and no mistake. A proper dastard. Ah, it's come to it when Scotsmen in their own land have to pay tribute to a damnt foreign infidel for building a village hall with their own wee hands, the souls, and him an Episcopalian into the bargain."

"Filthy beast."

"Ach, if there was an ounce of spirit in the people we would have the barricades up and make a unilateral declaration of independence," said Hughie bitterly. "It takes a darky like Ian Smith to make a proper job of it."

"Ian Smith's not a darky," Sally explained, "he's a white Rhodesian."

"Aye, so he says," Hughie muttered darkly, "but it amounts to the same thing except we haven't got the spirit left in us. By God, the Clearances have a lot to answer for, if that King George the Fourth was here now I would spit on his chin for luck."

"If the laird's going to put up the rent," said Harry, who had found his way through all this murky history, "why don't you build the village hall on a raft and anchor it offshore? That would fix his wagon."

"I was about to suggest that," Nat complained. "By God, everybody gets into my act, it's our own fault for feeding the kids all that orange juice and vitamin pills."

"Ach, no, by God it's a nice thought though," said Hughie. "But Geordie has enough trouble getting into the tin shed without drowning three or four times when he's playing the piano for the dancing. A raft would be the entire end of him. The barricades is the only answer if we could find enough old trees and upturned hay carts." Mary, suppressing her giggles because she felt she ought to go on feeling aggrieved about Louise, refilled his glass, and Hughie looked up at her and said,

"By Joves, you're a beautiful girl, Mrs. Boag, and I wouldn't tell you a lie and it's got nothing to do with the beer, there's not many of your kind about nowadays."

"She's not a girl, she's a woman," Sally corrected him, then, catching Mary's eye, added, "little girls should be seen and not heard."

"Thank you, Hughie," Mary said, but Nat didn't appear to have heard. He was sitting back with his eyes narrowed.

"We're spending too much time talking," he muttered. "We'll have to mount a campaign to drive Harper loony, Hughie. If I wasn't respectable and frightened I would make a quick tour of the village deflowering the maidens, to cheat him out of his droit de seigneur, for a start."

"There's not many of them," Hughie said doubtfully, "and I doubt if he's inclined that way anyway, he hasn't got the speed for it, whatever it means."

"You'd better take care of that end of it, Harry," Nat said seriously.

"It's too hot."

"That will be quite enough, Nat Boag," Mary said. "Now! Now! you've worn the joke out. I have spoken."

"It's bad for us kids to hear our parents quarreling in front of us," Harry complained. "There's a letter about that in the Oban Times this week. It distorts the emotional development of the growing child."

"Get out of my house!" Mary told him. He shrugged himself upright and immediately started walking down the drive. Sally leaped up and ran after him, and Mary could hear her muttering something about Rejection and Traumatic Shock.

"And clean out your mouth with soap and water!" Mary called after Sally. "Nat, you'll have to chuck it. Honest injun. If Louise hears the kids at the patter she'll go right round the twist. She's well bred."

"And am I not? Hughie, am I not well bred? Is it not true that kind hearts are more than coronets?"

"An honest man is the noblest work of God," Hughie intoned. "Right enough, you don't hear many kids talking like that, it's a fair education."

"I've got a good mind to set Sally onto Harper," Nat said, "she could destroy him slowly like that salamander she's got. God, woman, can't you see I'm in the last stages of dehydration? Don't give all that beer to these local scum!"

Mary smiled cruelly and threw the glassful of beer in his face.

"By joves!" Hughie was stunned. "You're a wonderful hand at the aiming, Mrs. Boag, and that's a fact!"

Nat was spluttering and hysterical — that was another thing about him, damn him, he couldn't help laughing at a man slipping on a banana skin even if the man was himself. If Hughie hadn't been there she would have kissed his beery face. She sank to her knees and laughed helplessly.

"I've trained her," Nat was gasping. "She knows it's the only way I'll drink beer pfrooff pooh hee hee." Before he could do anything desperate in retaliation she leaned forward and licked the beer on his cheek. By Joves, Hughie was thinking, a few more about like that and I wouldn't give a damn for the laird or the village hall either.

Sally was explaining to Harry that the human brain stops developing at the age of thirteen, and that accordingly he was incapable of any further development of any kind. They were approaching the bottom of the side road and nearing the butcher shop, and Harry had a mild quickening of the senses at the thought of Ada.

"You don't believe me," Sally nagged, "because you've got a vested interest in thinking that you're still developing at nineteen. You just shut your silly mind to it because you don't want to admit it."

"Drone on," Harry said wearily.

"People have a lot of scientific misconceptions about pubrity," she said. "It's got nothing to do with brains, it's purely psychological."

"Puberty."

"Pubrity!"

"Puberty."

"Pubrity!"

"Puberty. And you mean physiological, you ignorant twit."

"Smarty. I know more about lizards than you."

"Bully for you, mate."

"I know more about sailing than you. I can work a jib sheet."

"Oh, hooray."

"I can so! I worked it yesterday! It's a lot better than a smelly lot of pubrity, goggling at stupid dames, I bet if you had to work a jib sheet you would fall right over bam! Hello, Ada! Can you not say hello to Ada? She waved at you."

"I waved at her."

"Is Ada sexually attractive?"

"I've never noticed." Harry's face flushed hot, but they were past the shop and Sally wasn't looking at him. Ada's wave had been marvelously casual and uninterested. It was hard to believe that what had happened had happened.

She ought to look furtive, or triumphant, or something. *He* felt furtive and triumphant. And, he thought smugly, he had cut in there ahead of the laird's family too, whether Nat had been joking or not. At once he saw Linda, walking along the shore road beside her father, and he was completely confused again. If sex was at the root of it all, why did he get nervous and interested at the sight of Linda when he already had Ada?

"That's Davie Fitzgerald," Sally muttered urgently. "He's a neurosis."

"Neurotic," Harry amended, flicking his eyes briefly to the man approaching them at a rapid shuffle.

"He's got a prosecution complex. Hello, Mr. Fitzgerald," she added in a sharp shout, and Davie Fitzgerald jerked in stung terror as he passed them without slackening speed.

"You never even looked at him," Sally complained in a whisper. "You're too busy watching that stupid girl. Her old man keeps her on a chain." This was obviously a quotation from some overheard conversation. "His wife is dying a horrible death."

"What?"

"I mean Davie Fitzgerald's wife! He's got her locked up in a garret and nobody gets in to see her, wasting away and moaning and ooh, all putrid, ooh the smell of corruption and death, ooh."

"Oh, shut up — Nat's been up to see her."

"If Cousin Louise hears you calling him Nat she'll go straight round the twist," Sally told him in mincing beldam tones. "I bet I'm a better yachtsman than you any day, you don't know what lee-oh means, see!"

"Ha, ha."

"You don't, so don't kid on! People your age don't have *time* to learn anything useful, your kind gets stunted!"

Harry went through the quick flip sequence of Ada-Linda-Magda, and realized he had never noticed they all ended in "da," as if that was of any importance. Serve everybody right, he thought, and suspected that he was deceiving himself — if Magda hadn't gone to France he would never have looked at Linda, and if Linda had looked at him he would never have got mixed up with Ada. They all deserved what they got. Or, as the case might be, *didn't* get. If Magda were here right this minute, of course . . . but she wasn't, and neither was Ada, and Linda was there, walking too quickly so as to keep up with the aggressive stride of her father, and with her head cast down as if in disgrace. She really was so slim and sweet and soft and adorable that he was filled with a gentle melancholy and wondered what kind of mind he had that could produce so many confusions simultaneously, her calves so smooth and sweet, and her . . . but he didn't put any other anatomical details into words, even in his mind, it was really rather mean and sneaky to be aware of her hips at all when she didn't even know he was looking at her.

"I bet nobody would take you out with them for a crew," Sally was saying superciliously. "They don't want a lot of beginners mixing up the jib sheets and sinking the yacht and not knowing what lee-oh means."

With a small despair he saw Linda and her father sitting on a bench and evidently carrying on a one-sided conversation which it would be madness to interrupt. Her father was talking without pause and he didn't look cheerful or kindly, and Linda was letting his words flow over her and looking solemn. Rather than pass close to them, he turned off onto the beach and Sally trailed beside him, going on and on about jib sheets and lee-oh and yachting disasters. With one tiny corner of his mind he reflected that the sunshine must be deepening his color, and that when he got back to university he would be as brown as Magda anyway. But he couldn't picture Magda at all. When he tried to see her face, the slender sweet rear view of Linda blotted it out.

Sally was wrong about nobody being willing to take him on board a boat. As soon as they neared the water he saw that the gay beastly Don Juan Archie McBain was making adjustments to the rig of a sailing dinghy, and palpably waiting for somebody to help him to carry it into the sea. Another dinghy sat beside it, attended by his sister Dee and the sad English youth hosteler she had picked up the other night. Eric too was waiting for somebody to help him. Harry wondered briefly why Archie McBain hadn't volunteered, and decided that Archie wasn't going to help anybody who had found a girl when he, Archie, hadn't.

Harry advanced on Eric's boat, and without a word, he and Eric lifted it by a side each and struggled down the beach till it started to float.

"Can I come too?" Sally screamed. "I'm good at it!" Eric's face fell and he tried to remember that the boat was too small for three, but it looked remarkably big, and Dee turned to Eric with a melting smile and said, "She wouldn't be in the way, would she? She's very handy in boats, aren't you, Sally?" Sally's face was transfigured as she waded into the water behind the dinghy, clutching the transom and never intending to let go until she was aboard. Eric numbly helped Dee aboard, hoisted Sally over the stern and pushed off into the almost windless water. Harry thought, too late, of asking Archie McBain to take the brat. It was obviously no day for sailing, and Eric was merely arranging a lazy hour on the water where he could have Dee to himself. Life was going to be hell for everybody until Sally got up to the ears in pubrity herself.

"See these English blokes?" Archie McBain said. "No idea. See if that was a Scots bloke? He would have flung the kid over the side."

"Maybe he knew the kid was my sister," Harry said diplomatically.

"See sisters? A dead loss. You get a bird on a boat on a day like this, sisters, out." He had already taken the gunwale of the dinghy on one side, and seeing what was expected of him, Harry lifted the other side and started the stagger down the beach again.

"Fancy a go?" McBain asked.

"I'm easy." He decided he probably didn't like Archie

McBain at all, but he liked the boat, and it was better than walking the beach feeling sad about Linda. Archie shoved the boat out and leaped aboard in one movement, and Harry grabbed clumsily and pulled himself over the side with his trousers wet to the thigh. His head struck the boom with a smart clunk. Archie settled comfortably in the stern, cuddling the tiller under one arm, and lit a cigarette. He nodded in the direction of the other boat, drifting sideways out across the glassy water.

"See that bit? I thought I was in there, but Ginger turned up. The luck of the draw, try again next time."

"She is also my sister." With his skull still ringing, Harry felt that he was being pompous, but he wanted to avert any further talk in Archie's style about Dee. Archie took the news without flinching.

"Funny thing, that, isn't it? See sisters? You canny see it when it's your sister. She's all right. Is she steady wi' that English bloke?"

"Search me."

"Well, I mean, everybody's *somebody's* sister. No offense. Take in the jib a bit, we might get a puff."

Thinking fast, Harry took a rope and pulled it.

"Aye, that's fine, if it was on the other side," Archie McBain said, quite amiably. "There's nothin' in it when you've done it a few times."

"Sorry." Harry crouched under the boom and found another rope to pull. It was reasonable enough. The simple geometry of the arrangement clicked into place in his mind. Both sails same side of the mast. He was idly working out what to do if the boom swung over. Duck, let it pass, pull the other rope.

"See this weather?" Archie was saying. "A dead loss for sailing. The only thing it's good for is the birds. They like it in this weather."

"Oh, aye?" Harry wondered if he could get Archie off the subject. The crudity irritated him, particularly as he had just glanced shoreward and seen Linda again. But it was true, to his chagrin he found his mind leaping back to her, and this time with a sharp physical stirring. With ghostly clarity he heard Sally quietly saying,

"Are we ready to lee-oh yet?"

Archie laughed, and spoke in a low voice.

"See the sea when it's like this? You can hear miles away. It's like an amplifier. You've got to watch the old language. You can hear some funny things if you just sit still."

"Oh?"

"Here, you take the helm, you might as well learn when it's like this." Archie nimbly propelled himself forward, leaving the tiller, and Harry scrambled awkwardly into the stern and laid his hand on it.

"Nothing to it — look for a puff and see if you can drift into it," Archie went on. The odd thing was that when he was talking about the boat, he became serious and patient, and immediately switched into his gloating lechery as soon as he changed the subject. "No," he said, "take the sheet in your hand and feel it like a fishing rod — you get a nibble, you let it out a wee bit, just gentle, gentle. Jesus, we're away!"

With a thrill of delight, Harry felt the rope tighten in his hand, and there was a sudden slapping swishing of water as the dinghy sliced ahead.

"Down a bit . . . port, port," Archie was crooning, lolling very easily, arrogantly, near the bow. "See, there's the wind, don't run straight up it, gentle gentle, let out the sail a wee wee bit, ach, you cow." He had dropped his cigarette over the side. He lay back and lit another. The match hardly flickered in the light zephyr, but the little boat was definitely skimming across the water, and for a moment Harry decided

Sally was right, and that useful things like sailing were better than the confusions of pubrity. In answer, he heard a
shriek of joy from Sally in the other boat, now three hundred
yards away.

"We're losing it, losing it," Archie muttered. "Come
about . . . Oh aye — bring her round into the wind and
then ram the tiller across and duck. Tighten the sheet, nice,
too much, nice, okay any time you like." Stiff with excitement, Harry ducked and slammed the tiller across. The
boat hovered momentarily, then surged back toward the
shore, which was almost half a mile away. After a few minutes the rope went limp in his hand. The sail drooped, and
Archie McBain let got of the jib sheet and lay down philosophically on his back.

"Tell you a nice bit," he said thoughtfully. "Wee Stoddart."

"Oh?" Here it came again, and he had almost known it
would. "What is it like in a strong wind?" he asked desperately, dreading to hear Linda described by this loathsome
satyr.

"Just the same, only quicker," Archie dismissed the topic.
"See Stoddart? Funny thing, they've been here every year
for years, but nothing, a dead loss. See last year? A kid —
legs like two woodbine, never even knew she was female.
Different this year, it's funny, that — quite sudden."

"Some good-looking bits at the Youth Hostel." Harry
tried to match the tone and change the subject at the same
time. It was too far to leap out and swim ashore.

"Not bad, not bad. But see sudden? Never seen anything
like that. Just ripe."

"She seems like a nice quiet child."

"Yeah, *last* year a child. Funny, ever notice that? You get
a good bit like Stoddart, she always gets a pal like fat Retta,
I've seen it time and again, you always get it."

"Self-defense," Harry said weakly. "I don't blame her."

"Here, you fancy a bit there? I don't blame you. May the best man win." Harry could have torn off the tiller and smashed it into Archie's complacent mouth. He didn't, and the mouth went on. "Don't worry, there's a system for that — you take the two. See a bit like Retta — if she gets a cuddle at her door, she drops off, otherwise she knows she never gets another cuddle. She's slow, mind you — Stoddart, I mean . . . still a learner . . ." He closed his eyes and grinned to himself, and Harry said tartly,

"She's probably under the age of consent."

Archie sat up quickly.

"What difference does that make?"

"You try anything and you get two years." Harry tried to sound sad and sympathetic.

"Hey, what's the age of consent?"

"Eighteen," Harry lied. Archie relaxed.

"That's okay, well. Retta was at her eighteenth birthday party last month. Party! Five dames! What kind of party's that? Her old man's a nut, a complete nut. He hasny got the idea at all. I could tell him." Archie stretched, proud and vicious in his youth and strength, and Harry wondered if he himself was like that too, with nothing but a shell of inhibition or cowardliness to hide it. But no, he wasn't — he might do anything that the horrible Archie might do, but he wouldn't feel he had to *talk* about it all the time. If he did anything at all, it would be his own business, and the girl's and nobody else's. So he assured himself, and then defeated his own conceit when he heard himself saying,

"Ada Fraser's an interesting looking female."

"Uhuh, yeah." Archie chewed this thought over with pontifical interest. "But see Ada? I think it's all in the shop window and nothing in the shop. See a dame like that, that waggles it in front of you — when you get to it you're not on."

"Mm?" Harry had a small hard satisfaction in thinking that it must be all talk and nothing else, with Archie. Archie talked, *he* acted. This thought was succeeded by the miserable possibility that Ada might simply not go for Archie's type, but for his, Harry's. And that Linda might prefer Archie's. Life was going to be unbearable if the only girls who wanted him were the kind of girls he didn't really, madly, want.

"Now, see the quiet bits, the Sunday school teacher bits, they're the hot pieces, you only have to get them started. Hey, see these quiet bits, I was talking about the system. Funny thing that, you know brassieres have a snap-shackle thing at the back? If you've been about in boats for a while, you get the knack, you can snap it open right like that, snap accidental. See the quickness of the hand? Sometimes they don't even notice it. Funny that, you would think they would notice it, but no, half the times they don't. It makes everything jack easy."

Would it be possible to tip the boat over and drown him? No, he could probably swim like an olympic champion, and Harry couldn't.

"Well, you know what I mean, the gentle touch — hey, funny thing, if they're real prim they think it's an accident and they don't like to mention it. Never fails, you know. By the time they think they better mention it, they're getting to like it too much so they forget it."

"Okay, okay, talk about something else."

Archie was honestly surprised. He sat up.

"Do you not fancy it?"

"Everybody fancies it," Harry said heavily, "but it's all an old old story, I've heard this a million times."

"Aye, maybe." Archie sank back, rather sullen. "It's all right for you. See the big towns, it must be easy all right but it's different here, you've got to work for it. Hey anyway I discovered a funny thing — Wee Stoddart never wears one. It's the truth, you just run the hand up and down the back, no strap, nothing. Makes life easy, see? What a nice wee handful."

He had gone off into a half-dream and one of his hands was vaguely reconstructing the crime, and Harry felt sweat starting out on his head and a tight knot in his intestines, and at the same time he was staring past the bow of the boat and seeing Linda, sweet and fragile, a blur of yellow, still sitting beside her father on shore. Archie fell silent, with his eyes closed and a smile on his lips, and the boat drifted slowly toward the beach. The faintest breath of wind touched Harry's cheek and he teased out the mainsheet and steered for the old jetty. It might be quite nice, he thought, if he could step off lithely onto the jetty and then accidentally shove the boat as Archie was getting out.

But Archie's senses worked in tune with the boat. Ten yards from the jetty, he was already on his feet and lowering the sails, and as the boat approached, he was off in one spring with the painter in his hand. Harry numbly stepped off after him.

Sally was shouting at him from the other dinghy, which had followed their course, and he looked toward her blankly.

"The afternoon boat!" she was screaming. "Cousin Louise!"

It was true, they had timed everything well. The old tank landing craft, Geordie Mackay's hated mistress, was churning toward the slip. As Archie dragged his dinghy by the rope toward the beach, Harry waited to take hold of Eric's boat. Eric, not looking too sad in the circumstances, was standing at the bow and reaching out a hand, and Harry craned forward to take it and pull the boat toward him. Bursting with excitement, Sally put a foot on the gunwale of the boat and leaped the four-foot distance onto the slip. The dinghy rocked wildly and slid away from the jetty. Held together in a firm handshake, Harry and Eric slowly leaned nearer and nearer each other and then fell together, face-down, into the water.

As he came up choking, Harry had a whizzing panoramic view of a dozen people pouring out of the afternoon ferry and shrilling with ape-like laughter . . . a blank bit of beach . . . Martin Stoddart and Linda, now standing up and howling joyfully. He came up again and saw Eric's dinghy, with Dee standing up in the stern. She was shouting something.

"You crazy bastards, they're drowning!"

As his face went under again, he saw her leaping from the boat into the water. His feet touched something hard. He stood up, with water reaching his chest. Dee was thrashing face-down in the water a few inches below the surface and Eric was pulling her upright by the shirt.

"The boat, the boat!" he was spluttering. Without a pause, Dee leaped from his grasp and struck out toward the dinghy in a noisy crawl.

"They're here, they're here!" Sally screamed from the jetty.

"Aw, belt up," Harry muttered. He walked a few yards and then sat down waist-deep in the water and decided the time had come to cut himself from human society.

NINE

LOUISE'S FEET WERE as small as ever, and Nat thought that she was ever so lovely. She arrived, in the end, with family, by Hughie's doorless van, and the family consisted of her very tall, silent husband Sam and their son Timmy, a few months older than Sally. Timmy looked as if he ate too much.

Louise was enraptured with the casual homeliness of it all, free lifts in such odd ramshackle vehicles and nice friendly working-class people like Hughie. She was wearing a pale blue linen suit with a frilly blouse, and Mary was disgusted to see that she had kept her figure and her teeth and her sweet winning smile. She had hoped that Louise might by now be an obese bag, preferably with bad rheumatism and hammer toes.

"Oh, what a sweet old place," Louise said. "It must be full of possibilities. Oh, the things I could do to it!" Mary laughed in merry loathing, and Nat kissed Louise, who absolutely adored it. The lumpen husband Sam shook Mary's hand and couldn't find the courage to kiss her, and muttered something about hoping it wasn't an imposition. Louise trilled her laugh.

"You'll have to get used to Sam," she said, "he's quite capable of apologizing for being alive. Imposition!" She withered Sam with a look. "You'll never even notice we're here. Oh, it's going to be marvelous having good long chats; Mary, these are lovely slacks." Mary knew the compliment was sincere by the subtle change of tone and the hint of envy. She had a beastly impulse to say they had cost fifteen guineas, but she didn't.

"May I wash my hands, please, Aunt Mary?" The overfed Timmy looked at her in earnest respect. It was all a quiet placid nightmare in which the sole consolation was that there appeared to be only one child in Louise's family; but that child was obviously trained like a guardsman to good manners and gentle speech, he probably spent his time helping old ladies across streets and opening doors for adults, and no doubt played the piano like Mozart and was a whizz at maths and history. In contrast, Sally would seem coarse and ill-bred and cretinous, and Louise would have an absolutely glorious time making allowances for her and sympathizing with Mary.

"The bog's through the kitchen on the left," Sally said, obediently living up to Mary's prediction. Timmy looked prim and shocked and went into the house, bathed as he went in the light of Louise's smile. Sally went straight on talking like a fishwife.

"God, these nits," she said eagerly. "Bam bam bam, right in the drink, they're useless at yachting, hee hee! You should have seen Harry! He thought he was pulling Eric ashore and hee hee!" She held out her hand to describe the story in pantomime and leaned forward till she fell on the dry earth spluttering with the effort to stop laughing and tell the tale. Louise regarded her indulgently but without approval.

"That child is over-excited. Do you know what my mother always told me, Sally? She told me that if I laughed too much

I would end up crying. Oh, it was very funny all the same —
three of them all in the water *at once.* I don't think they're
very *expert* or they would know never to move about in a
boat."

"Who fell in the water?" Mary was firmly controlled, tight
patient smile, be amused, join in the joke, I would love to
slap your stupid face.

"Harry!" Sally squealed through her gasps. "And Dee!
And Eric hee hee hee. Bam! Splat! Bam!"

"I'd better go down and get them," Mary said. "They
could catch a chill." Or drown or be eaten by sharks and you
would stand there smirking, you bitch.

"I don't know, young people nowadays seem to have a
charmed life." Louise sat in the deck chair, back straight,
the whole movement copied from a mannequin . . . yes, as
soon as she had sat she crossed her ankles and looked smugly
at her little feet in their little shoes.

"Let them walk," Nat advised. "It'll dry them faster." But
Mary was already groping in her pocket for her keys and
walking toward the Land Rover.

"I have to get some more bread anyway," she threw over
her shoulder. She was unaccountably angry with everybody,
including Nat, and she warned herself to be calm and drive
slowly and not vent her temper on the car. Of course they
were right, Harry and Dee wouldn't have come to any harm.
But that was no reason for dismissing the accident, and whatever it had been . . . or maybe she was simply still angry at
the existence and the arrival of Louise, and she had to find
some excuse for her irritation. Or maybe it was because Nat
had kissed Louise. What was the harm in that? He was always kissing somebody, with no intention at all except good
humor. I don't care, she muttered to herself, alone in the car
and with the engine drowning the words. I don't care, he

should lay off — I don't go round kissing men, even if I felt like it.

She was momentarily horrified at herself, and stopped the car and breathed steadily to calm down and rediscover her practiced serenity. The sad thing, really, was that no matter how close you were to somebody, no matter how much you loved him, you could never know at all what went on in his mind, what idle meaningless ideas flitted through it when he wasn't thinking of anything in particular. There was no way of knowing whether Nat kissed women casually and openly from mere goodwill toward mankind, or whether he felt an illicit excitement when he did. The awful thing was that suddenly she wanted to know . . . but she didn't want to know, because the idle thoughts of an idle mind could be horrifying without meaning any harm.

How would Nat regard her if he knew that when he kissed Louise so lightly, she, Mary, had an involuntary vision of him lying with Louise, cloven to her? It was only a momentary vision, and it was ludicrous, it was a childish imagining. But it did present itself, and she wished it wouldn't. All right, then, she told herself, if my imagination is only harmless, meaningless imagination, why shouldn't Nat be thinking the same kind of thing, which would also be perfectly harmless and meaningless? Am I going to say, *Because I know he can be absolutely sure of me, but do I know I can be sure of him?* Or am I only an ordinary possessive female who would like to chain her man up where he could never see another woman? What you need, my girl, is a lot of cold baths and a lower-calorie diet.

She shook the whole thing out of her head and laughed because she knew herself to be inane, and started up the car again. In a few more years she would hit the menopause, and get past it, and wonder what all the fuss had been about . . . maybe . . .

She saw Harry first. He was sitting on one of the grassy dunes on the beach, rejecting the world with a towel round his waist and salt caking on his bare back. A few yards away, the red-headed boy Eric was hunched on the grass, and Dee, in damp shorts and blouse, was scrubbing his back dry. Harry looked up wearily at Mary and said,

"Yes, I fell in the water, no, I'm all right, yes, it was very funny."

"I know," she said, "it's unadulterated hell," and he decided to smile. All in all, she decided, it must be hell to be young and vigorous and not have a mate. Dee looked round, without pausing in the scrubbing, and said,

"This one should be in a warm bed. You should!" she said to Eric. "It isn't just the cold water, it's the shock."

"I often fall in," he said. "It wasn't even deep."

"What if you had hit your head on the bottom and knocked yourself out!"

Eric tried to shrug his shoulders as she scrubbed him mercilessly. His smile was embarrassed and vacuous and utterly self-satisfied.

"Will you be able to walk to the car?" Dee demanded, and he protested, "I don't want to be put to bed!"

"You're a fool," she said. "Turn over." She started to scrape the skin off his chest with the little towel and his smile grew even more vacuous. "You're not fit to be let out alone," Dee told him viciously. What a brilliant boy, Mary thought, to think of falling in the water. Now he had Dee properly hooked. The afternoon beach crowd had lost interest in the trio and were sitting on the sand or splashing in the sea, but Archie McBain, who looked like a rather dangerous boy, was sitting on the jetty and palpably wishing that he could be having his body scrubbed by a girl in damp shorts. If Eric had any sense, he wouldn't recover his health and strength too quickly, but deliver himself into the aggressive maternal care that Dee had suddenly developed for him. This was a shocking thing for a mother to be thinking — these laughable youthful adventures could be downright dangerous, especially in such hot weather. She looked affectionately at Dee and wondered what idle thoughts flitted through *her* ferocious little mind. The best thing to do was to get back to the car and buy some extra bread.

Before she reached it she was almost knocked over by a small man shuffling at high speed from the direction of the Tala. He bounced back from her, stammering and twitching, and spoke in a curious frightened half-whisper.

"Oh, sorry sorry sorry, Mrs. Boag. Oh dearie me, I think her time's come, eh, oh aye! Eh, it's awful, eh, well, she warned me, eh, oh dear! Eh, will you tell, eh, Mr. Boag? Eh, aye, that's right, Mr. Boag, he'll maybe, eh, want to see her. Oh dearie me, there she is again! Sadie Pringle! Eh, she's lookin' at me again! Oh dear, oh dear!" He had grabbed Mary by the arm in his confusion. Davie Fitzgerald, of course, and he must mean that his wife was finally deciding to die. A short, stout woman was sitting on the bench farther along the shore road, with her arms trying to fold themselves across her bosom. She was staring fixedly at Davie Fitzgerald, with her lips clamped tight. Mary tried to remember what this was all about, but decided she didn't know, and didn't want to inquire too closely.

"Do you want me to get Nat?" she asked.

"Eh, aye — well, eh, if he likes . . . eh, maybe it's another false alarm. Oh, it's a terrible worry, it's not good for me, this. I wish she would stop looking at me — I, eh, never done her any harm!"

"I don't think she's actually looking at you," Mary lied. The plump woman was giving a performance from some awful Victorian drama. If it hadn't been a beautiful sunny day, she would have been quite alarming with her unwavering stare and her impregnable silence. Davie Fitzgerald didn't appear to be listening. He kept his eyes turned away from Sadie Pringle and still clutched Mary's arm.

"Eh, oh, it's persecution," he almost wept. "I'm, eh, demented, everywhere I, eh, turn she's at it, oh dearie me, if you could give me a ride in your eh, motor, oh, we could whizz right past, oh, that would, eh, trick her, right enough, eh, would you do that? I don't like to, eh, ask you, oh, that would be good, whizz right past, she would never, eh, expect that."

Although he was standing still, he kept on shuffling, like an idling motor waiting to engage gear and blast off.

"All right," Mary said, hoping to calm him by her reasonable tone. "Jump in." He jumped straight into the seat and sat. The permanent shuffling motion transferred itself to his buttocks, and he squirmed in a mixture of nerves and relief. She climbed into the Land Rover, banged in the clutch and took off with a leap while Davie sat staring ahead through the windscreen and squirming and not looking at Sadie Pringle. Mary roared up to the Tarbie boardinghouse and Davie opened his door and did a backward leap, still shuffling but wearing an expression of gloating triumph. He threw one glance back along the road and took off for the open front door and vanished.

Ehe reversed and turned back toward the baker's. Sadie Pringle had left her place on the bench and was walking placidly in the direction of the boardinghouse. Nat would know what this strange affair meant. Actually, it was all very fascinating. Was the stout little woman going to take up position across from the boardinghouse and just stand there and stare at it? What strange impulse drove her to this silent vigil? What dark secret did it denote in Davie's hidden past?

Could our hero escape the clutches of the merciless Tong? Do not miss next week's gripping installment. She had entirely outgrown her silly introspection in contemplating the Strange Case of Davie Fitzgerald. There was no doubt about it, life in Ochie was a dilly.

As she came out of the baker's with a handful of paper bags, life became even more of a dilly. A tall blond young man who she knew must be the son of the odious Harper opened the door of the car for her and said, "You make a damn pretty picture."

She eyed him levelly and felt a smile growing in her. Nobody in this damned place behaved like a human being, she decided. Young Harper had stolen his remark from a really awful amateur drama production.

"You've very kind," she said, and tried not to sound condescending and indulgent. He was rather an acid-looking boy, but he probably had his own troubles — anybody with a father like that automatically had his troubles.

"You're Mrs. Boag!" he accused her brusquely.

"That's right. You're young Mister Harper."

"Not all that young." His reaction was prickly. She stepped into the car, but he kept the door open with his hand.

"We must get to know each other better," the boy snapped. Maybe he couldn't help his funny, second-lieutenant manner — some of these English public schools had weird effects on a boy's speech. Mary hoisted herself lightly across to the driving seat, and absentmindedly arranged the paper bags in a neat bundle on the middle seat.

"That shouldn't be difficult," she said lightly. "Ochie's a very small place." She gave him a smile that she hoped was motherly.

"Like to know people about the place," he gruffed. "No sense in being standoffish."

"I do agree." She kept the motherly smile going and got ready to turn the ignition key.

"Must do something about it!" His voice was still as clipped and stage-colonel as ever, but he blushed, and it came to her that he was probably fed-up and lonely and adolescent and that probably nobody talked to him very much.

"Yes, why not?" She delayed switching on the ignition. "We ought to be neighborly. It's a beautiful day," she added, frankly stuck for words.

"Yes! Yes, it is!" The boy smiled happily and her heart was touched, and she said, "Can I give you a lift?"

"Super!" He swung himself into the seat and closed the door and smiled happily at her. She smiled determinedly in return and started the motor. Oh well. She might as well get used to being everybody's Pollyanna. The kid probably had a million in his savings account and not a friend in the world. It wasn't costing her anything to be kindly, considering his gratitude, which was obvious enough to be embarrassing.

Winston felt that at last he had found a day that wouldn't be entirely wasted. His only worry was whether Tony Hammer would entirely approve of Mrs. Boag, who must be forty if she was a day. But hell, he didn't have to tell Tony she had been forty, and now he considered it, to hell with Tony, this was Winston's own worry. In fact, wasn't it in the best tradition to have a first work-out with an older woman, somebody with a bit of the old *nous?* And he was undoubtedly making the jolly old progress up this alley — Mrs. Boag wasn't one of your neurotic young pieces, she had got the message straight away, message received and understood. Women didn't fling that particular kind of smile at a man without knowing what the score was. *Can I give you a lift,* indeed! Yes, wench, all the way.

He wouldn't hurry it this time. He hoped he wasn't sim-

ply funking it in deciding that he shouldn't hurry it. But no,
it was only common sense. It was all very well, as Tony said,
to make the offer right out, without wasting a second — but
only if the time and place were convenient, and there wasn't
much convenience in a Land Rover in broad daylight. It was
okay, it was obviously okay, but the woman no doubt had a
lot of snotty kids waiting for that heap of paper bags, and he
didn't want to get her worried about her family responsibilities. This kind of enterprise needed single-minded concentration on the part of both parties. Yes, he would refrain
from hurrying it, now that he knew he was on. It was simply
a question of choosing the right time and place. And actually, if you liked the type, she was a bit of all right for her
age, if those weren't falsies. There was something very, very
. . . yielding was the word. To hell with your bony bints,
all teeth and angles.

"You look pretty good for your age," he said gruffly, anxious not to relapse too far into mawkishness. The woman
laughed.

"I do my humble best," she said, and glanced briefly away
from the road and toward him. "You look all right for
yours." She was still laughing, and although he hadn't expected this, he remembered that laughter was a symptom of
stimulation. He had to shift his position on the seat as his
physical responses ran ahead of his cool calculating mind.

"We must see more of each other," he said, and he charged
the words this time with the entire meaning. Mary hoped
the boy wasn't peculiar, or feeble-minded, as he fidgeted almost as violently as Davie Fitzgerald.

"Of course," she said kindly. "Would you like to come in
for a cup of tea now? There's a whole crowd of people already."

"No. Don't like crowds much." Winston laughed knowingly, and Mary decided that he was probably afraid of people. She stopped the car at the bottom of the twisting driveway.

"Well," she said, "I'll look out for you."

Thinking hard, Winston got out.

"Any particular time?" he asked, now feeling quite nervous.

"Oh, any time at all," Mary said, smiling brightly. "We'll recognize each other easily enough." She kept her hand on the gear lever and revved up a little.

"Soon," Winston said suavely. "Soon." He waved a hand and swung back down the hill. All right, the woman had decided to pick her own time — fair enough, really, with a husband and brats to think about. He would be ready. He couldn't imagine himself ever being more ready than he was at that moment.

There is something quite wrong with that child, Mary thought as she turned up the driveway. A bit of ordinary coarse company would probably do him good. But apart from that, she couldn't reasonably dismiss the flicker of suspicion that he had rather fancied her, in an innocent adolescent way. It was rather comforting to be fancied, even by a slightly odd adolescent.

TEN

THERE WAS A CATACLYSMIC thunderstorm which filled Mary with fear because as long as the sun kept shining, everybody was able to get out and scatter. If the regular boozers at the Tala were right, and this was the total end of the hot summer, she faced the unbearable prospect of being trapped indoors in a cottage overcrowded with Louise and listening to Louise's polite conversation forever. In self-protection she started to drag out the oilskins and propose a long walk.

"That would be quite nice," said Louise's silent husband Sam, and then immediately added, "when the rain stops . . . a bit . . ." He had caught Louise glaring swiftly at him and surrendered.

"Quite nice for ducks," Louise said, merry and hostile at the same time. "You know what Timmy's like if he gets his feet wet."

"Timmy's too fat to catch a cold," Sally said, and then caught Mary's eye and stopped talking. Suddenly a long walk in the rain was absolutely necessary. A whole afternoon in the moist kitchen was too much to face.

She made an effort to seem happy and matter-of-fact because she could feel Louise's resentment drilling through her shoulder blades as she sorted out the oilskins. It was impossible to know what to do with Cousin Louise. She considered herself to be on holiday and kept waiting for jolly outings and entertainments to be organized for her, but she didn't really like any when they were suggested, and most of all she resented being left alone if Mary did something selfish and amusing, like digging up tree-roots from the garden; and her constant demand was for everybody to take Timmy off her hands because she didn't want to be over-possessive toward him.

Okay okay okay, Mary was quietly seething to herself, Timmy can come if he likes or stay if he likes but away, away, liberation for this Mum. She caught sight of silent Sam, in his habitual pose of resignation and submission to fate, as he glanced at her wistfully and wished he had the viciousness to say he was going for a walk. He was clearly a beaten man without hope of rescue. "I've read all these comics," Timmy complained. "You can read them again, then," Louise silenced him. "Honestly, going out in this weather. Oh well," she forced a laugh, "I suppose it might be good for the complexion."

Harry got up from his uncomfortable chair, rather glumly, Mary thought, and said, "I'll take my books out to the pigsty and do some notes." Immediately Stacey chipped in, "I've got some chapter-polishing to do in my room, as a matter of fact . . ." It was interesting to see how mad the rush to escape. Sally and Dee were already pulling on oilskins like lifeboatmen hearing the maroon. Even Nat, who had been lying in a deck chair reading one of Timmy's comics, uncoiled himself and decided to visit Maggie Fitzgerald.

"Is it right to tire the old soul out when she's so near the end?" Louise asked, lowering her voice on the last phrase so that Timmy wouldn't understand it. Why is she so keen for Nat to stay at home? I'll scratch her eyes out, Mary reflected with some satisfaction.

"It's only my dirty jokes that keep her alive," Nat remarked, and Louise laughed and shrilled, "Oh Nat, you are awful." Nat could do no wrong, Louise had really gone a bundle on Nat. "That," he added, "and the oil painting. She'll never die happy till she sees herself in Technicolor in a gilt frame."

"What I'm going to do in that case," Louise said firmly, "is do a proper job on that old grate. I've been just itching to get it spick-and-span for days." Mary nodded in approval and didn't grit her teeth.

The rain was crashing straight down, truly delicious. Nat scowled at it and pulled his hat down hard, but Mary and the girls turned their faces to the sky and squealed as it ran down their necks. Sally kicked her way through a foot-deep torrent running down the hill and shot jets of water up under her coat and shrieked.

"It's good to be alone," Mary said.

"We're all insane," Nat muttered. "It's not bad — your relations are awful polite, you never told me you had polite connections."

"No."

"I don't mind them."

"Timmy is a carbuncle," Sally shouted. "A fat carbuncle."

"Don't put up with them for my sake," Mary pleaded with Nat, but all he said, was, "I don't mind them, honest." Maybe he didn't. He could blank off his mind. If he wasn't emotionally involved with people he just switched off. She pushed him into a puddle but all he did was jump up and down to watch the water spurt out from his boots.

"I think I'll go along to the hostel," Dee said casually. "They keep it open all day in this weather."

"Are you getting entangled with that red-haired wog?" Nat demanded. "You can't trust them, they're not like us, eating mealies and biltong."

"He's not a wog, he's a Yorkshireman." Dee smiled tolerantly.

"He's drippy," Sally yelled, and realized she had been witty and sniggered.

"He is a bit feeble-minded," Dee agreed, so genially that there was obviously something doing.

"I don't like it," Nat said, in character. "Red hair is a sign of debauchery. You'd better have that young man call formally till we inspect him."

"For prissy afternoon tea?" Dee asked, giggling and zigzagging across the streaming street with her arms out like wings.

"Yes," Sally giggled, "with the best china and tiny iced cakes."

"And toasted muffins!" Nat shouted.

"And 'Nearer My God to Thee' on the harmonium," Mary laughed.

"No," Nat yelled. " 'Less Than the Dust Beneath Thy Chariot Wheels.' "

"Yes, that's better," she agreed. "We'll make *him* sing it. And not iced cakes. We'll give him brittle oatcakes and treacle."

"In his hand!" Dee cackled.

As they passed the garage, singing "Less Than the Dust" in unison, Hughie Mackay looked out from the darkness and shouted, "Come in out of that, it's as wet as a . . ." his voice tailed off, but a practiced ear could have picked up the phrase "____'s ____."

"You go on," Nat said, "I want to talk to Hughie about

. . . gaskets and so on." He sounded utterly dishonest, and Mary said, "Just watch it, boy, I've got my eye on you."

"Very proper, too, in an adoring wife," Nat said with an evil smile. Through the rain, all black, there appeared the trundling figure of Tom Wishart on his bike, with rain gushing off his hat on to his black cape as his voice rose wildly in "Heigh-ho, Come to the Fair." He was like a dark lonely ship passing across a deserted ocean. Ochie was huddling in its parlors complaining about the weather and agreeing that all that sunshine hadn't been natural for July.

The Youth Hostel was an old rambling house over a mile out of the village. As they approached its front lawn, a hand could be distinctly seen wiping a clear space in the misted front window, and a few seconds later, red-haired Eric appeared at the door, in a shirt and slacks. Dee gave a wave of embarrassed farewell to Mary and Sally and walked up the path with measured slowness. Eric ran down from the door to meet her, and they stood talking.

"He hasn't got the sense to come in out of the rain," Sally said in disgust. With his shirt streaming, the boy turned and walked back to the door with Dee, bending toward her and talking eagerly. Ah youth, Mary thought. To hell with the shirt.

While Mary and Sally were scrambling over hill paths in the slackening rain, the three Bennets, Sam, Louise and little Timmy, were performing a Happy Families tableau in the kitchen at Kirk Cottage. Louise, having examined the old fireplace and decided that it wasn't quite ripe for cleaning, was relaxed in the best chair reading *Ideal Home*. Timmy had adjusted himself to rereading an old comic by discovering that he could reach a biscuit tin from his chair and work his way through the chocolate creams as he stared at the page. Sam was hunched over the *Daily Mail* crossword, solving it badly and very slowly and wondering if he could suddenly say that he must go for a walk without sounding as if he had been rehearsing the remark for hours. He decided he couldn't, and kept on hunching.

A man of limited imagination, he was practiced in resigning himself to sitting still when he would rather have done something. All the things he might want to do were nearly sure to irritate Louise and make life difficult. In a dim uncomplaining way he was able to enjoy the thought of going for a walk with his wife's cousin, who had badly upset his mental image of the married state. Mary evidently had some deficiency of morals or manners that allowed her to laugh and be casual and unworried, a condition he had come to associate exclusively with unmarried girls.

At the same time, he noticed again what a nice neat woman his wife was. It might be nice if she suddenly developed an urge for the old nonsense again; not that he could blame her, really, for not fancying it very much, it never seemed to work out very well for her. He seemed to have the urge, but not the knack. It was wiser not to bother, probably, than try and fail. There was a travel advertisement on the same page as the crossword, with a picture of a girl in a bathing suit. He shifted position so that he could keep his pencil poised on the puzzle and stare at the picture out of the corners of his eyes. Nice girl, very cheery looking. What would happen to Mary if Nat died? Who would there be to comfort her? He saw himself looking very grave and reassuring, not actually touching her — no, laying a gentle hand on her shoulder. She reached up her own hand and gripped his in gratitude. The girl in the swimsuit had a most fetching set of abdominal muscles. It must be interesting to be a photographer.

In the outhouse, Harry lay on one of the inflated air beds listening to the rain crashing on the roof and feeling relaxed and philosophical. There was no sense whatever in getting frazzled about personal relationships. The intelligent game was to stick to Ada, who was pleasant and stupid and exciting in exactly the right uncomplicated way, and forget all about adorable little Linda, and forget all about Magda too. There was no nervous apprehension connected with Ada. He would take a stroll later when the rain went off and chat Ada up and take her for a walk, or something, and talk endlessly about exams and Highland transport. He tucked his hand inside his shirt and rubbed his chest luxuriously.

In the unmarried females' dormitory in the cottage, Stacey sat up in her bed reading her typed sheets and correcting them with a felt-tipped pen that made lovely thick sensuous lines. There was a Roget open on the bed beside her, and she combed it meticulously for improved phrases and idioms. The book was taking a long time, but it was unfolding. *Miss Boag is a fastidious craftsman who will cheerfully spend days in polishing a single page of one of her enormously successful novels.*

If people only knew the enormous difficulty of simply getting the words put together, those easy flowing sentences that had to be chipped out of solid stone; not to mention the prodigious bother of working all the characters in and getting them into conflict with one another. And really, she *had* to get a Louise character into it. The precise, prim-mannered, um, teacher? no, married. Minister's wife! Yes, that was it, the touch of lace, the profound respectability, and underneath, the raging nympho — that degree of refinement was an absolute dead giveaway, it could mean nothing but the cover for a boiling passionateness. Actually, it was very interesting that Sam had so cheerfully accepted a celibate bed in the outhouse with Nat. These big-built men so often were undersexed, it must be a relief to get a break from the sheer exhaustion of the marriage bed, to have a holiday away from the quiet, refined, insistent cannibalism of a wife like Louise.

She picked up a blank page and scribbled hurriedly in case she might lose any ideas. A big dramatic scene — no, no! The very thing to avoid was that old cliché of the husband discovering the wife in flagrante delicto and thundering damnation at her. No, it was much more subtle and more dramatic. He would enter the bedroom and see them there, white limbs, hair strewn across pillow, face flushed in satiety . . . satiety? satiation? Anyway, face flushed . . .

Say the film rights sold for £100,000 — how much Income Tax would that mean? She would have to move to Switzerland, that was all. Or could she turn herself into a company? What was £100,000 invested at five percent . . . She scribbled some figures idly and smiled. Authorship was hell, but it had its joys, and the greatest joy was the seeing eye, the instinct for the hidden personalities that lurked behind ordinary faces. It was a bit frightening, really, like having second sight.

Mary wasn't surprised, when she came back with Sally in a fresh blaze of sunshine and steaming haze, to find that nothing had come of Louise's mad lust to clean the old grate. She had given up wondering how Louise contrived to pass the long hours of her days, because Louise never actually managed to do anything noticeable. Her cousin now rose reluctantly from her chair and without saying anything, conveyed her gentle reproach at the selfishness of people who went away and left her to take care of her husband and son single-handed. Stacey, who had stirred upstairs as soon as the outside door banged, came down and immediately filled a kettle for coffee. Good old Stacey, fat behind and all — Stacey *functioned.* In one quick glance, Mary saw that the biscuit tin she had left full was completely empty, and little Timmy was doggedly staring at his comic and looking virtuous and as shifty as hell. It was going to be too awful if she had to start caching all the food in the house every time she went outside.

With another stab of suspicion, or certainty, she sniffed the dense fragrance of Dior. Louise must have dabbed on an experimental half-bottle. She smiled determinedly at Louise and started peeling off her oilskins. Sam leaped up to help her, and Louise laughed and said,

"I've got him well trained!"

"Do you use a whip?" Mary also laughed, cozily.

"You rotten fat pig!" Sally was shouting, "you've scoffed all the damn biscuits!"

"The *what* biscuits?" Louise demanded.

"The damn blasted biscuits!" Sally had turned mutinous and ugly, and Louise shook her head and tutted. Very sweet.

"There's more in the cupboard," Mary said, to lower the temperature, and Timmy, with the open candid gaze of a born confidence-man, shook his head and said,

"I only had one or two, Aunt Mary, I never eat much." Mary couldn't quite muster the moral fiber to say she believed him. It was awful how crowded the kitchen became when it was full of Bennets as well as Boags. It was claustrophobically crowded.

"Will you have this chair, Aunt Mary?"

"No, I'll get cups," Mary said, and Timmy immediately sat down again permanently. But his eyes were following Sally, and when she picked up her box of lizard and marched out into the garden, he lingered for a moment, looking hard at his comic, and then very casually got up and followed her.

He came on Sally in the patch of fresh swamp beyond the

outhouse. She had had the notion that the lizard was probably ailing for lack of moisture, and the vanished thunderstorm had produced a beautiful squidgy consistency of soil
that must be good for amphibians.

"It's dead," she heard Timmy say. She breathed through
her nostrils and ignored him. She pulled back the chicken
wire and tenderly lifted the limp object out onto the rich
mud. Its tail moved a fraction.

"Smelly thing," Timmy said.

"You stink," she said absentmindedly.

"Don't be cheeky!" Unthinkingly he slapped Sally, not
very hard, on the back of the head. She turned round with
the face of a tigress and Timmy backed away. Sally remembered her mother's warnings about behavior, and turned
back to the lizard. It actually moved forward.

"They're poisonous," Timmy said primly. "You get germs
if you go near dirty things like that."

"Shut up," she muttered. Timmy walked away a few
steps, picked up a small stone and lobbed it at a nearby tree
with an unaccustomed, girlish movement of his arm. Sally
crouched over the lizard, which was decidedly beginning to
walk.

As she watched it tenderly, she was very aware of Timmy
standing and not looking at her, and lobbing stones at the
tree. The stones consistently missed the tree and fell nearer
and nearer the waddling little lizard.

"If you hit it I'll amputate you," she muttered.

"I'm not touching the smelly old thing!" His next stone
was thrown toward the tree. Sally stood up to let the sunshine get at the lizard, and it worked its legs briskly and advanced across the mud, then stiffened abruptly as a heavy
stone landed a foot from it. She turned round on Timmy
with her eyes screwed up. He was smirking, half-guilty and

half-defiant. She advanced and pushed him in the chest. He tried to slap her but missed. She grasped his arm and pushed again. Timmy breathed heavily and closed with her. They swayed together without speaking and she felt his fingers close on her flesh just below the ribs and nip savagely. She yelped and nodded her brow viciously into the side of his face.

Timmy fell back with tears starting, and tripped and fell against the outhouse. Sally glared at him, clenched her fists and took up a boxing pose.

Timmy stared up at her and a brilliant thought flickered across his face. He stood up shakily and drooped his head forward and let his mouth drop open.

"Wuh!" he groaned. Sally tried to keep her voice down. "Come on, if you want a fight!" she gritted.

Timmy said "Wuh!" again. His face had gone slack and vacant and his arms hung stupidly.

"Come on!" she ordered him. He stared at her as one stricken and said "Wuh!" She had a momentary panic.

"Crybaby!" she said, and when he gaped and said "Wuh" again, she said angrily, "Stop being a dope!"

"Wuh!" he said, and lifted his head and closed his eyes as the full effect of the paralytic stroke destroyed his nerve centers. "Wuh!"

Livid and frightened, Sally took his arm and shook him. He opened his eyes and stared blankly at her and let himself be shaken. "Wuh!" He pointed with a limp hand at his mouth.

"What is it?" she asked in a whispered yell. He kept pointing at his mouth and Wuhed a couple of times. His eyes were beginning to roll, and Sally shook him and pleaded, "What's wrong?"

"It's a simple case of cerebral palsy." Harry was standing

in the doorway of the outhouse with an open book in one hand, and Sally turned to him in love and relief.

"I never touched him, hardly!"

"I know," Harry said, "it's spontaneous degeneration of the riboflavin." Timmy was turning to stare slackly at Harry and shake his head in dumb denial. "The only cure," Harry said conversationally, "is to ram cold mud down the back of the neck."

Sally caught on instantly, and picked up a handful of watery earth, but instead of backing away, Timmy followed her movements with empty eyes and imbecilic mouth. He stood meekly as she lifted the mud toward him, and she looked at Harry.

"I'd better not," she said.

"No," he said, "maybe it's gone too far. I expect they'll put him in a home. Would you like that, Timmy? A nice home with a stone bed and cold baths every morning?" But Timmy merely waggled his head and looked like a calf.

"It's his own fault, he nipped me!" Sally was starting to prepare her defense against a charge of attempted murder, but Harry only nodded calmly and took Timmy by the arm and started to usher him toward the cottage. Timmy leaned heavily on Harry's arm and his head wobbled from side to side as they reached the cottage door. Louise, with a cup of coffee in her hand, turned toward them startled.

"You'd better look at Timmy," Harry said soothingly. "He was trying to kill the lizard and he slipped and hit his head."

As Louise jumped to her feet to deny the preposterous accusation, Sam, who was nearer the door, rose and towered between them.

"Did you?" His face was dark with anger and his big hand was rising.

"I never did!" Timmy yelled. "She hit me on the face, I never fell, she hit me with her head!" Sally, standing behind Timmy in the doorway, privately and ferociously nipped his bottom and he shrieked; but at the same moment Sam had grabbed him and was beginning to shake him, not quite sure what to do with him, and Louise was pushing between father and son to rescue Timmy from this unprecedented violence. In the confusion of voices, Timmy tore himself free and staggered into the open air and was spectacularly sick. Sally watched him coldly in the hope of confirming that he had eaten dozens of biscuits.

Timmy's effortless regurgitation provided a useful punctuation to the air of crisis and accusation. He ended in the best chair with Louise sponging his forehead and explaining to the air that it was all nonsense and that Timmy loved animals though it was doubtful if a half-dead lizard constituted an animal, it was probably very well in its own place but there was something creepy and clammy about lizards and the thing was probably dead of hunger in any case. Timmy, not pushing his luck too far, was agreeing that the whole thing was an accident and a misunderstanding. Sally was out in the garden shouting with excitement, and when Mary went out, she cried in triumph,

"It's gone, it's away home!" The lizard had disappeared back into the jungle. "Maybe that fat rat frightened it back to health," Sally opined judicially.

"That will be enough of that language," Mary said coldly. "And lay off the rough stuff as well. *I* know you hit him."

"He asked for it." Sally was sullen. "And it was him that fankled up Stacey's typewriter ribbon as well."

"What typewriter ribbon?" Mary was quickly suspicious.

"Oh, Stacey's old typewriter ribbon."

"Who fankled it up?"

"It was him!" Sally stared defiantly at Mary, who said, "It was you."

"I never meant to," Sally's face went closed and surly again.

"I've a good mind to slap you, hard," Mary said.

"I don't know how you always know when it's me," Sally complained bitterly. "He *was* trying to kill the lizard."

"You make me sick," Mary said. Sally started to walk toward the undergrowth weeping silently. It was all perfectly marvelous, Ochie, the cottage, the sea air, the sunshine, the happy family holiday, perfectly marvelous.

ELEVEN

THE NIGHT of the crime began like any night. Nat came home from a long session with Maggie Fitzgerald and reported that the old dragon was holding off death with both teeth and that her picture was progressing finely. By unspoken agreement, nobody mentioned the strange incident of the lizard and the children, and he was in good insulting form, almost hectic, Mary thought.

"What a festering shower," he protested. "Nothing but ravenous maws everywhere I look. I'm telling you, we'll have to move into a barn if we breed any more of you. My God, prime stewed steak again, it's enough to grow horns on a man. When do we get lobsters?"

"When you catch one," Mary said weakly. It was bloody fine for Nat to go off gallivanting with old Maggie Fitzgerald and his paints while she wrestled with the villainies of mankind and the smell of cooking.

"Don't think I couldn't," he said, "I've got a permit for fishing the Tarbie Burn."

"What, freshwater lobsters?" Harry asked with interest.

"It could happen," Nat insisted. "Just because nobody

else catches freshwater lobsters is no reason why it can't be done. Or eels, giant conger eels. You'll have to starve that kid, Louise, he's beginning to come out rectangular."

"He's got a good appetite, haven't you, Timmy?" Louise asked fondly, not at all put out by Nat's jollity. Nat had a license to be funny.

"He's got a ravening maw," Nat said. "What have you got, Timmy? A ravening maw. You look like a whited Rubens. A few dishes of eel is what you need, my lad." Timmy, who had failed to figure Nat out, smirked uneasily.

"Do you eat eels alive?" Sally inquired hopefully, and got the response she hoped for in a retching noise from Timmy and a horrified cry from Louise.

"Sure," Nat said. "Give them a sporting chance. Eat or be eaten, that's what we mean by British fair play, Timmy."

Throughout this, Sam Bennet smiled amiably and a little enviously. It would never do to talk the way Nat talked, but it did make life easy for Nat, he could say anything that came into his mind instead of considering it carefully and then not saying it at all. Stacey and Harry washed the dishes after the meal, and Louise sat with an assumption of conscious self-sacrifice on one of the hard chairs and told Nat,

"You're a very lucky man, Nat, you married a good plain cook."

"She's not as plain as all that," Nat said, and Mary would have wrung his neck if he hadn't. Louise, who didn't catch on very quickly to rapid turns in the conversation, went straight on.

"Father always said that a good plain cook was a pearl above price. He was always laughing at me for my French cuisine, ha ha."

"Great!" Nat said. "Can you do a Wienerschnitzel? I could eat Wienerschnitzel all night."

Louise looked eager and earnest.

". . . Is that French? I don't think that's French." She waggled a corrective finger at Nat.

"I like sausages best," Timmy announced, and Sally muttered under her breath, "You *are* a sausage."

It was Stacey who broke up this witty badinage by calling for volunteers to join her in a pint. Sam perked up into sentient life, just as Louise was saying thoughtfully,

"I don't think so," and looking firmly at Sam.

"We'll all go down and drink ourselves to death." Nat was arrogant. "The brats can stay here and murder each other." He seemed not to notice the sudden silence that this remark provoked. "You'll come as well," he told Louise. "It's time you tried reeling about the streets singing."

This changed Louise's attitude somewhat, and she feebly suggested that she would stay in the cottage and let Sam go out, now that it was clear she wouldn't be allowed to stay. Unfortunately, this suggestion triggered off one of Sam's reflexes and he dutifully offered to stay at home, and this might have happened if Mary hadn't suggested that she would wait with Louise to see everything tidied and settled before they came down to the Tala. Then Harry offered to take Sally and Timmy for a walk along the beach.

By this time Nat had gone gabbling down the hill with Sam and Stacey, and Louise lingered and fussed over what to wear for a formal visit to the hotel. Mary held herself in patience and tried not to hurry her. Not a pint, she was thinking, but a thumping neat whisky and a loud conversation with a non-relation — even Geordie Mackay. She washed her face at the sink while Louise moved about quietly in the bedroom upstairs. This was really the greatest puzzle of all: how she came to be sharing a bedroom with Louise while Sam and Nat were sleeping in the studio. It had all happened while she, Mary, had been down at the beach to rescue the drowned mariners, and the arrangement had the stamp of Louise's fine little hand. In one way, Mary decided, Louise was bent on a return to carefree youth, sharing a room with another girl and having good giggles, while the sordid male sex was banished elsewhere. Certainly Sam didn't seem like a stimulating roommate, but it was ominous to see how briskly Louise banished him. They probably had twin beds at home, it was difficult to picture Louise yielding her brittle privacy every night.

Louise came downstairs in a tweed suit and started to make up her face lengthily at the mirror over the sink. She plucked her eyebrows.

"We don't see much of Dee," she said roguishly. "Has that young lady got other interests?"

"She probably ate at the Youth Hostel," Mary tried to finish the topic.

"O-oh! I suppose Youth Hostels are all right, really. There's a warden, or something, isn't there?"

"I have no idea."

"Oh, there would have to be. Though I don't know, young people today seem to get all the freedom they want. Personally, I'm a bit old-fashioned about these things."

"What things?" Mary asked mercilessly.

"You know."

"No."

"Of course, I always say, if a girl's well brought up, her parents should be able to trust her. I expect Dee's got a good head on her shoulders, although she's so quiet."

Quiet, Mary thought, was really very funny.

"But boys of that age," Louise droned on, "Well, I suppose they've always been the same. Man is the eternal hunter, father always used to say. It's all right for them — they're not going to suffer."

"No, it's very irritating," Mary said calmly, "having your daughters coming pregnant every night."

"I didn't mean anything like that!" Louise cried in protest. "Still, it must be a worry. Although really, it is very sweet, at that age, isn't it? Lord, remember those dances? Wondering if *anybody* was going to take you *home?* I wouldn't go through that again for a pension. Remember that boy Harrison? The one with the reputation? I was always *terrified* he would ask me to dance. He was probably all right, really. Of course, parents were stricter then. Half-past ten on the dot. Sometimes I wonder if it wasn't the best idea."

"Where did you meet Sam?" Mary asked, in the hope of shutting her up about those dances. To her surprise, she saw a blush on Louise's half-turned cheek. Louise laughed shakily.

"Sam! Oh, I just . . . met him. He worked in Sowerby's, the drapers. Still does, of course. Of course, I was quite grown up then. *Not* that I didn't have my chances, as you well know. But frankly, I was never in any hurry . . ."

How sad, how damned sad, Mary thought. Too true, Louise had had her chances, dozens of them. She must have turned down one too many and discovered that the chances were thinning out while ordinary girls like Mary had jumped at offers and used up the supply of men.

"He's got funny ideas, like the rest of them, of course," Louise said defensively. "But he's very well fixed at Sowerby's. Maybe it's not very *exciting,* but it's dependable. They think a lot of him."

"What funny ideas has he got?" Mary asked. She couldn't believe that they could be wildly funny, definitely not Marx Brothers standard.

"Oh, you know." Louise plucked several hairs in succession, rather fiercely. "Going into business on his own. That's all right with a lot of money. What if you fail? Know when you're well off, that's what I say." She plucked another hair as a full stop.

The sheer din surprised Louise at the Tala. She had probably expected a softly lit lounge with a lot of rich old leather and a quiet Highland waiter. Apart from the general babble, Geordie Mackay was trying to sing, and Andy Anderson had a fat forefinger two inches from his nose, telling him to shut up or be thrown out, and young Archie McBain was conducting a discussion about eight-meter boats at the top of his voice with an invisible friend. The family party was sitting round a worm-eaten table with Hughie Mackay and Denis McBain and Martin Stoddart, who was looking pompous and self-satisfied because Stacey was jammed beside him on a bench with one arm lying across his shoulders for balance. Once Louise had sat down, there was simply no more room, and Nat pulled Mary onto his knee.

"Mind how you distribute your pointed bones," he muttered. "I still have my manhood to worry about."

"I've been wondering if you had," she said into his ear, while Louise tried to smile tolerantly at this Bohemianism and Martin Stoddart's left ear tried to extend like a tulip-stalk to catch the conversation. Nat's free hand dug into her waist.

"Are the young people not with you?" Martin Stoddart shouted genially, "or do they prefer, ha ha ha, water, ha ha ha?" Mary smiled sweetly in return, and Louise laughed and laughed. Even Nat grinned his appreciation, while he murmured through unmoving lips,

"You're bloody female, did you know that?" His fingers squeezed her with loving concentration. "Why don't you and I get the hell outa here and bundle in the heather, babe?" Without looking at him and without moving her lips, Mary said, "Any time you like."

"Honest?" He turned to face her.

"Honest."

"Well for Pete's sake and the land o' Goshen. Now?"

"This very moment."

"Let's go," he muttered, and they looked at each other and she said, "Oh hell," and he said, "Oh well."

Hughie Mackay was reacting with quick instinct to Louise's aura of delicate sheltered femininity and offering her a port and lemon.

"Oh, I think an orange juice will suffice," she pleaded. "What are you drinking, Sam?"

"A whisky. And a beer." Sam was firm in the courage of companionship, and Louise did no more than purse her lips.

"Spike the orange with vodka," Nat muttered in Hughie's ear, and when Hughie looked shocked at this villainy, Nat added, "or you and I are finished." Mary giggled happily. Now it didn't matter that she and Nat couldn't rush out into the heather at that very moment. It was enough that they felt like it, that they both felt like it; and that cousin Louise was very likely to be roaring mortal drunk.

She was, too. When they all stood up to go, she suddenly looked stricken and dazed and said, "You sure that was orjuice? Onjuice? Mus' be the smoke."

Mary noticed that Stacey was sauntering out with her arm in Stoddart's — not that she was drunk, because she had a hard head. In fact, she was partly supporting the little schoolteacher, and listening to his babblings in a spirit of generous indulgence as they strolled off along the shore road. Louise was falling against Sam and accusing him of being the worse for liquor.

Louise reacted to the drink with giggles, but behind the giggles was a kind of hostility. She seized hold of Nat as they walked up to the cottage in the mild evening breeze, clung to his arm and took support from him, and babbled incoherently about artists and models. "*I* know! *I* know! Can' pull wool over *my* eyes!" she cackled. "Glad I'm not married to you, Na' Boag, wouldn' truss you f'a minute. Ar'ists? Th're all overset. Sect. Sexed. Did I say overslept? Ha ha ha. Don' truss you at all!"

She lurched, and Sam obligingly moved to take her other arm, but she flailed out with it, quite ferociously, to ward him off.

"I've got a partner f'this dance!" she said coldly, and then sniggered. Sam shrugged his shoulders and left her alone and fell back to walk beside Mary.

"She's not used to it," he said protectively, and Louise cried, "Whad he say?" angrily, but Nat merely laughed and kept her going. Louise had now put her arm round Nat's waist and was leaning her head awkwardly on his shoulder as they walked, and Sam was staring dumbly at them from behind. Mary decisively put her arm through his and squeezed, and he appeared to lose interest in Louise. He daringly patted Mary's hand without looking at her, and thought of stories he had read about husbands exchanging wives on holiday. He didn't actually enjoy the idea of lending Louise to another man, even a pleasant man like Nat, but there was a horrified kind of excitement about it, added to the dizzy thought of being Mary's temporary husband and having Mary all friendly and helpful and cooperative. Such an improper fantasy was novel to him. He was surprised at himself, but he held on to the thought muzzily and felt quite pleased. Mary took longer steps than Louise, though she wasn't much taller. It was easy to walk arm in arm with her, and he wasn't sure whether it excited or soothed him. He felt very strong and muscular.

Louise's giggling phase progressed rapidly into urgent fatigue. By the time they reached the cottage she was hanging heavily on Nat and yawning rather crossly, and this time she accepted Sam's support on the other side without actual resistance.

"Beddy-byes for you," Nat said amiably, and she tried to give him a leering smile, but her eyes were drooping, and she allowed Sam to help her up the steep staircase to the bedroom. Timmy and Sally were mercifully still out somewhere with Harry. Without conscious thought Mary started to make tea and Nat lolled smugly in the armchair in the kitchen. The shuffling of feet upstairs was amplified by the wooden ceiling, and then they heard Louise's slurred angry tones.

"Take your hands off."

"I'm only trying to help," Sam muttered.

"Never think about anybody but yourself . . . I'm not supposed to have any rights."

"Ssh."

"I'll ssh if I like, I can manage it myself, I'm going straight to sleep."

"Good idea."

"Yes, it is! Sleep, straight away. Some people don't seem to know that's what beds are for."

"Yes, I know. Ssh, Louise."

"Ssh! Ssh! Zat all you can say? I'm so *tired.*"

Nat looked up absentmindedly at Mary and said, "A virtuous woman is a pearl above price, I always think. What do you always think?"

"I always think you're a callous sod," she said. "At least I'll have no all-night sessions of girlish reminiscences."

"There's something very cold and practical about you, and I deplore it," Nat said. He reached out as she passed him with the teapot, and gripped her thigh. She stopped. He moved his hand up and down and then dropped it.

"I must cure myself of my evil thoughts," he murmured. "A boy can go blind that way, did you know that?"

"You could always get a job selling matches," she said thickly. Then Sam came, stooping awkwardly, downstairs. He coughed twice, sagging at the shoulders.

"Quite a nice night for a walk," he said and cleared his throat again, and to Mary's dismay, Nat immediately agreed and started to get up. It was true that Sam looked so embarrassed and vulnerable that it was only decent to be nice to him, but she had simultaneously thought that it would be nice to go for a walk with Nat, alone, before the kids came back home.

Outside she heard a thin voice shouting, "Ah ha, your stinky old lizard got away," and another thin voice shouting, "Fatty! You're a fat fatty!" She breathed out philosophically and started to look for the biscuits she had hidden.

Harry had failed after all to catch sight of Ada Fraser, and spent the evening walking and teaching Timmy and Sally to skim flat stones across the sea. As twilight, the late northern twilight, was approaching, he met Dee walking alone from the direction of the Youth Hostel, and the younger children started running home ahead, inseparable in hatred.

"That Timmy kid is a horned toad," he remarked to Dee. "How's Eric?"

"Oh, all right."

"Does he let you walk home alone?"

"I'm not fragile, am I? Anyway, it's nearly locking-up time at the Hostel."

"Locking, schmocking." Harry wasn't really too interested.

"He is a bit of a softy," Dee agreed. "Have you seen Linda?"

"No. Have you?"

"No, I just wondered. Do you fancy her?"

"I don't know her, actually. She seems all right."

"She's a bit soft too. Do you think we've got an affinity for softies?"

"Dunno." Harry thought of Ada Fraser and wondered . . . and thought of Magda. No, not a softy, and neither was Ada. The question intrigued him intellectually.

"Well, he's better than nothing," Dee said vaguely, and they walked in silence. Harry felt pleasantly fit and relaxed and cheerful. It didn't really matter that he hadn't bumped into Ada, she would always be there. It was a pity he hadn't met Linda, but he couldn't make up his mind whether she was going to be as fascinating and intelligent as he thought girls ought to be. He found he could contemplate her with detached pleasure and wait and see.

"Say you got to know Linda better," Dee said suddenly.

"Uhuh?"

"Nothing. I expect she's all right."

"She's not bad-looking."

"No, she's quite pretty," Dee agreed handsomely. "Eric's a paint salesman."

"Oh."

"House paint, I mean. Enamel and so on."

"Good."

"No — say . . ."

"Yes, say I got to know Linda better, uhuh, you said that. Spit it out."

Dee laughed, not too confidently.

"It's only a holiday, you'd probably never see her again."

"Uhuh."

There was another silence.

"How far would you expect to get?" Dee suddenly demanded, almost angrily.

"I don't know. How far where?"

"Sexually, dope."

"I don't know, dope. What is the latent import of this periphrastic interrogation?"

"Nothing."

"Not very far," Harry said firmly, answering a previous question. Dee looked at him scornfully.

"That is big brother talk."

"So? I'm Big Brother."

"I wish you would tell me. It's a damned bother." Dee had nearly regained her customary briskness. "Are you a virgin?"

"That is Big Brother's business."

"I bet you are," Dee scoffed. "I don't know, maybe you're not. Answer to next question, yes, dope."

"I knew you were."

"That is simply ridiculous. I'm not afraid of mice, am I?"

"My God, what has that got to do with anything?" Harry asked.

"Sally's right," Dee said. "You *are* ignorant. It was Sally that told me about mice. If you let a mouse loose in a roomful of women, the ones that jump on chairs and scream are virgins. It's nearly a hundred-percent accurate."

"Where do you dames get that rubbish? Is that true?"

"So Sally says."

"That kid is ruined," Harry said amiably. "Mind you, it figures. Phallic symbolism? But Sally doesn't worry about mice, so what does that mean?"

"Oh, honestly. It means it isn't exactly a hundred-percent accurate. *I* don't worry about mice."

"I don't know why you brought them up, then."

Dee abandoned mice.

"Oh," Harry said. "Answer to question one. Don't go any distance at all."

"I never asked that question, and you don't sound like yourself, either, you sound like Big Brother. Honestly, it's ridiculous. What if I was Linda?"

"I would say the same thing."

"Ho, ho."

"If I was Linda's brother I would say the same thing," Harry said unhappily. "Honest. Think of the trouble."

"It's different for boys, of *course*." Dee picked up a pebble and threw it aimlessly at the sea. He understood that there was no argument in process at all, that she was thinking out her own thoughts and would make her own decision about whatever it was.

"It's all very well," he said lamely, "talking about doing anything you like, but who takes care of the bastard?"

"Oh, don't be medieval. You're right. I could always ask the old lady for a pill."

"My God. Steal one, if you like."

"You mean it's okay?"

"No, I never said that! I suppose you'd be better having one than not, if you're afraid you might do something loony."

"I don't know!"

"I thought you could always hold the boys off with one hand, two-gun Boag. Eric shouldn't be much trouble. He *is* a softy. Does he drive you mad with forbidden passion?"

"No." She sounded quite matter-of-fact. "I think I drive him, a bit."

"That's his funeral. Dammit, these young fellas should take more cold baths, it always worked in Poona."

"It's different," Dee said with surprise. "When you know somebody. Boys aren't any bother, you know what they're after and they're not getting it. When you know somebody, you don't like to be lousy to them. I don't mean you have to . . . I don't know — what do people do?"

"You mean *you're* not keen," Harry said desperately. "So? Don't do it."

"Tell that to Linda. I'm not frigid, you know. I don't think I'm frigid."

"All right." Harry felt he was sacrificing his ambitions with some nobility. "I won't do it to Linda, and you don't do it with Eric. I swear."

"Huh. Do you mean Linda isn't going to let you, anyway?"

"I am not," he said loftily, "without some skill in these matters."

"Maybe that swine Eric is the same," she said moodily. "Maybe the softy act is the whole act. But he *is,* you can't help feeling . . . sorry for him?"

"Maternal?"

"I don't know."

"Junk the tragic routine. Plenty of girls would like to have your problem."

"I know," she said with a happy smile. "It's very . . . very problematical."

"Here, I tell you what, ask the old lady about it."

"Kindly, drown yourself, along the dotted line."

"She's not decrepit, you know."

"No, I know, but she's not young either. *Young.* You know what I mean, it's just a giggle with them. They've got past the Big Problem Phase years ago."

"Mm, I suppose so. I wish I had. Here, ask Cousin Louise for *her* advice."

Dee held on to his arm and shrieked.

Night fell softly on the peninsula, where the summer sun-light lingered faintly till almost midnight. Harry stolidly settled to sleep on the sofa bed beside Timmy. Stacey lay happily on her bunk scribbling some notes about her new character . . . a retired university don, she thought, had more kick than a schoolmaster . . . rather desiccated and pedantic, but with a turbulent history of sensuality and even brutality behind him. She wondered why she had paid so little attention to Martin Stoddart before, with his prissy but really quite attractive manners and the accidental revela-tions of his wild past, and perhaps even wild present, as a relentless pursuer of feminine virtue. He hadn't actually claimed this, and if he had she might have dismissed the claim as a boast; but so often he stopped himself just on the point of a disgraceful reminiscence that she had analyzed him unerringly.

In the bunk below, Dee lay on her back with open eyes and enjoyed the delight of wrestling with a crucial problem of life. Sally was sprawled in bed at the other side of the room, face-down and in deep coma.

In even deeper coma, Louise snored indelicately next door, and Mary lay awake in the bed above, grateful not to be en-gaged in conversation for one night at least, and resolutely thinking about methods of reflooring the kitchen, so as not to think about other more urgent and infuriating things.

It was past one in the morning when Sam, uncomfortably dozing on an air bed in the studio outhouse, felt a hand press-ing on his shoulder and shaking him gently. His eyes opened at once and he saw Nat's face, slightly evil in the light of a candle, above him.

"Ssh, Nat said. Sam stared up at him and sshed.

"Are you awake?" said Nat, in character tones of awe, "or have you died in your sleep?"

"I'm awake," Sam whispered, uncomprehending.

"Good. Do you like salmon?"

"Quite well."

"Can you stick to a lie when they're beating you with rubber truncheons?"

Sam sat up as a gasp collided with a yawn and threatened to choke him. He blinked rapidly and beat his chest to relieve the blockage.

"Have no fear," Nat said, banging him absentmindedly on the back. Nat then skipped to the window of the outhouse and surveyed the cottage, and came back in loping strides. "I'll have to take you into my confidence, Sam. I'm leaving right now for a secret mission, unknown to medical science, and I need an alibi. Will you stand by me in the witness box? We played pontoon all night? No, not pontoon, Old Maid — I don't know how to play pontoon."

"Eh, eh, eh, oh. You goin' somewhere?"

"Good, good, intelligence, I like that. *Secret*. The future of the galaxy hangs in the balance."

Sam started to disentangle himself from his sleeping bag.

"It's none of my business, Nat," he said timidly. "You shouldn't do it, it's not right. I quite see artists and that are different, but Mary's a nice girl. It's not for me to judge — no offense, mind you. I suppose it's got nothing to do with me." He sat up and looked shattered. "A nice girl like that, she's that nice. I wouldn't take a girl like that for granted."

"What the hell are you maundering about?"

"Sorry, Nat, it's none of my business. But honestly, no offense. What time is it? No, honest, Nat." Sam was out of his depth and pleading. "There was a girl in the cash desk once . . . but what I decided was, what's the use? I said, no, stop, it's only a . . . after all, for better or for worse. Maybe I was wrong. I'd be frightened."

Nat had started to snicker very quietly as he moved about

the studio and pulled on canvas shoes. To Sam's astonishment, he rubbed his fingers on the back of the dead fire and rubbed soot on his face.

"You're sex-mad, Sam, did anybody ever tell you that? This is a secret mission behind the Iron Curtain. Strike hard and melt into the everlasting snows. You sure you like salmon?"

"Poaching!" Sam was horrified.

"Did the laird give birth to the salmon?" Nat asked loftily. "Does the good book not say the earth and all the fruits thereof?" He laughed and came over and patted Sam on the pajama shoulder with a black hand. "There, there, try and get some sleep, and remember, I was here all night."

Sam watched him wistfully as he decanted whisky from a half-full bottle into a hip flask and stuffed it into a pocket.

"Can I come?" he asked humbly. Nat turned with surprised interest.

"Can you keep your head when all about you have lost theirs?" he asked in wonder. "Never mind that, can you run?"

"Oh, I keep pretty fit," said Sam.

"By God, you're deputized," said Nat. "If you fall into the hands of the enemy we disown you, you know that? Damn, we've got no suicide pills."

"I've never done much fishing," Sam said, in ecstasy. "But I could carry things."

"Stout chap." Nat patted him on the other shoulder as he hoisted himself clear and reached for his trousers. "Just as long as you can run like a whippet." Sam dressed in a frenzy of haste and joy and liberation. There was nobody present to look at him and make him sit down while everybody else went to the circus. His apprehension had gone. He was being allowed to join in something, in the anonymous dark of night, something absolutely forbidden. In a daze, he rubbed his hand on the sooty fire-back and massaged black into his face.

The house was dark, but they crept down the driveway without a whisper, and Sam fell dutifully in beside Nat as he turned up and headed for the skyline. In ten minutes they left the road and began to scramble through gorse and heather, heading south. Suddenly there was a low cough, and Nat froze. Sam cannoned into him, but avoided falling.

"Don't say ccchic or ochic!" Nat whispered violently, and a voice answered, "Eeechie or ochie! By Joves, man, I was beginning to think you had drowned at sea or gone for a sodger. What was keeping you at all?" In the vagrant light of the sliver of moon, Sam saw Hughie Mackay rising from the gorse, his face unblackened and glimmering.

"We had to drug everybody's tea," Nat muttered. "Sam came. He can run."

"Ach, who wants to be running when a bit of military strategy can make it a walkover, a veritable walkover," Hughie said calmly.

"I can't fish," Sam apologized, now suddenly worried that somebody might give him a rod and expect him to know what to do with it.

"To hell, the fish don't know that," Hughie soothed him. "They'll be jumping into your hand before you're an hour older. Just a wee clout of the sound waves and they'll be queuing up for the smoking." He turned up the hill and Sam loped behind as they flitted through the beginnings of a scrubby wood. From time to time Nat, in the middle position, looked over his shoulder and swung his hand in an arc to keep the cavalry charge moving forward.

The wood became impenetrably dark, and Sam found himself cannoning into small trees, comforted by the muttered curses of Nat who was doing the same thing a few paces ahead.

"Ssht." Hughie Mackay stopped. Sam stopped, and listened to his own breathing. There was the faintest glimmer of water ahead, and the small sounds of water.

"It's the grand night for it," Hughie muttered. "It's as dark as a ——'s ——."

"It's a —— sight darker than that," Sam whispered, and felt overjoyed with abandonment. He felt Nat's hand patting his arm in approval, and blushed.

"We'll just stroll along like gentlemen to the other end," Hughie remarked, but still in an undertone, "and take what the good God has been saving up for us. Ssh."

There was the distinct sound of movement somewhere among the trees.

"It's only a Bengal tiger," Nat whispered, and Sam held his mouth to stifle a giggle.

"There is no Bengal tiger about here," Hughie muttered. "Maybe it is Hughie McVain and him getting the courage to come and steal our bloody fish."

Somewhere in the woods, somebody coughed, once, twice. Then Sam leaped three inches in the air as a voice crashed through the darkness.

"Vide o mare quantu bello, Spira tantu sentimento!"

The noise came off the water as off a sounding board, bizarre and terrifying in the dark solitude of the wood; a reverberating tenor, cracking slightly on the last high note and then coughing and sailing away with the next line.

"By the living ——'s ——!" Hughie croaked. "It's the operatic polis!"

"Did you bring your mandolin, Sam?" Nat asked. Sam shook his head. His heart was still pounding.

"The Lowland bastart," Hughie muttered fiercely. "Up

here committing diatonic incest with himself when he should be seducing his landlady like an honest man. Oh, I hope it never takes me like that, damn him for a —————'s ————!"

"What'll we do?" Sam asked in a trembling voice, and Hughie turned round in disgust and muttered, "Maybe if you could do the soprano part you would lure him away like one of those laurel-eyed women you hear about." Hughie sat down against a tree. "He'll have us here for a month before he runs out of symphonies, and I still say the bugger's sherp on his high notes."

Nat sat down, and Sam sat down beside him, praying that the expedition would be canceled now that he had had all the excitement he needed. The soaring voice farther along the pool had finished "Sorrento" and was now launched on a selection from *The Desert Song*.

"He's trying to sicken the fish to death," Nat suggested.

"Ach, no, the silly hoor has to practice somewhere," Hughie said tolerantly. "No decent citizen in the village would stand for that noise."

"Sam!" Nat had clutched his wrist and was leaning toward him. "Can you do funny accents?"

"No."

"You're useless, do you know that? Useless. Never go poaching without learning funny accents. Hughie!" He leaned toward Hughie to whisper urgently. "You take Sam and get off the path and don't breathe. I'll get Sherlock Holmes away. Ssh!" He raised an imperious hand to silence questions, and turned and loped back through the woods in an Indian crouch. Sam found himself being hustled into deep undergrowth, and squatting in soft leaf mold with bushes jabbing his neck.

The Riff Song was reprised by the vibrant tenor of Tom Wishart. Then he cleared his throat. Sam and Hughie sat tensed, and growing colder, and to their disgust the voice swelled again in the big chorus number from *The Student Prince*. It went on and on and on.

But as the last note died lingeringly away this time, there was a fresh voice added, from far away to the north.

"Bi the howly saints, yez are mortherin' me! Ah, would yez now! Moind the knoife! Aaargh! Oo! Thod!" All this came piercing through the trees in a shrill sequence, followed by gasps and grunts and thumps. Any of the Boags would have recognized it as Nat's famous version of the Dublin Amateur Players enacting the French Revolution. Sam didn't recognize it, and he felt the sweat starting out on his chest and his wrists prickling.

When the performance reached a dramatic pause, there was a pause too from the direction of Tom Wishart, and then the constable's voice, embarrassed, shouted, "Pardon?"

"Ow moy God, oi'm dead for shure! Take that!" A crashing in the undergrowth.

"Who's that?" Tom Wishart yelled, and started his own crash through the undergrowth. The confused shouts from Nat continued, now extending their vocal range to include a squealing woman and a groaning bass. Sam found his faint view of the water blotted out as a big black body thundered toward him and a great boot flashed past less than a yard from his head. He stiffened in anguish. Was it a fine poachers got, or years and years in jail? Sweat was trickling down into his eyes, but he was terrified to raise a hand to wipe it off.

"By Joves," Hughie Mackay whispered, "what do you think of that for initiative, man?" Above the steady crunch of small branches there came the clear sound of a bicycle bell. Sam Bennet tried to smile in the dark and took comfort from the evident joy and assurance of Hughie, who was

shaking his head and muttering "Man, man!" He had to
endure the suspense for nearly half an hour before twigs
started to snap again nearby and a voice muttered, "Eechie
or ochie!"

"Man," said Hughie, "it was a pantomime and no mistake,
you'll have to teach me the Irish or maybe the Pakistani, was
it not a joy to listen to, Sam?"

"But what if he comes back?" Sam asked nervously.

"Ach, we'll think of some other brilliant performance,"
Hughie said recklessly. "We have the heels of him when it
comes to military strategy, and only one of him chasing us in
different directions at once."

"Ten years," Nat said, "positively no more than ten years
and then I do my farewell tour. Don't worry, Sam," he added
kindly as he sat down to breathe, "he'll not be back. I drove
his bike like Paul Revere nearly to the beach and then got
up on the bank and spied on him. There's a good place for
illicit houghmagandy down there," he remarked to Hughie.
"You can see for miles and nobody can see you and the grass
is nice and soft."

"Ach, the very place, I know it," Hughie agreed. "It's a
wonder there's a blade of grass left on it."

"None of your revolting reminiscences," Nat said. "He
picked up his bike and rode along the shore in both directions at once."

"He'll think you were a crowd off a foreign yat," Hughie
opined happily. "He'll be getting out a dinghy and quarter-
ing the Irish Sea for you. Come on."

Slightly less unhappy, but with a prickle in the shoulder
blades, Sam followed them to the edge of the Long Pool and
along to the far end, and watched numbly as Hughie Mackay
took a white stick out of his knapsack and heaved it out into
the water on the end of what looked like electric cable. His

eyes glazed as Hughie lit a match and touched it to the end of the cable. The cable burned steadily till the flame reached the water, and then kept on burning beneath the surface.

"Where will we shelter?" Sam asked in a hoarse whisper. Hughie patted his arm.

"Man, we're not going to explode the peninsula," he said. "It's only a gentle wee squib to tell the fish it's bedtime."

At that moment a voice, subdued but clear, floated across the water.

"They're lighting a fire."

In the open air by the pool it was possible to see several yards in the dim dark, and Hughie and Nat and Sam turned to stare at one another.

"The Martians!" Nat whispered.

There was a loud splash in the distance, and an English voice called, "Who's there?" Then somebody said "Oh!" and there was another splash. There was another splash, and a girl laughed.

"Bi the holy hooly!" Nat whispered. "There's some silly sods swimming, the filthy naked beasts."

"Aye," Hughie muttered in admiration, "and by Joves, though, you need to be young and fit for that up here."

"But you'll blow them up!" Sam gasped, and Nat said, "You might, at that, Hughie. How strong is it?"

"Ach, a man can't live for people overrunning the woods! We'll have to think."

Without waiting to think, Sam jumped straight into the water and gasped as the cold hit his waist. He thrashed about a few yards from the shore, and a few seconds later came wallowing up to the bank holding a sputtering light in front of him.

"You mad bastard," Nat said approvingly. "Get rid of

it!" But Hughie was meeting him at the edge and taking the sputtering fuse from him.

"Dammit to hell," he complained, "it's a dear stuff nowadays and there's another ten feet of it. Let me get my knife."

"Just a minute," Nat whispered. He turned his head toward the sound of splashing farther down the pool, and yelled,

"Oi can see yez, ye poachin' spalpeens! Get out of there or Oi'll give yez both barrels. Yez are surrounded!"

"Oh God!" somebody squealed. There was a chorus of splashes and gasps.

"Ten seconds and Oi foire!" Nat yelled, and whispered, "how long will it burn?"

"Ach, minutes yet, but it's us that are surrounded," Hughie said. "There's an entire herd of them."

"I want your names, the intoire lot of thim!" Nat bellowed, "Yez'll pay for this noight's work!"

From far up the pool, the splashes had stopped, but there was a babble of low voices and the clink of glass, and a girl's voice squealing, "But my *clothes!* I don't care, I want my clothes!"

"Ach, to hell with it," Hughie said, and threw the sputtering end of the fuse back into the water. From the noise farther up the pool, there could have been perhaps three hundred people scrambling in the darkness to get dressed and falling over one another and not getting anything done well or quickly.

"Stand back a wee bit," Hughie muttered, and Sam, dripping and aggrieved at not being applauded as a hero, shuffled back in dripping trousers as the little light under the water inched downward. Slowed down by shivers and the weight of his wet clothes, he was still in the line of fire when a deep report thundered from the pool and a wall of water crashed over his top half.

The silence that followed was deep and tingling.

"Bang," Nat said in quiet bliss. A babble burst out from farther up the pool, in which the words dynamite and poachers and salmon recurred. Hughie and Nat were already at the water's edge, scooping joyfully with nets and piling stiff dead fish on the bank. Sam, useless and wretched, and without a net, thought of wading in and picking up fish with his bare hands, but he couldn't see how they could carry much more, so he beat his arms round his shoulders to keep warm while Hughie and Nat stuffed salmon into their rucksacks.

"He'll get your fingerprints off the bike handles, man!" Hughie suddenly said. After a thoughtful pause, Nat replied, "You're not thinking right, Hughie, not thinking right, know that? He's got his own prints all over it now. Stop giving us heart failure and let's get the hell outa here before the posse."

The babble at the other end of the pool had changed in tone, swelling in a chorus of delighted shouts and splashes. Without discussing the next move, Nat and Hughie closed the rucksacks, stowed the nets and set off through the wood, and Sam shambled behind, reflecting that it was handy to be wearing Terylene trousers and nylon socks, since they would dry out before Louise saw them. As they were nearing open air, Hughie stopped and motioned for silence. He didn't need to. There was the unmistakable shrill of a police whistle.

"The polis in front and Jamieson the keeper at the back," he said philosophically. "Let the swimming team make all the noise."

It was hard to tell how far or near the noises were, but the wood was alive with crunches and shouts and mutters. The whistle sounded again, a little farther away, and Tom Wishart could be heard shouting "Stop, stop!" A dog barked, and Hughie cursed briefly and plunged on again.

When they reached open air they could see a torchlight swooping and waving away to the left, and most of the voices had stopped. Hughie ran at a gentle trot and the two others followed. They reached a little plateau overlooking the string road, and Hughie sat down and to Sam's horror, lit a cigarette.

"It's safe as Gibraltar, man," Hughie comforted him, "we're the invisible men up here." He held the cigarette in a cupped hand behind him and lay face-down and looked over the edge, and Sam and Nat followed. Down the string road came two bikes, each ridden by a young man and each with a girl in shorts perched on the crossbar. One of the girls was waving a salmon eighteen inches long. The police whistle sounded again.

"Joves, a nakit girl in the watter and a salmon in the hand the same night," Hughie whispered enviously. "It's a fair bonanza for the hostelers this night."

A fat young man came pounding down the road with a salmon swinging from his hand and his breath in painful gasps. He looked round in despair and threw himself, rolling, into the ditch, as another bike whistled down from the direction of the wood. Tom Wishart's legs flashed as his bike swooped round the curve, skidded, and slid away from him over the edge of the shore road and on to the beach. His voice carried clearly back up the hill.

"It's a ——'s ——!" It sounded almost like weeping. He got up and scrambled down onto the beach and threw the bike bodily up onto the road. The fat young man lay gasping in the ditch. Tom heaved himself up onto the road, kicked the bike brutally, threw his leg across the saddle and started to pedal listlessly along the shore road. There was a musical ping of broken spokes as he went.

"If I was a religious man I would think we was being taken care of for sure," Hughie said. "For God's sake, wash the scales off yourself when you get home, they'll be out with an amplifying glass and mine detectors tomorrow. No, give Sam the first pull, the poor man, I never saw such a grand piece of heroics as that, and it's a fact."

Nat handed his whisky flask to Sam. Sam took it and poured the hot neat stuff down his throat. He had never drunk neat whisky before. It almost dried his socks instantaneously.

"Too right," said Nat, "definitely mentioned in dispatches — jumping into that perishing icy water on a night like this!" But he smiled and punched Sam on the arm, and Sam glowed and choked on the whisky. The fat young man got up cautiously and started trotting down the road, still clutching the salmon. Other members of the swimming party, which was probably only twenty strong in spite of its noise, flitted down the string road and across the hills making good speed. One of them was a girl in a bathing suit with a coat thrown over it, and light hair flopping on her shoulders.

"I wouldn't mind a midnight swim with that one," Sam said, letting himself go entirely. Hughie said, "And Joves, I would warm the pool for you too!" Warmed with the whisky and drunk with the excitement, Sam felt that if only Louise was lying in a double bed instead of a bunk at the cottage, he would have gone home and thrown back the covers and wakened her up and shown her what a man was really like and to hell with how tired she was. They left a fish at Martin Stoddart's door — to get the guilt distributed, as Hughie explained before he vanished toward and beyond the Tala.

Back in the outhouse, Sam found himself amazingly un-
tired and unshivery, but Nat lit the oil stove and got it roaring, and blandly poured the rest of the bottle of whisky into
two great helpings. Then he meticulously went over his
clothes for fish scales, and did the same for Sam's, while Sam
sat smiling helplessly in his sleeping bag with his face still
streaked with soot.

"Death to the infidels," Nat said, drained his glass and said
"Ouch." He switched off the stove and lay down, and Sam
sipped his whisky and then lay back and flexed his muscles,
suddenly slightly dizzy in the darkness.

In the morning, Louise looked horrible. Her eyes were
deeply shadowed and she moaned from time to time; and
glaring at Sam with open loathing, she told him he would
have to amuse Timmy because she was definitely ill and
would have to rest.

"Tripe," Nat said brutally. "A good jag of whisky and
you'll be singing bawdy songs again. And Sam and I are going fishing today without any accursed brats tripping us up.
I've got to get my money's worth out of my permit."

"Sam," Louise said grimly, the test of wills, the moment of
truth, "will stay in this house today."

"You will get back to bed," Nat said, "till you feel you can
eat a greasy chop like other people. Come on."

Louise was not really enjoying Nat's offensive charm as
much as she usually did. There was a definite possibility,
Mary thought, that Nat was going to have his first failure
with Louise. But Louise also didn't have the vigor to fight
back. She was pushed upstairs, and Nat left her and came
back down and said to Sam, "Over the top, men!" Sam
meekly stood up and got ready to go, and the eye he fixed on
Timmy silenced the little boy's whimpering complaints before they were uttered.

"Frankly," said Mary, "I hope you both catch your death of cold."

"We will catch five salmon. I guarantee it, I, Chingachgook, mighty hunter, ugh."

"I'll buy some roast lamb," she said. He kissed her and said, "Oh? Does that go with salmon?" She returned the kiss.

"That goes with anything," she said.

Nat and Sam walked along the shore road to the Tarbie Burn, carrying a legal rod and a permit from the Ochard Angling Association and a clean rucksack. Tom Wishart was sitting on a pile of tires in the morning sunshine in the forecourt of Hughie Mackay's garage, and Hughie was snipping wire spokes and fitting them into a half-empty bike wheel.

"Ach, that polis job of yours is a ——'s ——," he was saying. "I wouldn't be surprised if they *was* Irish, or maybe a boatload of these delinquents from Barra, they have a terrible Irish way of talking in Barra being Catholics. And what was you doing up at the Long Pool anyways? Did you have a tip-off from the Interpol?"

"Ach, — " said Tom. His character had been deeply changed. He looked sourly at Nat's fishing rod and wished he was working traffic duty in Edinburgh.

TWELVE

As HUGHIE MACKAY always said, it only needed one clype to ruin a whole village where salmon were concerned. But the great crime finally had to be put away in the files of the police and the splenetic laird as unsolved. One of the people who might well have clyped out of duty and a hunger to please the laird was Martin Stoddart, and his conscience was no match for the discovery of a two-pound fish on his doorstep. He immediately adopted his other conscience and spoke of the nobility of least-said-soonest-mended, and Isa made a really beautiful job of cooking it and burning every scrap of evidence afterward.

Tom Wishart was nearly sure that the great fish robbery was the work of touring professionals, and there was suggestive evidence in the presence of nine or ten motor cruisers in the bay. It had been a quiet month for visiting sailing boats, with the absence of a decent wind, but any of the motor cruisers might have been the headquarters of an international gang of salmon-dynamiters, and he couldn't see how he was going to investigate this possibility. He had never been sure how far his authority extended out into the water,

and he didn't want to phone Oban for advice from his supe-
riors or from the Customs man, whom he disliked as an imitation type of police official.

He hadn't noticed the fact that during the next day, a fat
young hosteler had spent a lot of time in a dinghy, with sails
up but using oars on the windless sea, and had cruised in-
quisitively around several of the motor cruisers. The fat boy,
never particularly popular with the hostel crowd, had now
become a power in the little community by having the nerve
and the business instinct to undertake the export of the entire catch of dynamited fish to the yacht people, who bought it
and paid for it and said nothing except when drinking in the
Tala, where it didn't matter.

Tom had one small consolation in not having to report
that he had smashed the County Constabulary's official
bicycle. Hughie Mackay, who wasn't hard-hearted in spite
of his foul tongue, had repaired the broken wheel, in his own
words, as an experiment in a lost mechanical art, and
wouldn't take money for it. If everybody in Ochie had been
like Hughie Mackay, Tom thought, a policeman's lot would
be a lot less hard.

The laird, of course, felt the poaching as a mortal wound.
He didn't, himself, enjoy fishing much, but the fish were
his, and he had often computed the exact cash value of the
Long Pool at a given moment and felt cheered by it. Not
only that, the fish were an essential part of his hospitality to
people who mattered, buyers and bottlers and political people who had an entrée to the Honours List; and every fish
stolen was a guest disappointed. Arnold had a long noisy
session with Cully Jamieson, his gamekeeper, who was quite
infuriating in pointing out that he couldn't patrol 18,000
acres every night and that there were plenty of salmon left
for anybody who had the wit to cast a line.

More infuriating was the calm, placid way Jamieson explained all this, as if he wouldn't be worried if the laird immediately fired him. More infuriating still was the fact that this was true. If he fired Jamieson he would get somebody worse and Jamieson would pick up another job the next day.

This was one of the occasions when Arnold longed sentimentally for the good old days of his ancestors, the hereditary Lairds of Ochie, with power of fire and sword, life and death, and a private gallows in the courtyard for clansman or stranger who offended the peace of the house.

Mrs. Harper was quieter but if anything, more angry than Arnold. A magazine writer from Kingston, New York, before she became Arnold's second wife, she had adopted Britain with delight as God's own country because of her impression that class still counted there and that a woman could rise to the top and be recognized as a top woman. Like Arnold, she had thrown a haze between herself and her ancestors, who had run a drugstore in Kingston, and often thought about her grandfather the great Indian fighter; a totemistic figure in her imagination, and dead against the sickly sentimentality of modern times and the uppityness of inferior races and social groups.

At the same time, for we all have our inconsistencies, she had a pleasant ambition to return, very briefly, to Kingston as Lady Harper, or Baroness Harper, let some of her old friends see her, and depart at once for the Olympian joys of noble society in England again.

"Well, it's *your* welfare state," she accused Arnold, quite unfairly. "All you do in this country is encourage the poor white trash to get above themselves." Her rather agreeable natural accent moved several states south when she thought about poor white trash. "Why don't you lay bear-traps or something? I don't trust that gamekeeper and never did.

He's one of them, isn't he? I think I'll go and lay down for a while."

Joyce spent quite a lot of time lying down when they were at Ochie. The stresses of being a vivid hostess in London brought out all her organizing energy, but when she came north, there was no incentive to sparkle, and she treated Argyllshire as a rest cure when there were no friends visiting. She had agreed to entertain the Boags for simple and practical reasons. If Arnold got his title . . . *when* Arnold got his title, it would be impossible to delay any longer having a proper portrait done of her, and she was attracted by the possibility of getting a good one cheap.

A Boag portrait would be good. When Arnold had mentioned the name, Joyce had at once called friends in London to have him assessed, and had learned that his portrait of E. M. Forster in the last Academy had been the only portrait worth a damn. And it would obviously be cheap, since Boag, in spite of his London reputation, was nevertheless one of the local tenantry, sworn to loyalty and servility to the hereditary laird.

Arnold was surprised when young Winston offered to deliver the invitation to Nat Boag. The boy usually shied away from any helpful activity and was in fact not much good for anything, his education having apparently destroyed his capacity for work without putting anything else in its place.

"Just the two of them, mind," he told Winston. "I'm not serving good food to a crowd of kids, you know?"

"Really, do you *mind?*"

Arnold hoped Winston's languid manner wasn't a symptom of queerness, but he never had the nerve to say so. He was going to feel happier when the guests arrived for the birthday celebrations and there were some young women about the house and the boat to waken the kid up out of his apathy.

Winston, utterly confident and utterly uncertain, was glad to find on arriving at Kirk Cottage that there seemed to be nobody about except the tolerable Mrs. Boag.

Winston was wrong. Nat was in the studio with Ada Fraser; but everybody else was away from the house, and Mary was pleasurably occupied in soaking the dense thicknesses of wallpaper from the kitchen walls and stripping down the bare wood. All the internal walls of the house were lined with the same grooved pine, and she had positively decided to expose it and do something clever to bring it up pale, and then seal it and wax it. After that was done, she could start wondering about how to replace the uneven flagstones on the kitchen floor with something bright and simple . . . unshiny tiles, cork, something.

It was a relief to be working at her present useful drudgery. But for the arrival of Louise and family, she would have started on this a week before. There was something delicious, almost sensuous, about finding the occasional piece of wall where three thicknesses of ancient wallpaper peeled away in one great piece.

She had started the job in sweater and slacks, but after half an hour of exertion, had taken off the sweater, and after another ten minutes, had taken off the slacks too. Her hair was wrapped in a scarf to keep out the drips as she flung water on the wall with a distemper brush, and her feet were in tattered canvas shoes. When she heard the sharp knock on the door she suspected instantly that whoever was knocking had probably first of all had a good look through the kitchen window. Chiding herself for such a maidenish thought, she grabbed a smock and pulled it on and buttoned it before she went to the door.

The first thing Winston's eager eyes saw when the door opened was not Mary's face or the scarf or the smock, but the sweater and the slacks casually flung across the kitchen table, and her bare legs showing beneath the smock. His heart thumped faster.

"Hello," he said, with a sinister undertone that nobody could possibly mistake.

"Hello." Mary held the wet brush aside to avoid dripping water on him. He leaned against the doorjamb and tried to eye her speculatively. Mary was irritated mildly at being caught in the smock and tattered shoes; not for the reason Winston would have expected, but simply because she felt she wasn't skinny enough to wear a loose balloony smock elegantly and she hadn't expected to meet anybody at all. As he stood there, obviously tongue-tied, she dismissed these vain reflections and said, "Come in out of the heat."

Winston sauntered in on the balls of his feet and looked round the kitchen. Nothing to lie on, and it was an inch deep in water in places . . . an open staircase . . . zounds, it was like a set for a French movie.

"Jolly decent little nest," he said kindly. "All alone, hey?"

"Yes, it's not bad, or it will be." She was flushed. She rubbed one cheek with a damp hand. "Can I do something for you?"

"Oh, that." Winston perched one buttock elegantly on the kitchen table and rested his hands on the crumpled slacks. "Yes, a bore I expect, my people would like you for dinner as a matter of fact."

Nat would have said "Oh, fried?" but she decided not to try this on this humorless boy. He was right, the prospect of dinner with the Harpers *was* a bore. But in a place like Ochie you couldn't plead fifteen previous engagements.

"Thank you," she said. "When?" She was going to lay down the dripping brush, but out of the corner of her eye she saw his hand idly fingering her discarded slacks, and in a first twinge of suspicion, she kept the brush in her hand. It

was ridiculous, of course, elegant young men however
tongue-tied didn't pursue her; but she held onto the brush.

"Oh, tomorrow night." He flipped a limp hand to dispose
of that topic. "Informal, of course," he added tolerantly.
Mary smiled a little smile and refrained from letting him
have the brush across his silly condescending face. She had
a picture of Nat turning up at the big house in shorts and
gum boots, and kept herself from laughing aloud.

"Hard at it, eh?" Winston asked, his eyes flickering up and
down the buttons on the smock. There was no possible doubt
about it, he thought, as one of her legs moved and a flash of
bare thigh showed, the invitation cards were positively out.
"Hardly an amusing pastime for a jolly afternoon . . ."

He was rubbing one of his sweating palms on his jacket,
and Mary realized that her suspicions were dead right. Having decided that, she relaxed entirely. Her only problem
was going to be how to beat him off without letting him
realize it. The boy was decidedly an odd one, and probably
very easy to wound.

"Oh, I like it," she said. "About eight o'clock tomorrow?
I really must get back to this." She picked up the bucket of
water and poked the brush in it.

"Jolly interesting," he said in a suave voice. "I'd like to
watch it."

It was going to be difficult. She turned her back on him
without quite letting him out of her sight, and started
to paint water lavishly onto a dry stretch of paper; and as she
did this she thought of Tom Sawyer and of how irresistible
a wet brush was to anybody watching.

"You've got the knack," she heard him say, and knew that
he had moved. He towered over her from behind and she
resolutely carried on.

"I don't suppose I'd be any damn good at a thing

like that," he breathed shakily. "Mind if I have a try?" And instead of taking the brush, he reached over her shoulder and imprisoned both the brush and her hand and moved them up and down.

"Yes," he muttered, "you're jolly good at it." His left hand slipped from her shoulder and insolently closed on her breast. Without letting it linger for an instant she said, "More water," and stooped sharply down and sideways to the bucket. Surprised, he almost shot over her back. He released her hand and stretched out an arm to support himself on the wall as he almost fell, and Mary smoothly straightened up with the brush clutched in her hand and drove the handle upwards into his mouth.

Winston jerked back and clutched his face, too agonized to cry out.

"You poor child!" she cried, "have you hurt yourself?"

"I may have broken a damn tooth!" he yelped.

"How awful! I'll call my husband from the outhouse — perhaps he could pull it for you," she added wildly. "What a beastly thing to happen to you." Winston had put his elbows on the table and was crouching with his mouth in one hand, and she patted his head as she sped for the door. She was relieved when Winston bolted after her.

"Don't be a damn fool," he shouted politely. "Never mind the damn tooth. Damn." She let him brush past her into the garden still holding his mouth.

"I do hope it's better by tomorrow," she said. "Will you thank your parents for us?"

"Oh . . . !" He turned and stamped down the driveway.

He was still slightly confused. It was true the whole affair had been a bungle, but the damn woman hadn't actually complained, she couldn't have been nicer, for her sort. Maybe she had simply failed to get the message. Tony Hammer was undoubtedly right, the straightforward style was the only way. And yet, and yet, the insolent bitch had called him . . . he tried not to remember it, but it stuck . . . *child.* Maybe that was just the silly damn way these people talked. And also, as the awful pain in his gum settled to a sickening ache, his left hand remembered taking a hold of her and the quite fantastic mixture of firm and soft. That was supposed to get them raving for it like squeezing the old trigger . . . no, wrong, that was where you needed a spot of patience . . . damn, damn damn. In fact, ——! And it was damned offensive, when you thought of it, that the parents had actually invited that pair to dinner on equal terms. It distorted everything. They'll probably use the wrong forks and sit like dummies and not say a word all through the meal, he thought, and knew this wasn't true, and hated them.

Mary waited till Winston was properly down the driveway and safely away before she relaxed and left the doorway. For a moment she had contemplated having to shout for Nat, because the boy was clearly so odd that he might have done something genuinely silly. It was going to be a scream sitting down to table with him in his own home.

She was pondering the incident quite calmly now that it was over, and refusing to feel flattered that a lad of twenty should have made a pass at her, because this was no ordinary lad of twenty. She warned herself that she must warn Dee about him. She would not, of course, warn Louise. Anything that might frighten Louise into going back home to Bathgate would be a social boon. How frightful, she thought, suddenly thinking seriously about Dee, if something like this happened to Dee and she didn't manage to squirm out of it. Sex was all very well, it was all very glorious when you could get it, but it was terrifying too, it could be as destructive as a coronary.

She thought of telling Nat and decided not to. Since the night of the crime, which she knew all about (everybody knew about it, in fact, except Louise and Timmy) he seemed to have acquired a new enthusiasm for work, both with the old woman Fitzgerald and with Ada. She knew by the quiet way he behaved that he was working well and she was determined to keep him safe till he broke out of his own accord. Anyway, if they had to dine with the Harpers, and Nat knew, he would be sure to conduct a Grand Guignol performance with his tongue on Winston, and that might snap something permanently in the boy's brain.

What she did was to tidy her clothes away and sweep out some of the water from the floor and put on a dress to go to the baker's for more of the bread that the household consumed by the ton. She didn't bother telling Nat in case he was at a tricky point in his mastery of Ada.

On the way down the hill she met Louise and Sam coming up; Sam looking as always polite and resigned and silent, and Louise as always slightly bored and petulant.

"Not a care in the world!" Louise accused her admiringly. "You look so cool, I don't know how you do it."

"Thinking noble thoughts," Mary said, quite cheered by Louise's flushed face and tired feet. "I'm just going for some bread. There's cold beer under the sink, Sam."

"You know this, I believe I could drink a glass of beer myself," Louise said, wondering at the progress of her own wickedness. "Just a small glass, of course."

"A dirty big pint," Sam said, his recklessness having also progressed, and Louise did no more than nudge him impatiently and say, "Men!"

"Is er, Nat in the house?" she asked Mary, very uninterested.

"No, he's in the studio with Ada."

"Oh!"

It was a mark of Sam's growing education that he looked weary and contemptuous at Louise's tone. Louise, not entirely a fool, switched tones and said roguishly, "Oh, I'm only joking! But really, an *attractive* man like Nat . . . and that girl! Talk about obvious! I would be frightened to trust her alone with Sam, even."

"So would I," Mary agreed. "Sam's a dark horse."

"O-oh? What's this? Sam Bennet?"

"There's always something about men with grey eyes," Mary said archly, rubbing it in.

"There had better not be!" Louise was somewhat flattered by the suggestion. Sam was trying to look dangerous, and looking quite sweet, actually, considering what a helpless soul he was. Louise was saying to him, in good humor, "I'll have to set a watch on you, my lad," as Mary left them and went downhill.

Louise nearly always spent her first minute in the kitchen, when the house was empty, airily touring the room and looking into all the cupboards and drawers, a habit Sam detested. He didn't say anything, but took out two cans of beer and opened them and hungrily drank one straight from the can, while he was pouring the other for Louise.

"I think I'll . . . sit in the garden," she said casually. Sam opened another can and obediently followed her out. She wiped her face with a tissue and said, "Of course, beer only brings out more perspiration . . . It's really quite nice, though, isn't it . . . Isn't it silly, we're always *praying* for sunshine and then when we get it, what do we do? Complain! . . . Drinking beer, really, at my age, I feel quite fast . . . I think Mary's taken on an awful job with this place . . . Quite nice, though . . ."

The aimless banality of her remarks was downright suspicious. She was establishing her sense of relaxation and her lack of interest in anything outside herself. She kept glancing involuntarily over at the outhouse, from which no sound could be heard. After a few minutes she said, "Er, maybe Nat would like a glass of beer . . . maybe not, of course."

"He's got beer in the studio," Sam said, hating this. He wondered if he had the audacity to stop her from bursting into the studio if she made up her mind. Now that the place had been mentioned, Louise felt free to stare at it thoughtfully and say, "I don't suppose Nat is *susceptible* to a girl like Ada. She's terribly fat, it's ridiculous."

"She's a bit fat." Sam's response to Ada was mild and sluggish, as was his response to most women out of his reach, but he considered Ada in the light of Louise's private thoughts about nude poses, and decided that she wasn't *terribly* fat, she wasn't bad. Quite nice, in fact. He wondered if she sagged a lot with her clothes off.

Ada didn't sag very much with her clothes off. She bulged, but she didn't sag much. Her main complaint at that moment was that nobody knew how little she sagged, because the posing sessions had been a great disappointment. Mr. Boag had done a lot of quick drawings of her, sitting down and standing up and cutting bread and opening windows, and she had accepted this dull stuff because it was only the preliminary. Today he was going to begin a real colored painting, and she expected to get into the job properly.

Ada, for all her mental simplicity, was fairly complicated temperamentally. She enjoyed having men look at her, any men at all, and it pleased her to think that she didn't look at them the way they looked at her. When she did see a man she wanted to look at, she tried not to, with the elementary motive of being always hard to get. She liked men often, but being the shape she was, and not liking every man, she had developed a simple direct defense. If a man tried to get through to her with the silly things men said, she blandly cut him short. If she liked him, she would get to know him when she chose to, and she didn't like a lot of smutty talk because it was sometimes over her head and she couldn't think of an answer.

This habit was so ingrained that she had come to reject any kind of persuasive talk at all, and her dislike of it was her armor and her proof of her virtue. She would consider the act of doing *anything* with a man in broad daylight to be nasty and dirty, because it was the same kind of thing, in a way, as talking out loud about . . . that kind of thing. In the dark and in silence she knew where she was, and it was all right as long as you didn't look and you talked about something else, something ordinary and not dirty.

But posing for an artist was different. It was respectable, some film stars had done it. It was the one chance a girl had of doing *everything*, right out in the open, with permission. She quite liked Mr. Boag, but even if he didn't *do* anything, anything *wrong*, she was mad with impatience to show everything and enjoy this holiday from the proper rules and regulations of life.

When she arrived for the sitting, she found the easel at one end of the little studio and a workbench at the other end. Nat waved her toward the bench, and she decided that this was supposed to be something different, a grand piano maybe or a marble pillar. She had her shoes and skirt off before she reached it.

"What's wrong, it is too warm?" Nat asked blankly.

"No, it's nice and warm, I would hate to pose in the cold!" She unbuttoned her blouse slickly and started to pull it off. Nat stared at her and held up a hand like a traffic policeman.

"Halt, I say!" He shook his head and smiled. "Put that blouse on at once, quick quick chop chop!"

She found herself hurrying to put the blouse back on.

"I thought you were going to paint me today," she said sulkily.

"You're a good kid, Ada, a good kid. Don't worry, I can *imagine* what you look like underneath."

"Imagine? Huh! I might as well go back to the shop and you could imagine I was here."

"A pretty wit," Nat said vaguely, lifting the easel and moving it. "The skirt too."

She picked up the skirt sullenly and let it hang from her hand.

"I don't like this skirt, I would have wore a nicer one if I had of known."

"It's lovely and you're lovely, put it on or I'll lose my head and skelp you."

"Just you try, you wouldn't dare, I would tell Mrs. Boag, I can take care of myself, you know." But in a dull heavy excitement she was fingering the waistband of her pants. Nat loosed one of his explosive laughs, grabbed the skirt from her and wrapped it round her waist and fastened the catch. She stood sleepy-eyed and heavy and then said coyly,

"People can get into trouble touching a girl all over like that without permission."

Nat slapped her sharply on the tight seat of the skirt and said, "I'm not people, I'm an inhuman monster. Button up and put this on." He picked up a striped butcher's apron from a chair and thrust it at her. Ada stared at it dumbfounded.

"This is my day off, thank you very much! You'll be asking me to chop up meat next."

"How did you guess?" Nat grinned. Disgusted, she threw the apron on the floor.

"What kind of picture will that be, you're only making a fool of people, I suppose you think I want everybody to know

I work in a butcher's, that's not the kind of thing a girl likes people to talk about, I thought you were going to do a nice picture of me." The skirt was still fastened only at the waist, and she was lifting it to one side and looking down wistfully at the rich thigh that the world was never going to see. Nat had started to heave the workbench into a new position.

"Ach, away you go," he said. "The world's rotten wi' nudes — it's the only way they can attract attention. It takes a real glamor puss to look sexy in an overall, kid. Every man in the world will be slavering to tear it off, see? Keep the bastards unsatisfied."

"Real models don't do it in overalls," she persisted, "and I don't like that kind of language, Mr. Boag." But her will was crumbling.

"You'll have to shut your wee ears in that case. My God, you're a prude, Ada. What are you? A prude. Who ever heard of a nude prude?"

"Huh! What's the difference if I'm not going to be . . . what you said."

"Shut your stupid mouth," Nat said callously. "And don't kid yourself, everybody's nude, inside their clothes. You're walking about Ochie nude all day, inside that overall."

"That's not a nice way to talk," Ada said, savoring the revelation. But she was defeated, and she was surrendering her lust to strip, with some fortitude since this new light had been shed on the situation.

"Could I not just do it in the blouse and skirt?" she pleaded hopelessly. Nat surveyed her.

"Christ, you could do it in an asbestos suit, Ada. But you're in the hands of the Philistines, come on, get into disguise." He was fitting the apron over her head. In dull resignation she tied the tapes round her waist, and Nat eyed the effect critically. He untied them and took them round her body twice, once at the waist and once tightly over her ribs just under her melodramatic bosom.

"That's it, kid, you got 'em, you show 'em," he said happily. "Here," he handed her a cleaver. "Get behind the counter and chop. We'll put in the meat later if we can afford it." She stood reluctantly behind the workbench and brandished the cleaver, squinting down at the swelling contours of the striped apron.

"I don't usually tie it like this," she complained, and pushed her chest out a couple of inches.

"Don't shove it too far when you're waving that chopper about," he muttered as he stooped and undid the bottom button of the skirt.

"Here! Right enough!" she protested, afraid to move in case she blurred the picture.

"Feet wider apart, good."

"Will that be in the picture?" She tried to sound scandalized as she squinted down at her knee and six inches of thigh.

"Sure thing, all prime Scotch meat is what the customers want, kid. People'll want to eat you, do you know that? Grrr! They'll be swimming to Ochie like lemmings wi' their wee teeth twitching for a bite."

Utterly overborne, Ada let him push her about and move her and say awful things about her stomach and her hips that she would never have stood from another man even in the dark. Her mind had sunk into a dazed hum, and she stood dumb and unthinking as he worked at the easel and muttered such a lot of absolute nonsense that the best thing a girl could do was ignore it.

This was the position that had been reached when Sam and Louise sat in the garden with their beer and Louise's aimless talk. Sam now moved his deck chair so that he could close his eyes without being accused of falling asleep. Louise read his mind easily, and didn't interfere. By turning away from her he had also turned his back on the outhouse. She stopped talking and sighed and lay as still as she could until she heard the breath of a snore from Sam. Then she put a finger delicately to her forehead and performed the gesture of somebody who has just this instant thought of something.

She got up silently from her chair and walked quickly to the door of the outhouse, where she faltered. She put her fingers to her mouth and performed the gesture of somebody who has thought of something and can't for a moment remember what it is. Then she opened the door of the outhouse and went in.

"Oh," she said in surprise. "Are you here?"

"Get out." Nat didn't look up from the easel.

"Oh! Nat! It's me, Louise."

"Get out," he said in a singsong voice. Her eyes still dazzled by the sunshine outside, she couldn't take in a full picture of the studio. Nat was half-hidden by the canvas on the easel, and since she was facing in his direction, Ada was half-behind her, and she didn't want to turn her head too quickly and nosily to look at Ada.

"I wondered if you would like some bee-eer," she crooned, and laughed nervously so that she shouldn't quite hear him snapping, "Later!" She had no idea why she should be feeling jittery, she wasn't breaking any law or anything, there weren't any *secrets* in the outhouse, after all it was Sam's bedroom as well as a studio, it was part of the house.

"Shut that door," he said tightly, still without looking round the easel. "It's spilling light!"

"Yes, silly of me!" She shut the door with painful care, staying inside, and was now able to turn slowly to see Ada . . . no, a butcher . . . a girl . . . yes, Ada, looking half-asleep and leaning on the bench with a washed-out blouse and a striped apron.

"You can sit down for ten minutes, Ada," Nat said, and

emerged from behind the easel. "Sorry, Louise, we're busy, I'll see you later."

"I don't mind." She waved her hands in forgiveness. "I'll be as quiet as a wee mouse."

"No, just go away, Louise." Nat was calm and friendly, and she took courage and laughed merrily.

"It's all right, I don't mind, Nat. I'll get you a glass of beer if you haven't started yet." She looked round quickly to see where the beer could be. Ada stretched her limbs and sat dully in a chair.

"We have started, Louise," Nat explained gently. "I'll have a drink later on."

"Oh, really!" Her laugh was quite charming. "You men would starve to death if somebody didn't take care of you." Nat's smile was so boyish and friendly that she knew he had been putting on one of his "characters." "And I know perfectly well . . ." she moved swiftly toward a cupboard where the beer must be, ". . . you haven't really started, I mean, Ada hasn't even cha — "

"Louise, go away, go away at once."

"Honestly, Nat, you're not — " Louise couldn't understand why she felt so cheated, almost disgusted. " — You're not painting her in that horrid apron! I may not know much about art, but really!"

"You mind your own business!" Ada showed the first energy she had demonstrated for an hour. "It's none of your business." And as Nat turned to silence Ada, Louise turned on her coldly and said,

"Don't use that tone to me!"

But as she was about to demolish the impertinent butcher-girl, Nat had already moved to the door, opened it, and was taking her by the arm and forcing her quite brutally outside.

"Nat! Let go!" She tried to laugh. "Don't be silly!" She

was standing outside and the door was shut. She laughed uneasily and made to knock on the door, but stopped her hand halfway.

"Honestly!" she said, quite loudly, and laughed. Sam was still lying in his deck chair, unmoving and perhaps asleep. Louise shook her head at the absurdity of people, the childish absurdity of people. She stamped into the cottage kitchen and opened and shut several drawers. "Never!" she muttered with lips tight. "Never in my life, never never *never!*"

Sam lay in the deck chair and listened to the slamming of drawers and kept his eyes shut and breathed noisily.

Inside the studio, Ada was sulking in the chair.

"Come on, be a good little girl," Nat said impatiently. "You look great."

"Even her," Ada sulked. "She thinks it looks stupid. I never wanted to wear it, you talking about glamor, huh, I'll look a right fool."

"Stand behind the bench," Nat said in a feeble tone Mary would hardly have recognized.

"I don't like it."

"All right, take it off and go home." His face was white.

"Are you not going to do a picture?" Ada was confused in her resentment. Nat quietly said a rude word and she ignored it. He went to the cupboard and took out a can of beer and bashed it open and drank from it, breathing deeply and relaxing between gulps.

"I'll go away well," she blustered. "See if I care." She moved unwillingly toward the door, but he merely stared at her bleakly over the beer can.

"I'm going away," she threatened.

"Well, how would you like it?" she said. "I thought it was going to be a nice picture as well, butcher's aprons, a girl likes to make the best of herself."

"I wish you weren't such a festering cretin, kid," Nat said emptily. "In that getup you're as hot as a blow-lamp."

Ada had paused in her slow progress to the door and her lower lip trembled.

"*She* doesn't think that 'well!"

Nat said a still ruder word.

"Neither do you," she muttered desperately, "dressing me up like this as if I *lived* in a shop or something, you look at me as if I was a bit of meat or something."

Nat put down the empty can and squared his shoulders.

"Button the lip and get back on the assembly line," he said. "If you were a bit of meat I would get my teeth in you raw, do you know that?" Ada stood sullenly halfway to the door, and he took her arm above the elbow and started to shove her back to the bench. She lifted her other hand to fight him off and he caught hold of it. She stood breathing heavily and scowling and he slowly loosened his grip and patted her shoulder.

"It's not any fun at all!" she sobbed. Nat put an arm round her shoulder and patted her soothingly. She stood close to him sniffling and he patted her vaguely with his teeth clenched and she leaned her head on his chest for a few seconds and quieted down. Then, almost like a robot, she put her arms round him and tilted her head and kissed him. Nat's arms tightened across her back and she groaned and strained closer while his fingers dug into her skin. When he let her go she was panting.

"You've got your apron all crumpled, kid," Nat said, and whistled a little tune. Ada quickly smoothed out the apron and said wildly, "It wouldn't be fair to Mrs. Boag, would it? Even when you canny help it, it's not right, I'm not like that, you know, it's all right posing but I'm not a girl like that, I don't go in for that kind of thing."

"Normally," Nat suggested.

"No. Honest, is this apron all right, does it not look stupid?"

"Would you rather strip?" Nat moved himself carefully back to the easel and Ada thought hard and regretfully.

"Not on your life — and have her coming in to look at me! No, thank you! I know what she would think, her! I don't know what's wrong with working in a butcher's, it's a free country, isn't it, it's not a crime or something!" She felt heavy and weak and was reminding herself that she wasn't a girl like that, that nice Mrs. Boag, it wasn't fair, a girl had to be careful, maybe Harry would be back and offer to walk her home before the picture was finished, maybe if the picture was nice Mr. Boag would do another one some time, a right one, his fingers were awful hard. She couldn't for a second remember the name of the song she was humming. Oh yes, it was "Climb, Climb Up Sunshine Mountain."

THIRTEEN

MARY KNEW THAT Louise's change of manner must have something to do with Nat, because Louise kept not looking at Nat. What had happened she would find out soon enough because Nat would inevitably tell her, but she was quite satisfied with the abrupt issue of a reprieve in Louise's decision that it was time she and family were going home, they had imposed on Mary's hospitality long enough. Mary made conventional sounds of protest, but there was no heart in them.

When Nat went to the studio the next day, she waited for a convenient moment and followed him.

"Come in, come in," he said, "I thought for a minute it was the dreaded Jivaro Indians, egad, they ooze out of the plaster if you don't keep your shotgun on them."

He was working on the small canvas of old Maggie Fitzgerald, which he had brought home after every session so that Maggie wouldn't get a look at it. Mary sat in the old chair and sagged in relief. Nat had his face close to the canvas and his tongue poked out.

"When I've knocked off Maggie and Ada, finish, mate," he

muttered. "This primeval forest is no place for a highly-
strung brush man. Do you fancy a sailing dinghy?"

"It might be all right," she agreed.

"Has it come to your attention?" he stopped painting.
"Has it brought itself to your notice that this is the first time
I've seen you in years without human ants crawling over us?"

"I've been wondering when you would notice," she said
drily. "You've been too busy blowing yourself up and leaving your wife and kids starving. For God's sake, Nat, you
could have got *jail* for that. You're an irresponsible bastard.
All right, all right, the subject is closed. You never even
asked me to come," she added plaintively.

"Man great hunter, squaw sit home make wampum," he
said absentmindedly and pushed his face toward the canvas
again. "It was good for Sam's character, honest. I just don't
like that sod Harper, but I'll be good, I'll wash my hands for
dinner and everything and not call him a swine more than
twice. I want to let old Maggie see this today, she's practically ready for Boot Hill, the old bag."

"Don't be horrible."

"Ah, shut up, I love her and you know it."

"You love everybody."

"I think my passion for Cousin Louise has cooled to something akin to respect, or maybe the dry vomits."

"She's decided to go home."

"Issue rum to all hands," he said, looking up, and then
started painting again. "This is a bloody fine picture."

"Are you giving it to her?"

"Are you insane, woman? I'm giving her the life rent of it,
which should be about eight minutes, and then flogging it
pronto to a rich imbecile. So you want to know why Cousin
Louise is going back East, well, I was nice to her, I was really
helluva nice to her, you wouldn't have known your uncouth

barbarian. I asked her to get the hell out of the studio so sweetly I nearly sickened myself."

"Did she go?"

"After some social chitchat and a cuddle."

"While Ada was here?"

"I have put the sixteen-cylinder intellect to work on why she popped in, incidentally. She's got a lesbian streak, know that? Sad, I believe there's a lot of it about nowadays, it's these chemical fertilizers I tell you."

"Ah." Mary wasn't sure whether she had suddenly made the same deduction or whether she had taken it from Nat by telepathy. "She expected to see Ada in the buff."

"With horny slavering artist astride her, maybe — let's not be mingy about entertainment, madam, we have standards to keep up. This is a damned good picture, I don't know where I get this talent."

"Poor Louise, she gives me the creeps," Mary said. "You're a good kid, kid, do you know that, Nat? I hope you spat in her mascara."

"I didn't, honest, iron self-control, I smiled all the time and combed my hair over my horns."

Mary didn't care. She was almost inclined to believe that Nat had been nice and sweet to Louise, although she knew how dangerous he could be if somebody intruded on him when he was working. It was enough that Louise was positively going, because her own character was deteriorating under the strain. She had taken to hiding perfume and lipstick and anything else that might be used experimentally, and tucking food away in furtive places just to keep it from vanishing.

But what was worse was the skin-crawling feeling that had become habitual because she was sure that nothing was secret from Louise, that handbags and drawers and cupboards were under endless surveillance, underwear was constantly inspected, and the comings and goings of everybody were noted and resented. She had come to feel guilty every time she did anything without telling Louise first. She found herself to her dismay thinking nostalgically of being home in the city, with ordinary dull housework to do and meals to cook in the sensational privacy of her own family and nobody else.

She was interrupted in this agreeable review of her troubles by the wailing voice of Timmy as he flounced out of the cottage and into the garden, and she wondered sadly why she had never had enough character to rattle his teeth when there was nobody about.

"I don't care!" he was yelling, "I want to see the fireworks! Ya, shut up skinny!"

"Shut up, fatty! You're going home and you're not coming back!"

Louise had a talent for not hearing this kind of recurring crisis. Although she was so sensitive and detested scenes, she could switch off her ears when Timmy and Sally started a noisy fight, and Timmy and Sally had been going in more and more for noisy fights over the past week. Louise only smiled, and managed to convey that children *would* be children, and that as a guest, she hardly had the right to interfere, and that Mary really ought to avert this kind of nastiness, and that it wasn't surprising since Sally had a violent nature and was always picking on Timmy, who wasn't used to bullying. The awful thing was that Sally *was* showing signs of a violent nature. It was possible that she really was a nasty little girl when she was among other children, though Mary had never thought of such a thing before Timmy came into their lives.

She got up from the chair, and Nat looked over and said, "Let them get tore in, maybe they'll kill each other." He

could switch off too. She went out to the garden and found
Sally and Timmy circling each other and occasionally feinting and pushing.

"I'm seeing the fireworks!" Timmy snarled, "and you're
not going to stop me!" and under his breath, not noticing
Mary, he added, "You're a bugger!"

"You're a fat bastard," Sally said, right out loud. Louise
had come to the cottage door and was looking disgusted and
world-weary, and at this last remark, petrified.

"Sally!" Mary's voice was sharp and hard, and Sally glared
at her. Timmy turned to her too, and wailed, "She said a
bad word, and I want to see the fireworks, Aunt Mary. I've
never seen fireworks before." With smooth facility, he had
begun to weep and blubber.

"The fireworks aren't till Friday, and you're going home
tomorrow." Sally maintained the contempt and viciousness
of her tone in open defiance of Mary's presence, and Mary
felt she could cheerfully have beaten her senseless for men-
tioning fireworks, and then for being so blatantly delinquent
in front of Louise.

"Please, Aunt Mary," Timmy wailed, "I want to see the
fireworks!"

It was hopeless. She didn't have the mettle for this kind of
crisis. She tried not to look sick as she said, "Well, maybe
you can stay for the fireworks."

"Yes," Louise chimed in from the cottage doorway. "We'll
stay till Saturday as long as you're good, and don't cause a
nuisance or get led into any fights."

Mary forced herself not to react to the brazenness of this.
Damn and blast, Saturday was still only four days away, you
could live out four days as long as you knew they were going
to end, it was like suffering a horrible train journey and
knowing that you must arrive in the end. Timmy's weeping

was cut off and he turned triumphantly to Sally and sang, "I'm going to see the fireworks, I'm going to see the fireworks, fireworks, fireworks, I'm going to see the fireworks."

Sally bared her teeth at him and disgustedly stamped down the drive into the street. He followed her, skipping clumsily and shouting "Fireworks, fireworks!" Sally broke into a run, her only escape as Timmy wasn't hot on speed, and his voice could be heard diminishing in the distance and yelling that he would tell her mother and that he was going to see the fireworks.

"It's only a day or two more," Louise said, once more her sweet self, "and it would be a shame to deprive the wee soul, really."

Mary smiled in return and calculated four days, three people, thirty-six meals, a bagatelle that any hostess would take in her stride. The studio door opened and Nat, the traitor, the deserter, the craven coward, came out jauntily with the little canvas carefully held in two hands and went straight to the Land Rover with it and climbed aboard. He didn't even say anything, he just waved blandly and started the motor and reversed down the drive with the wheels spinning.

"The artistic temperament," Louise said irrelevantly. "It must be very hard to live with."

FOURTEEN

DINNER WITH THE HARPERS was expected to be a big laugh, but Mary had gone off the idea badly after thinking about fat little Arnold and the nutty young Winston, and the prospect bored her to a degree that drove Louise insane with disapproval.

"What are you going to wear?" Louise asked breathlessly. "Will I lend you my pearls? Not that it matters, of course — really important people don't *care* about these things, I've always noticed that. The simpler, the better. There's nothing worse than being ostentatious and just looking vulgar. I wonder what the Big House is like inside! Oh, it must be marvelous. You don't know how lucky you are."

"No, I don't," Mary agreed listlessly. "I expect they've got fitted carpets on all the ceilings."

"I don't think landed people go in for vulgar things like that," Louise said huffily, and added in a wistful tone, "I've never even *seen* them."

"They go about in full evening dress all the time," Nat mumbled, his mouth full of one-inch nails. "Even when they're playing tennis." He was setting a new window frame with a big pane of glass to replace the dark little window in the kitchen. "When it rains they put suits of armor on top, the craven swine."

Louise had positively lost her adoration for Nat. She turned away from him and said to Mary, in cloying pity, "I hope he isn't going to talk a lot of nonsense like that in front of them. It's a pity they hadn't known Sam and I were here. I'm sure they would have invited us too. Are you sure they haven't got a title?"

It was almost a physical pain to Louise to stand idly by and watch people like Nat and Mary, who had no grasp of the important things of life, whisking off to mix with landed people and deprive her of an evening in which she would have glittered and laughed gaily and been the delight of the upper set.

Mary had been sure that no Harper could affect her composure, but she found herself cringing under the fishy stare of the mistress of the Big House. Joyce regarded her as a sociological curio. Luckily the gin cocktails that Winston served, rather sullenly, were big and strong, and she took two on the principle that drunken disgrace was better than discomfort. Hard pressed for anything to say to the handsome Joyce, she made polite and lying comments on the house, which she thought was horrible.

"It has no grace," Joyce drawled, rejecting the compliment. "It has no . . . *persona*. The fabric is nineteenth century, an age of uninspired architectural pretentiousness."

"That puts old man Nash in his place," Nat said, but without his usual bite. He had come from the Fitzgeralds' rather gloomy, and Mary suspected that he was brooding about death, which he did from time to time in depressive fits that nothing could lighten.

"Nash was the late flowering," Joyce went on fluently, "of an earlier phase of creative vitality."

The woman was obviously not a fool. Although she sounded like a guide on a conducted tour of a museum, she radiated a supercilious confidence and had learned her script thoroughly. And Winston, on his home ground, seemed somewhat different; not erratic and adolescent, but the entrenched young lord and master. When he did look at Mary, his eye was cold and commercial. She looked forward unhappily to long conversations about architecture and all the other cultural subjects that Joyce would certainly have studied and where she herself had nothing but ignorance and instinct to guide her.

"Joyce does go on," said young Winston, "but it's all Grade-A certified material. Do let's you and I talk about something else, Mrs. Boag." He moved her toward a sofa and sat beside her, and she realized that his cold clinical performance was something he could maintain only when he was silent. When he spoke, there was an awkward experimental child inside him, striving to attain the dignity of manhood by using the right tricks. She smiled vaguely at him and inched away as he sat too close beside her and idiotically tried to pat her knee.

Nat, in an unusual condition of surrender, was letting Joyce wash him under with a three-volume summary of the aristocratic tradition in English history, which overlapped cocktail time and flowed smoothly over a rather indifferently cooked dinner. Winston had quite definitely stopped patting her knee and was resting his hand on it, and she removed his hand with a firm maternal gesture, after which he glowered into his drink and his food.

"There's a rather interesting correlation between humor and creative art," Joyce was saying through the sweet course. "Evidently a negative correlation so far as I have established in my own personal researches into the subject, if you consider, for instance, poor Van Gogh, who was only able to create out of a pathological internal conflict, and even Leonardo — Leonardo da Vinci, that is, of course — whose most strenuous endeavors were consistently, that is, they consistently eventuated in failure and disaster . . ."

Mary had not, she realized, uttered a remark since dinner started, and she had the suspicion that Arnold was asleep with his little eyes open; that he had heard all this before and was placidly proud of his wife's erudite noises without going so far as to listen to the actual words.

"Or take for instance jolly old Bach," Mary said wildly, as Joyce paused. And Winston turned to her and said, "I don't think German composers are quite what Joyce was talking about." His tone was a mixture of condescension and resentment.

"That's a good point, Winston," Nat said at once. "It shows you've been listening."

Winston glared at him, unable to analyze him and therefore apprehensive and hostile.

"Talking about art," Arnold said, jolted awake by the interruption to Joyce's built-in tape recording. "You lost one of your subjects, know?"

Nat looked polite.

"Dying for months? you know?" Arnold demanded. "I hear all the gossip, know?"

"Music is, of course, a rather different field of study," Joyce intoned. "But on the other hand, if you consider Chopin and that perfectly wretched Georges Sand affair . . . well . . ."

"Do you mean Maggie Fitzgerald?" Mary asked Arnold, rather rudely but urgently because she suspected that Nat would want to know about Maggie.

"I wish you wouldn't interrupt," Winston said.

There was an instant of embarrassed silence, during which Nat turned a kindly smile on Winston and said,

"Winston, I do declare I had forgotten you were there — you must speak up oftener, boy, we're anxious to have your ideas. Do you mean Maggie Fitzgerald's dead?" he asked Arnold, without pausing, while Winston grew pale at the nostrils.

"Dead as a doorknob, you know? Seven o'clock." Arnold was brisk and satisfied. "Good property, that, know? Might get that back into the estate, you know? Build a real hotel?"

"Poor old Maggie," Nat said to himself. It was true, he must have been brooding about her. The face of death always struck him harder than it did most people. "I knew I should have stayed with her."

"Oh, one of the tenants?" Joyce found this mundane interruption tiresome.

"But Maggie has a husband," Mary objected. Arnold waved a podgy hand.

"Know all about him, you know? He's the village idiot? He'll be glad to take a cottage? Too many of these old tenants, no go in them — hold up development, you know? Only way to develop the Highlands, do it in big sections, if the lairds were left to it they could make a proper business of it, you know?"

"Yes, there's something in what you say, Arnold," Nat was so respectful that Mary knew he must be feeling vicious. "The old Countess of Sutherland had the right idea."

"The Countess of Sutherland." Joyce rolled the title round her mouth like an oyster. "The family was united with an English noble house, of course. Was it the Staffords?"

"Take the old road, you know?" Arnold was now himself wound up. "Always moaning about it, some people? It keeps the wrong people out. Build a good road? They come in like locusts — all got cars now, you know? Make the place like Coney Island."

They were going into the lounge for coffee, and Arnold had unexpectedly taken Mary's arm and was eyeing her with approval; possibly enjoying the presence of a fairly silent woman.

"The Countess of Sutherland," Joyce cooed as she poured coffee. "Ah . . ."

"Was she the one," Mary asked, "who burned the cottages down while the tenants were still inside them?"

"Do you have to talk rot?" Winston asked her icily. Winston had carefully recapitulated the events of the day, and incredible as it seemed, he had decided that the Boag woman had made a fool of him.

Mary stared at him, speechless. Nat, who was sitting beside him, turned to stare too, but with an expression of thoughtful interest and attention. Arnold, startled by Winston's question, was beginning to splutter into gear when Nat reached out in a smooth casual movement and poured his steaming coffee over Winston's pale blue trousers.

"You've got coffee all over you," he said. Winston leaped in the air howling. Nat leaned back and smiled up at him, like a child enjoying a conjurer. Winston's fists clenched and he glared at Nat and at the smile, and stalked from the room.

Nat made Mary drive the Land Rover home.

"What's wrong, are you drunk?" she asked him.

"No, but in my present condition of bile I might run it into something for a laugh."

"They're so mean and *small!*" Mary said. "Surely they can't all be like that — landlords, I mean. The dinner was awful."

"What's with that pimply infant?" Nat wondered. "They should keep *that* one chained to a ring in the cellar for a start."

"You never even discussed painting that American drone."

"She's made of soap, did you notice that? What has Winston got against you?"

She concentrated on the road ahead and said lightly, "I *think* he made a pass at me yesterday, and I think I made him feel daft."

"Mary!" Nat recovered some of his spirits. "You shouldn't do that to young masters, you should be respectful and help them, pull their teeth out and so on."

"I nearly did," she giggled.

"It's the heat, you know, it's got everybody as randy as — "

" — don't dare say it!"

"They must die, you know that? What must they do? What must the tyrannical landlords do?"

"Die."

"Very good, go to the top of the class. Why the hell doesn't Sam sleep in the other bunk and you in the pigsty with me? Dammit, I paid for a license to sleep with you."

"Are you feeling filthy?"

"I'm only trying to be kind."

"No," she said.

"No what? This is your lord and master speaking."

"I'm not going to change the beds now. I just couldn't stand Louise rolling her eyes and twittering and *thinking.* Thinking *Oho!* It's like having her in the bed along with you."

"She might even burst in to ask for a match or a cup of

sugar," Nat agreed bitterly. "At that very second. Why don't you stop the car and gambol among the nettles?"

"Yes."

"Right."

"I mean it."

"Right!"

"Who's that?"

The headlamps picked out Harry and Dee standing on the roadside and thumbing.

"I always think a family's nice," Nat snarled. "It keeps you young and vibrant."

"Yes, it's nice," Mary moaned. Dee squeezed in beside Nat and Harry heaved himself into the back seat.

"I hope you puling brats haven't gone kinky," Nat said. "Roaming the hills with your brothers and sisters. I don't like it, there's too much of it about."

"She got the waggle," Harry said mysteriously.

"The brush-off," Dee corrected him, in too calm a tone. "Eric's girl friend arrived from Doncaster."

"I hope you horsewhipped him." Nat turned to Harry in the darkness of the back seat, and Harry said curtly, "I couldn't find the horse."

"I honestly don't understand it," Dee said, wonderingly. "It's not as if I was crazy about him, but I wouldn't do that to a dog. Not even a mongrel."

"I would do it to a basset hound," Nat said. "Basset hounds have it coming to them. These foreigners all have a touch of the tarbrush, did you know that? They file their teeth and eat ants."

"And blubber," Harry added gloomily.

"So would you blubber if you ate ants," Dee said, and her voice didn't break, but slid smoothly into weeping.

"Daddy will buy you a big doll that walks and talks and

wets its nappies for Christmas." Nat used his horrid child-film-star voice. From the slight movements beside her, Mary divined that he had put his arm round Dee and that she was weeping quietly on his shoulder.

"Will it vomit too?" she moaned.

"It'll come out in hives."

"You heard him promise, Harry," Dee wailed.

FIFTEEN

IT HADN'T OCCURRED to many people that Maggie Fitzgerald might have timed her death to throw a blight over the Young Master's big birthday celebrations. Louise was quite upset when the coincidence emerged, and expressed the considered opinion that the funeral should be hurried up by a day or put off for a week out of respect for the civic celebrations.

"No!" Stacey cried joyfully, "there's something poetic about it!" She was now sure that she had envisaged this all along, the grim contrast of festivity and morality. She was almost sorry it had happened, because if it hadn't, she would have been able to invent it as a fabulous piece of dramatic structure . . . contrapuntal was the word, merry reckless faces laughing and dancing in the village square (she had equipped the village with a square) and beyond them as they laughed, the small silent procession of death and the stricken face of the husband listening dully to the lilting music.

"I don't know much about poetry, of course," Louise snapped, "but it doesn't seem very *nice,* forcing people's grief on people when they're entitled to enjoy themselves. It's not very nice for the children."

"Ah, kids love a good funeral," Nat said unfeelingly. "Sally would walk miles for a look at a corpse."

"Sally might." Louise sniffed, and Mary laughed, drunk with the knowledge that after one more night, the house would be private and Louise would vanish into the unknown forever.

"If they held up the funeral the body would go bad in this weather," Sally said solemnly, and shuddered. Louise turned her head away, and Good, good, thought Mary, get to hate us entirely, shake us from your feet and go, in the name of God, go.

"You'll be coming to the funeral, Sam," Nat said, and Louise answered.

"I don't think so, I don't think it's very suitable."

"Well, Davie and I can't carry the coffin — a flaming heavy thing, a coffin."

"Okay, I don't mind," Sam said.

"You didn't even know her," Louise told him sharply, and Sam turned and said in a mixture of fear and sullen defiance,

"Somebody's got to give Nat a hand."

". . . Oh, don't mind me!" There was that in Louise's face which plainly said Wait till I get you alone, just wait. Sam slunk out to the outhouse to find a dark tie, and Nat refrained from making any comment on his mutiny.

The Tarbie boardinghouse was a sightless frontage of curtained windows, and everybody in the village seemed to be making for it, except the guests who had been picked up that morning in Oban by the Lady Joyce to be brought to the celebrations. A few of them watched with idle curiosity, strangers cut off from the quaint everyday life of the village, rather like expensive youth hostelers, Nat thought. The hostelers were sunbathing and paddling around the bay in sailing dinghies hoping for a breath of wind for the regatta.

Davie Fitzgerald grabbed Nat and Sam at the door and

hustled them through the hallway and into the kitchen, where Hughie Mackay was looking solemn in a stiff black suit and trying out the whisky.

"She's eh, here, she's eh, upstairs," Davie babbled. "I couldny keep her, eh, out! She's been here, eh, since, eh, wan o'cloth . . . *lookin'*."

"Ach, she's only a daft auld bitch," Hughie comforted him. "You pay no attention to her, you're the boss. Did you see the rare job we've made of the van, Nat? Black velvet curtains all over the damned thing, it's just champion, I would be proud to ride in it to my own funeral as long as the clutch doesn't burn out, that clutch is a hoor in this weather."

Davie was pouring whisky into two glasses with shaking hands.

"So are, eh, the Jacksons, oh dear, they give me, eh, palpitations, so they do, eh, they just, eh, sit there."

"Fine big strapping lads, the Jacksons," Nat said. "They can take the heavy end of the box."

"They, eh, they came in a *cart*," Davie stuttered. "What, eh, would they want to do, eh, a thing like that, eh, for?"

"They have no sense of the right way of things at all," Hughie agreed tolerantly. "There was only the wan brain between the two of them when they was born and that's the truth, it's all perverted snobbery like Sadie Pringle turning up in her cousin's pick-up. She's a bad case of the depressives, that wumman, she should take a tonic or something."

"Oh dear, oh dear I, eh, wish Maggie was, eh, here!"

"Ach, away with you, Davie man, she was drinking your blood right up, you'll have the high old jinkies now you're a free man — the lassies'll be fair after you like whippets."

This prospect plunged Davie into a terrified silence, and Ada tiptoed into the kitchen. She was sewn into a dress of black satin and a solemn expression.

"You should be upstairs," she whispered hoarsely.

"Man, lassie." Hughie looked owlishly at her. "That frock fair suits you, you could go dancing in it a treat." Even Sam's sluggish responses were drawn like his eyes to the shimmer of light and shade as Ada's person flexed inside the satin.

"I don't like that kind of talk, Mr. Mackay," she whispered sternly. "This is a house of death." And she drooped her head and squinted down at the pleasing sheen of the cloth. Davie Fitzgerald did a skip and shuffle past her, and they followed him upstairs.

The Jackson twins were easily recognizable, big and bony and identical in their features and their vacant gloom. So was Sadie Pringle, in a heavy black coat, sitting with a handbag clutched fiercely in her lap and darting her eyes endlessly round the room. The minister, a slim rather elegant young man, stood up and coughed. The Jacksons glowered at him. Sadie tutted and stood up, bowed her head slightly and kept it moving jerkily in all directions.

"Friends and brethren," the minister began suavely, "we are gathered together today in this house of sorrow . . ."

There was a general nodding of heads in agreement, and a shifting of feet as new mourners started to squeeze into the room. A splendid turnout, Nat thought. Maggie would have laughed her head off. Jenny McNeill, forcing her way through the crush, tripped and squealed, and the minister spoke smoothly on above a chorus of disapproving tuts.

"You haven't sprained *your* ankle!" Jenny snapped at somebody.

"You have no manners."

"Ssht!"

Nat became aware that Ada was standing on tiptoe and stretching up dangerously to signal to him with a jabbing forefinger. He looked a question at her as the minister turned toward her, and Ada lowered her head reverently and kept her arm up and her finger jabbing the air.

"The coffin, the coffin!" Jenny McNeill barked at him, as she plowed her way back through the crowd toward the door. "It's time for the coffin!"

"Ssh!"

"Ssh yourself!" she half-turned in defiance to whoever had sshed. "How can you have a funeral without the coffin?" Nat found her podgy little hands pushing him in the chest and he staggered backward onto the landing. Hughie Mackay burrowed through the crowd with Sam behind him, and held a finger to his lips and then muttered,

"Murdo MacMillan should be here, the hoor, it's his job to supervise — he'll be at the whisky for sure. Where in the world is the dampt coffin?" He started to tour the landing, opening and shutting doors.

"Upstairs?" Nat whispered.

"Ach, it's a ——'s ——!" What for can people not die on the street level in this weather? That Murdo MacMillan is no administrator of funerals at all!"

Nat was followed upstairs by the muttering Hughie and Sam and the muscular young Archie McBain, who kept spitting on his hands and clapping them. The coffin was indeed in the top-floor room where Maggie had died. The picture Nat had painted was propped on a table beside it, and somebody had draped it tastefully with black velvet swags.

"By Joves, you've made her a fine-looking woman," Hughie cried. "She never had hair like that on her in her whole life and that's a fact."

Nat looked at the picture and said sadly,

"Well, she should have. It suits her."

"Ach, there's good and bad in us all," Hughie said philosophically. "Give me a lift with the dampt thing now and don't drop it because that MacMillan is no more a good joiner than a mackerel is a bird, it'll be stuck together with potty and cellophane."

"My God!" Sam gasped. Archie McBain arrogantly put his shoulder under the heavy end and started to hoist.

The staircase was too narrow for four men and a box. Sam and Archie McBain carried it down the first flight with Hughie and Nat backing before them in case they fell headlong. Sam's face was white with the terror of maybe seeing Maggie pitch bodily into sight among a heap of splintered wood. They reached the door behind which the minister was praying on with his ears sharp for the progress of the coffin.

"Rest it now," said Hughie breathlessly, having carried it single-handed in imagination. "No, not on the banister, you daft hoor, my God it's over!" Nat made a wild leap and grabbed one of the handles as the box tilted fearfully and started to slide.

"See these old houses? They should have lifts," Archie McBain muttered angrily. "This is a dead liberty."

"By Joves," Hughie said, "another inch and we would have had to dribble her to the graveyard like a football and no mistake."

Nat and Archie and Hughie were able to squeeze together down the second flight, with Sam backing ahead of them in numb fear. Hughie moved some of the old tires and tools in his dreadful old van and they slid the coffin aboard. At once there was a thunder of feet and the mourners spilled out into the sunlight. There was a diplomatic impasse, when Davie tried to insist that the minister should ride in the van, and the minister, after looking at the van, insisted that Davie should ride while he walked. It was settled when Davie miserably sat in the tail of the van, with his feet hanging out, and the minister took the seat beside Hughie. A cloud of poisonous smoke from the exhaust half-hid him as Hughie started up and began a slow drive to the graveyard two hundred yards away. It was astonishing how many people had assembled for the walking procession behind. Geordie Mackay, genially drunk, shambled to the front rank and grinned and nodded comfort to Davie as the van bounced horribly and the smell of burning rubber started to drift back from the slipping clutch.

"Thassit, Davie lad, keep your spirits up," Geordie exhorted him. "The Lor' giveth 'n' the Lor' taketh away, eh? You'll be a' ri', Davie, you've got plenny friens, lad, jus' you sit there and don' worry." Cries of "ssh" came from the stern mourners behind. Davie gave a sickly smile and inhaled a lungful of exhaust smoke and swayed dizzily. He couldn't drag his eyes away from the Jackson twins, clumping stolidly along in the second rank and glowering at him without blinking.

It was at the graveside that Davie first started to lose his air of oppression. As he stepped back from the lowering of the coffin, he whispered to Nat, "Oh, eh, they're eh, away . . . eh, I hope that's them away for, eh, good!"

Nat didn't pay attention at first, because a discussion had sprung up actually inside the grave at the time. Murdo MacMillan, standing up to his shoulders in the hole and sweatily leveling out the bottom to take the coffin, had exposed a length of crumbling black wood and a dark skull, which was jammed on the point of his little trenching spade, and the mourners had crowded to the edge of the pit to get a good look.

"My God, it's Dod Pringle!" Geordie Mackay breathed in delight, and Davie Fitzgerald jerked in terror.

"Where's your powers of discernment, man?" Hughie demanded. "There was never a Pringle with cerebellums of that dimensions, he has the look of an educated chap, that."

"Dod Pringle had black hair," somebody objected. Geordie Mackay craned forward for a closer look and was grabbed by fellow-mourners as his feet slipped over the edge of the hole.

"The hair is the first to go," Murdo MacMillan said with solemn professionalism.

" 'S'havers!" Geordie Mackay mumbled, swaying in the grip of his rescuers. "Worms don' eat hair. Eyes is the firs'. Eyes!" He swiveled his head round the crowd with his eyes open wide to demonstrate.

"He's drunk," somebody explained, and Hughie blinked his resentment.

"Dod Pringle's sober," he muttered triumphantly.

"That is never Dod Pringle," his brother insisted. "There is a great bliddy brain chamber there big enough for Karl Marx or Epstein, and by Joves, you've made a fine crack in it, Murdo."

"It looks like yon baker," somebody said importantly, "the wan that fell off the horse, Mackintosh he was."

Murdo obligingly raised the spade to provide a better view, and said,

"Ach, away man, Mackintosh's head was all nothing but splinters, they had to fasten him with Seccotine before the doctor could even diagnose him. This is a wumman, a fine-looking young wumman."

"Poor girl," Hughie muttered, quite moved. "It's a bliddy dull place to be in if you're young and no mistake."

The young minister, who had been suffering the discussion with resigned tolerance, interrupted.

"Dust unto dust."

"Aye, sorry, sir," Murdo said quickly, awkwardly pushing the skull off his spade with one foot and throwing a quick spadeful of earth over it before he reached up for a hand to help him out. The coffin was lowered and lay at a grotesque slant which everybody courteously ignored. The minister opened the book.

"I, eh, don't see them," Davie whispered to Nat, who suddenly became aware of him. "The, eh, Jacksons . . ."

"Good," Nat whispered. The minister was intoning with unusual speed, and Davie was startled to find that the service was over.

"Do you, eh, see them, eh, anywhere?" Davie asked Nat, and Hughie interrupted in an urgent whisper, "Aye, by Joves, and they're up to something! My God, the furniture!"

The Jacksons hadn't actually vanished, but while the other mourners were lingering respectfully near the graveside, the twins were obviously, almost blatantly, sliding toward the rear of the crowd and the cemetery gate, and making an unfunereal turn of speed.

"They'll be first back at the house, man," Hughie said, "if we don't head them off." He took Nat by the arm, and Nat, mystified, allowed himself to be hustled toward the gate. The Jacksons saw them coming, and at once turned and broke into a lumbering canter in the direction of the boardinghouse.

"The van, Hughie!" Nat was now running, with Hughie panting alongside, and there was another burst of blue smoke as the engine started with a roar and took off. Hughie drove with the horn blaring and the Jacksons swerved aside to let him overtake. But they were only twenty yards behind when Hughie braked in front of the boardinghouse and made for the door.

Once there, he couldn't think of what to do. Nat sauntered up to his side, and the Jacksons arrived seconds later.

"Did you chaps want something?" Nat asked in his Etonian character.

Jackson One, as he was known in the village, lowered his head for a charge and said, "Baked ham!"

"He's right," Nat said helplessly to Hughie. "Baked ham is the inalienable right of every freeborn citizen."

"It's a hoor," Hughie said.

"The Lord will smite thee," Jackson Two grunted, and pushed past him into the hallway. One of the downstairs rooms was loud with the chatter of women and the clink of china. Ada came briskly from it with an empty tray in her hand.

"Ah, you're a kind lassie," Hughie said vaguely, "Davie was right to ask you to take charge of him."

"I didn't need to be asked." Very dignified. Davie Fitzgerald came shuffling at speed through the door and gasped, "Where did they go?" Hughie jerked a thumb at the door of the downstairs room, and Davie swayed on his feet with his mouth open.

"Come on," Nat said, "the kitchen, quick." He propelled Davie through the hall and Ada clipped along ahead in her high heels.

"I've got sausage rolls in the oven," she said. "They're lovely." Nat closed the kitchen door as the main mass of mourners swarmed through the front door.

"It's too bad you couldn't ram the Jacksons in the oven," Nat muttered, and Davie uttered a little moan and sank onto a chair.

"Huh, the Jacksons! I wouldn't see them in my way. What have *they* done?"

"Ach, man, you should have guessed, Davie, it's the furniture," Hughie said, reaching instinctively for a whisky bottle from the dresser. Davie's head came up in bewilderment, and Nat patted him briskly on the shoulder.

"He's right, Davie, you've got the invaders inside the wall red in tooth and claw. You may have to die fighting."

"Man, man, Davie, weren't we the gomerils not to suspicion them straight away, them and their tractor with the cart and Sadie with the pick-up! They'll redd the house before your eyes, Davie."

"Get Tom Wishart?" Nat suggested.

"Ach, he's no more use than a . . ." Hughie bit back the phrase in deference to Ada. "He'll be away up some mountain practicing the whole of Puccini and Robinson Caruso for the concert, and every dampt high note sharp!"

"Well, while you're talking I've got the sausage rolls," Ada said firmly, rather peevish because she had no idea what anybody was talking about. She straightened up from the oven with a full load and swayed out of the kitchen to feed the mob.

"That lassie should be forbidden by Act of Parliament," Hughie muttered. "She's got my hormones fair dizzy racing round and round the veins and no way out. I wouldn't like to face a Jackson single-handed on a warm day like this, and that's the truth. They're terrible heavy in the hand."

"You could disconnect their cart," Nat said. "By Gad, we must be a match for any fuzzy-wuzzies."

"Joves man, you've got the brains — I'll do better than that if I get a hand on their tractor engine!"

He bolted through the back door and into the yard. Nat stood shaking his head sympathetically at Davie, and finally poured him a whisky and pressed it into his limp hand.

"No, eh, no' the whisky, the vodka hasn't got, eh, a smell!" Davie said cunningly. "She could, eh, smell the whisky . . ."

Nat fed a glass of vodka into his hand without remark.

"Right, to the barricades," he said. He had to lift Davie by the elbow to force him toward the room where the mourners were drinking tea and eating ham sandwiches and rolls and wondering in alarm if there was going to be no whisky course. Already there were hints of strife. The voice of Sadie Pringle, which he had never heard before, cut shrilly through the mixture of reverent mutters and cheerful guffaws.

"Aye, they're lovely vases, I bought them myself in Wylie and Lochhead's in Glasgow — I lent them to Dod when he got married, the biggest mistake of my life!"

She already had one huge figured vase off the mantelpiece and under her arm, and was picking down the other. Davie, faced at last with action, gave a startled cry.

"Eh, that's mine, you!"

"We'll see about that! Right's right!"

"Eh, eh, eh, I bought it, I bought the, eh, pair in Dunoon for a, eh, present!"

"Zright there, I mind it fine," Geordie Mackay said thickly. "They cos' two quid, izznat right, Davie?"

Sadie Pringle was confused. "They're very like the ones I lent Dod," she said angrily, and then conceding victory, put the vase carelessly on the hearth. "But you never bought that — that's one of our heirlooms, Dod should never have took it out the house. *She* made him!" As quick as a snake, she threw herself at the ormolu clock on the center of the mantelpiece and clutched it fiercely to her. She fixed glittering eyes on Davie, who fell back stammering as she marched to the open door. Somebody laughed hysterically and somebody else said it was disgusting; but nobody moved to stop her until she reached the door, which was suddenly full of one of the Jackson twins. He reached out a great paw toward the clock and spoke in a rumbling bass.

"That's Charlie's."

Sadie screwed up her face and stared hate at him, and pressed the clock to her bosom.

"Don't you touch me! Don't you dare touch me, Jackson One or I'll have you for assault and battery! Charlie's!

Charlie never had a clock like this in his life and you know it, it was my grandmother's."

The twin looked puzzled and resentful and said,

"I'm Jackson Two." And weakened in his resolve by the mental effort of this, he let Sadie squeeze past him into the hall.

"That's my clock," Davie sobbed. "It's no' fair!"

The hubbub that was about to break was silenced by a sudden movement as Jackson One detached himself from the crush with a little Indian table lifted in one hand.

"Charlie's!" he intoned. Davie backed against a wall, dumb, as the twin clumped out into the hall. Then Davie spoke.

"That's a, eh, fib! Maggie's first man got that in, eh, Hong Kong!"

"Chris' almigh'y!" Geordie Mackay said, looking round the company. "Did she have *another* man?"

"Aye, a Mister, eh, McConnachie, he was a stoker!"

"Righ' enough!" Geordie cried. "You gotty hand it to 'er!"

"It's a public scandal!" said a thin woman with a sausage roll in her mouth. Davie slumped onto the lap of a plump lady and put his head in his hands. Nat was regarding him with a benign smile, grateful for the bizarre entertainment, when Hughie Mackay materialized at his elbow.

"The sparking plugs are in my pocket, Nat, and by Joves it was a near thing, if Jackson had seen me I would have an oriental coffee table fitted round my ears at this very minute. Have you got a strategy?"

Nat shook his head helplessly. It was too fascinating to interfere.

"Think, man," Hughie said, disillusioned. "They'll have the place as bare as a ——'s —— in three minutes."

Sadie Pringle suddenly scurried back into the room, did a

two-second survey, and seized a two-foot bronze statue of
Minerva from the sideboard.

"*This* is going back where it belongs!" she snapped at
everybody, and set off on a staggering run for the outside
door. There was a hush as the ceiling shook. Something
heavy was falling in the room above.

"They're eh, taking my eh, bed!" Davie cried, broken.
Hughie looked appealingly at Nat, who said,

"These Jackson boys, Hughie — what did they feed them
on? Have you noticed the size of their mitts?"

"Aye, man, it would be a right idiot that would try the
judo on that pair, it's the strategy we need." Through the
open door to the hallway, they could see the Jackson boys actually running downstairs carrying a massive mahogany chest
of drawers. They stopped in the hall, maneuvered, and lumbered out of the house with the prize. An instant later Sadie
Pringle shot back into the house and into the room of mourn-
ing.

"Who did it?" she screamed. "Who stole my clock?
There's a thief in this house!"

Nat saw young Archie McBain delicately ramming a ham
roll into his mouth and smiling slyly and looking flushed.

"It is a judgment on you, woman," Hughie declaimed,
"for defamatin' a house of death this day. The Lord giveth
and the Lord taketh away. Man, he's a good man, the Lord!
He's the boy for you!"

"Think black burning shame of yourself, Hugh Mackay,
for soiling your lips with the Lord's name! It was you that
stole my clock!"

"Ach, shut your face, you silly auld bitch," Hughie said.
The audience, unsure of the proprieties, was beginning reluctantly to enjoy the entertainment. Mourners had started
to drift out into the hall carrying cups of tea and sandwiches

in their hands, to watch as the Jacksons lumbered back inside and vanished upstairs again.

Sadie Pringle, snapping like a piranha, was crouched beside a display cabinet in the room across the hall, loading her arms with decorated china. Guests listened to the crashes from upstairs and speculated on what was coming next. What came was a bulbous wardrobe, carried at a gallop with clothes falling out of one of the swing doors. The Jacksons crashed their way into the daylight, and Sadie tottered behind them leaving a trail of saucers.

It was clearly going to be a race, since the Jacksons would start on the light stuff once they had cleared the heavy cargoes, and Sadie had to scoop up the best before that happened. Davie Fitzgerald had been pushed, kindly enough, off the plump woman's lap and was now standing against a wall with his head resting on his forearm and his body shaking with quiet sobs. Hughie started to dig Nat in the ribs in a frenzy of impatience. But at this moment Ada appeared beside them, sniffing contemptuously.

"Could youse not stop them?" she demanded. "It's daylight robbery, so it is. I've bolted the back door."

"Ah, you're talking to two fragile men, Ada," Nat said.

"Men! Useless!" Ada followed in the wake of Sadie Pringle and firmly closed the front door and locked it. A small cheer rose involuntarily from the munching mourners.

"By Joves, you never thought of that!" Hughie said, and Nat muttered, "No good, they'll starve us out, Hughie — when the sausage rolls are done it's a lingering death."

The door handle rattled, and the mourners in the vicinity backed away quickly. The doorbell rang. The handle rattled again.

"Open up!" The bass of Jackson Two, whose body blotted out the light against the stained-glass door panel. Only Ada

Fraser remained in the neighborhood of the door, and Nat's eyes glazed as he saw that she was hefting a meat chopper in her right hand.

With a horrifying crash, the great fist of Jackson One came through the glass. Ada immediately turned the key and swung the door open. Jackson One was towering in the doorway looking sullenly at the hand that had broken the glass.

"The funeral's finished!" Ada shouted at him.

"Charlie's bed!"

"Try and get in!" Ada raised the chopper. Her shoulders were thrown back and her splendid legs braced apart and bulging against the black satin.

"Bravo!" Nat shouted. The hand holding the chopper moved up and down experimentally.

"Just try!" Ada shouted again, and advanced six inches. Jackson One backed, and Sadie Pringle, running up from behind, bounced off him and sprawled in the path. Jackson One's face was baffled and resentful as he backed another step. Sadie Pringle, with her hat hanging from one ear, looked round him and screamed.

"This is family business, you keep out of it, Ada Fraser!" Ada made a quick feinting jab, and Sadie squealed and fell back. With a theatrical toss of her head, Ada slammed the door again and locked it. Sadie Pringle put her face to the hole in the glass.

"You've got no rights in this house, Ada Fraser, I'll thank you to get out of it."

"When Davie tells me to get out!" Ada's voice rang like a clan rally. "Do you want me for to get out, Davie?" she demanded. Davie raised shaking hands.

"Eh, naw! Naw, naw, Ada, it's eh, all right, honest."

Ada, still brandishing the meat chopper, surveyed the throng of mourners in the hall with a challenging eye, and they tried to look away and seem uninvolved.

"You stick wi' Davie!" Geordie Mackay babbled. "At's what poor sowl needs, a bodyguard!"

Davie tried to straighten his spine, and said wildly, "I never liked that wardrobe anyway!"

"You better serve the whisky, Davie," Ada said, and her voice was a curious echo of Maggie Fitzgerald's. After a moment of hesitation, Davie obediently shuffled toward the kitchen. The atmosphere in the house brightened at once as mourners made haste to get rid of cups and saucers and listened for the merry chink of glass.

"By Joves," Hughie said to Nat, "he never even saw it hitting him, she'll eat him like a pomegranate."

"You never see pomegranates nowadays," Nat said wonderingly. "They must have moved their breeding grounds."

SIXTEEN

Two men had been transported all the way from the English Midlands to assume command of the crate of fireworks that was to be the climax of the Young Master's twenty-first birthday celebrations. Various half-formed plans for kidnapping the crate had been discussed by the more subversive villagers, including Hughie and Nat, and by some of the hostelers whose taste for danger was inflamed by the night of the Great Crime. But the crate was impregnable in the cellar of the Big House, and the village resigned itself to a mere efficient display of the things, without the possibility of aiming them at anybody.

Owing to the imperfect system of communication between the laird and the peasantry, the rest of the celebrations were a list of rumors rather than a formal program. Denis McBain, always a gentle and trusting man, was convinced that there would be a mass issue of free beer in which to drink young Winston's health. Andy Anderson regarded this story with doubt and apprehension; doubt because it seemed

out of character with Arnold's resolute business principles,
and apprehension in case he was going to have a village full
of free boozers and an empty pub.

Geordie Mackay, using his appetite as a barometer, advanced the theory that beer was English and alien, and that
Harper would have the decency to issue a bottle of whisky to
every man, woman and child in Ochie. Hughie, disgusted at
this show of greedy servility, assured him that if anything
was issued, it would be Blue Water Gin, which the laird
could get for nothing and which was known in the village as
Harper's Harpic, ideal for cleaning round the bend of lava-
tory systems. Even Geordie, who had been known to try anti-
freeze in extreme need, turned white and sober at Hughie's
prediction.

There was some talk of the laird's inviting his old tenants
on board Lady Joyce for a social orgy, in order to raise the
tone of the stockbrokers and other inferior foreigners who
had arrived as his house guests. Nat was careful to warn anybody in sight that such an invitation could only mean a dastardly plot to drug everybody and slip downriver for South
America and the white slave markets on the morning tide.
Even Sadie Pringle, he insisted, could fetch a sound price
among the sex-mad merchants of the Mato Grosso.

It was known that Tom Wishart was taking the awful risk
of promoting a Grand Concert in the village hall, in aid of
the rebuilding fund and as a compliment to the young master; two terrible risks, in fact, because he would be diverted
from his duty at a time when constructive hysteria was likely
to rage among the populace, and he would also be singing
openly and exposing his official status to the savagery of an
Ochie audience.

Apart from that, the villagers didn't know what delights
the night would offer, and the laird didn't know they ex-

pected anything more than fireworks, and damned expensive fireworks at that.

By the early evening, there was a feeling abroad in the place compounded of festivity and unhealthy anticipation. Maggie Fitzgerald's mourners had been turned out into the open air by Ada Fraser, and they went willingly enough because it had been a good funeral and the whisky was finished. Three men in dark suits and black ties were baking in the sun on the sand dunes while they slept it off. Ada was still in the boardinghouse, and there was some speculation as to whether she was washing the dishes or putting Davie to bed, or taking Davie to bed. Most of the mourners, apart from the thin woman with the lust for sausage rolls, felt that after her bravura performance in routing the Jacksons, she was entitled to any perquisites available; and the thin woman was not so much disapproving as disappointed.

The postman arrived in the village on foot to add to the sum of excitement with the report that his van had been stopped by a wee landslide on the far side of the Devil's Drap. This might have been caused by the thunderstorm of a few days previously. It might, Hughie Mackay thought, have been caused by subterranean shock waves from the dynamiting of the salmon.

"A man with a scientific training never overlooks a possibility," he told Nat and Sam solemnly as they sat in front of the garage and drank some flat beer he had found in a tool chest. "It is a known fact that if you play a fiddle in the Alps you can drown an entire community under thousands of tons of snow, and a bit of dynamite is as noisy as a fiddle any day of the week."

"Is this the first time there's been a landslide?" Sam asked, worried.

"No, it is not, it is not, I admit that," Hughie said airily.

"But it isn't the first time I've blown up the Long Pool either. I bet you if I was a statistician I could manufacture a correspondence between the landslides and the free salmon."

"The obnoxious thing about you, Hughie," said Nat, "is that you want to take credit for acts of God — you can get a thunderbolt right up your nostril for that, it's happening all the time. You would need a dozen sticks to blow the road up."

"And by Joves, I've got a dozen, if I ever got the notion of it," Hughie said warmly. "But who would want an old lump of basalt for breakfast when the world is full of good fish?"

Nat pondered this, eyeing Hughie with eyes screwed up against the evening sun, and finally said, "There's a lot of iron in basalt, it's good for the sexual development — the great Fingal used to chew it all the time while he was building his cave."

When Nat and Sam arrived back at the cottage, Louise had already shut Sam out in the darkness of purgatory for attending the funeral against her wishes, and the whiff of whisky on his breath completed his rejection.

"There was a fight at the funeral," he said timidly, hoping that his story would readmit him to grace. But she gave her head a sharp little shake and muttered, "I don't want to know anything about the funeral, thank you very much." As she clip-clopped from the garden to the house and back again, pretending to arrange small items of clothing for the next day's trip, Sam trailed pleadingly after her; but eventually he gave up, and sat in crushed guilt on a bit of stone wall and sighed. The postman arrived a few minutes later, with a bundle of letters for Nat and one for Harry.

Stacey was out for a walk and had accidentally met Martin Stoddart. More and more she considered she had underestimated Martin. He had a fussy manner, but he knew all about Jane Austen and several plays of Shakespeare, the plays that figured in the school curriculum, and he could listen intelligently to talk about plot construction and dramatic irony and characterization. His sharp, slightly acid manner, she decided, was the product of a troublesome virility carefully suppressed, and as she drew him out with artistic cunning, he dropped more and more hints about the women he had known . . . "known" . . . The word had a hidden fascination, and she said slyly,

"You *knew* that girl, Martin. I take it you mean you knew her carnally . . ." Yes, she was right, he blushed.

"Now that is a question that no gentleman would answer!" he laughed a nervous laugh, but his chest expanded. Oh yes, the roaring sensualist carefully concealed under the schoolmaster exterior was somehow more true to *life* than a stock muscle-man with the mat of black hair showing through the half-open shirt.

"I had occasion," he changed the subject *so* obviously, "to attend Mrs. Fitzgerald's funeral today. A very distasteful experience, distasteful in the extreme. To put it briefly, that woman left a legacy of family bitterness."

"What happened?" Stacey was eager for the dirt, but Martin shook his head firmly.

"Even a broad-minded young lady like you — and you *are* broad-minded, admirably broad-minded — " he looked at her boldly, " — even a broad-minded young lady like you would hardly find it edifying. It reached the extent of physical conflict among certain members of the family. A mockery of death, I assure you, Miss Boag."

"Stacey."

"Stacey, then, since you are so kind." Martin wondered if it would be amusing to recount the events of the funeral, but decided that it was so sordid that he would probably lapse from the correct literary manner of speech that he enjoyed so much. "Stacey — may I inquire if that is a contraction of Anastasia?"

"How perceptive of you, Martin," Stacey replied ambiguously. What the hell was the use of saying it was a contraction for Agnes? Her mind was racing over the obscure story of the funeral, and clarifying it. The old woman, with three husbands . . . probably a very dull bitch, it was interesting how often men married dreary women . . . but they probably projected some romantic ideal of her ordinary personality . . . was she one of those stupid women with an unconscious fascination . . . possibly a string of lovers as well as husbands? My God, could Martin himself be one of the string? These "family" squabbles, like all squabbles, always had some undetected sexual motive . . . the assembly of mourners, some of them women whose husbands had been lovers of the dead woman . . . the women hating her and feeling glad she was punished with death . . . and the men, surprised to find that even after all these years there was a deep terrible sadness in her death . . . two of the old lovers suddenly each realizing the other's secret, like a thunderclap of betrayal . . .

And Martin, with his carefully built shell of pride and correctitude, not even wanting to talk about it because the sudden flare of violence between the two lovers suddenly told him that he, too, had been betrayed, that he had not been her only secret passion.

The implications made Stacey dizzy with joy. The true, the unseen, the deep undertones of grim respectable life in the hamlet were like the rumblings of a great volcano . . . volcano? subterranean river? . . . no, volcano was all right. A great volcano ready to roar into horrid life. The violence at the funeral was no more than a preliminary bubbling, a geyser? no, a bubble of lava . . .

And all this on top of her other character, the wanton wife

of the minister . . . Not an eternal triangle, but a maze . . .
an electric circuit! She was tempted to write the phrase down
at once. A tortuous electric circuit in which, if two wires
crossed for an instant, the volcano would erupt. Mm, cir-
cuits and volcanoes didn't go too well together. Bolts of light-
ning . . .

With another part of her mind, which she mostly ignored,
she was thinking that Stoddart, in spite of the dangerous way
he pushed the conversation toward carnality, was never in a
hurry even to take her arm. It was all there, she knew that
she was desirable, she felt desirable, but he was probably
timing his moves with all the cunning of his experience. She
wondered, she couldn't help wondering, about the absolute
basic mechanics of how it would happen . . . would he
bring the conversation back again to something or other, and
then take her hand, as it were unthinkingly, and then squeeze
it, and take it from there? Or would he stop suddenly and
clasp her? And after that, could there possibly be a way of
progressing smoothly to the moment of passion?

It was all very well to gloss this over in writing about
it . . . *dazed and ecstatic, she found herself beneath him,
while his strong hands* . . . but hell, she wasn't in the habit
of getting dazed, and there had to be a moment when somebody said *okay, lie down there,* or even started *shoving.* No
matter how she thought it over, she kept running into the
undignified scramble between the first glance of mutual
recognition and that prostrate position on the grass, or the
divan, or wherever it was. Not to mention a lot of ludicrous,
farcical business with suspender belts. She wanted it to happen even just once, to find out how people got over such social disasters without looking idiotic.

The easy way out, in the book, was really to abandon the
heather and the open-air thing and stick to simple situations

. . . as she wheeled in surprise from the sofa, her robe splayed open and he realized she was wearing nothing beneath. Then you knew where you were, except that even then, what was *he* wearing, unless this was in some improbable mixed Turkish bath? He was probably wearing a mass of buttons and zipp fasteners and there could be nothing in the world so silly as a man taking off his trousers. People didn't realize what a tough business it was writing true-to-life realistic novels.

Martin, happy and expansive, knew the temptation to touch Stacey's hand, to grab that strong bare arm. But of course, his interest in her was, truly, honestly, intellectual, and he *was* a man with responsibilities and honor. It would be different, of course, if she stopped and threw herself into his arms, and in the most friendly way, realizing that it just wouldn't do, he were to clasp her and sit down with her and, er . . . he would hardly be able to blame himself, after all. But such thoughts really were rather undignified, and unless she started something, he certainly wasn't going to risk his self-esteem by being snubbed, or even slapped. This hot weather was really rather a nuisance, it distracted one's mind from interesting conversation.

Mary fancied that both Nat and Harry had found something interesting in the mail, but in the eternal presence of Louise, she had no intention of raising any questions with either of them. Nat had flipped through his letters with the contempt that he always brought to letters, handing bills to her with a snarl; and then looking stern at one sealed letter and shoving it in his trouser pocket without discussing it. Harry had opened his letter at once, in the garden, and pored over it in puzzlement, and then wandered away with it still in his hand, obviously to read it again somewhere else. If he wanted to say anything about it, he would say it tomorrow. She had the pleasing suspicion that it might be good news.

He wandered back a few minutes later and said vaguely, "Magda's got appendicitis."

"Magda?" She kept her interest casual.

"A girl."

"There's a lot of it about," she said.

"What, of girls?" he asked absentmindedly, and wandered on toward the street. She caught the distinct flash of his pale shirt through the shrubbery and knew that he had stopped just outside the garden to read the letter yet again.

He hadn't been able to make out the signature at first. She had never written to him before, and the handwriting was both strange and illegible.

"Dirty dog," it started, and the phrase warmed him absurdly. *"While some dirty dogs are* something something *South of France and* something something something *death's door with appendicitis and not* something *a postcard* something something *phoned and phoned* something something *absolutely flinging myself at your* something something *no right to be* something something *girls while I lie pining for you in my bed of pain* something *actually up and raring to go where is Ochie for God's sake?*

And then, printed in block letters:

SIGNED. A FRIEND.

And then the scrawling signature which finally emerged as Magda.

Poor Magda. Within two minutes his entire feeling about Magda had turned itself upside down — or at least, his firm rejection of Magda had. What an unfeeling swine he had been, and what a fool to entertain a lot of childish jealous fantasies when the girl was ill in hospital and thinking of nobody but him. In fact, even if she *had* gone to the South of

France, she wouldn't have done anything silly. That was the thing about Magda, she was absolutely reliable and straight, and he was a dirty dog.

He would go home tomorrow on the same boat as Sam and Louise and filthy Timmy. In fact, he could even take Magda to the house at home since it was empty, and nurse her and make beef tea for her and wait hand and foot on her. That was loony, of course, her parents would never let the poor girl out of their sight when she had just had an operation. Maybe he could bring her down to Ochie, since that would be respectable — as long as she didn't go and get a crush on Nat, which some girls did because he was taller than Harry and thin or because he was a rich painter or something.

Harry pondered all these possibilities, including the crush on Nat, in a cheerful dream. In fact, she could get a crush on Nat if she liked, as long as she did all her serious pining for him, Harry. He felt a twinge of pity for Dee, who had been ditched by a cloth-headed English paint salesman, but now he was sure she would get over it. He thought he would go down to the Tala and maybe have a pint with Archie McBain, and listen to Archie's banal lechery with a tolerant smile, even encourage him for the hell of it. He might even chat up one of those two blonde hostelers whose legs had been bothering him all week, and let them know, kindly and subtly, that if they fancied him, they were not on. And they *would* fancy him, they couldn't help it.

He actually saw Archie, sitting on the concrete boat slip with Dee, of all people, and as he came down behind them, tentatively so as not to disturb them, he heard Archie saying, "See a boat like that? That's not a sailor's boat at all." He dismissed the Lady Joyce, riding opulently at anchor, with a wave of his hand. "But see women? You get a boat like that, women go for you, it never fails. Brass buttons and a big diesel job and they go for you straight away."

"You're a sex bore," Dee said. "Did you know that? A sex bore."

"I do all right," he said sullenly. "See fellas like that Winston? No use. Brass buttons and bullshit."

"What an elegant turn of phrase," Dee said in lofty distaste. "Oh, Harry. Good!"

Archie McBain scrambled to his feet, glancing shiftily at Harry and trying not to look like a sex bore.

"I thought we might have a pint, Archie," Harry said kindly.

"You two do that," Dee said airily, and Archie turned to her and said, "Aw!"

"I'm too young."

"Not at all," Archie protested. "See you? You look maturer than these bits on that diesel boat, honest. See debutantes? Dead loss. You don't mind, Harry, eh?" he pleaded.

"Jack-easy," said Harry.

"Oh, all right," Dee said, humoring the children. She strolled up the slipway, ignoring Archie, who came up behind trying not to look at her back view.

On the Lady Joyce, Tony Hammer was leaning back against a bulkhead to steady the hands that held a ten-power binocular trained on Dee.

"Now that looks like good nourishing food for growing boys," he murmured. Winston Harper curled his lip.

"Very short of the old calories," he objected. "Not to mention a perfectly frightfully rudimentary grasp of technique."

Tony lowered the glasses with interest and respect.

"You haven't!"

"I wish I hadn't. The mother is marginally better, as a matter of fact, but definitely not five-star material."

"Well, well." Winston almost felt guilty at the ease with which he had deceived Tony. Obviously, Tony didn't find such claims hard to believe, they agreed with his own experience of life.

"I don't usually deal in secondhand material," Tony mused, with the glasses at his eyes again. "But one must ingest where the nourishment is. I think, yes, I rather think. Our friends in the salon," he added briskly, "are definitely non-starters. Selling-platers, Winston. I fancy a return to the jolly old peasant soil is indicated, the rich fertile loam. Mother, eh? Broad-hipped yeoman stock?"

"Quite broad-hipped." Winston uttered a reminiscent chuckle from some histrionic talent he hadn't known about. "Broad is as broad does."

"An epigram, lad! Well well. I see we have a dark horse in old Winston. Cooperative? Ready and willing?"

"Hard to tell." Winston adopted a tone of earnest meditation, suddenly frightened of going too far. "I rather fancy they might be *rather* choosy. A certain period of gentle persuasion was required."

"It usually is." Dee had now vanished into the Tala, but Tony kept the glasses poised and slowly surveyed the landscape. "Sometimes it can take, oh, *days*, damn their dear little proley prejudices."

This admission relieved Winston's fears and aroused his suspicions. In the long saga of Tony's venery, no interval had ever occurred between the request and the conquest. It was just possible that Tony was capable of elaborating his recitals.

"However," Tony was murmuring, "the wine and wassail of the young master's natal day should have a perceptible solvent effect. The grape, my boy, the grape that doth with logic absolute."

Winston's fears began to return. Brought up in an atmosphere where liquor was in lavish supply night and day, he had accordingly grown up abstemious. Now he rather fancied he might have rather a lot to drink at his birthday party. He wasn't too sure if he was quite, entirely, enjoying the arrival of Tony; but his resolution remained, stronger than ever, not to enter into his majority without an experience that he could relate with absolute truth.

SEVENTEEN

THERE WAS NOTHING greedy about Tom Wishart's ambition as a singer. He didn't want a job in the Scala or even the Palladium, he didn't even mind if audiences never rose to him in cheering ecstasy. He simply loved singing and he wanted to do it all the time. Faced with his first really public performance, he wasn't keyed up with nerves and hope; only weighed with the gloomy certainty that it would go wrong.

The arrival of a score of people from the Big House at the village hall didn't excite him. He knew they wouldn't stay long enough to hear him in any case. The program had opened with a Welsh boy whom Tom had winkled out of the Youth Hostel crowd, and he was still going strong, playing a guitar and singing Irish rebel folksongs in an American accent. He knew nearly a hundred Irish rebel songs, he had told Tom three minutes before the concert started, and Tom had already counted eleven and the man wasn't even tired.

The party from the Big House were talking casually among themselves, as if the Welsh boy weren't a live performer but a television commercial. They were massed at the rear of the hall, convenient to the door. At the front, the raggle-taggle of local rowdies and hostelers had started to stamp their feet, out of time, and shout for "Mingulay."

"I don't know it," the Welsh boy shouted, and strummed a long G chord and shouted, "Now folks, my next number is that good old oldie, 'The Wild Colonial Boy.' "

"Give us 'Mingulay!' "

"The Wild Colonial Boy" and "Mingulay" started more or less simultaneously, and "Mingulay" soon won by weight of numbers. The Welsh boy gritted his teeth and sang bravely for three verses, and then in disgust stood up and took a bow. Half of the audience applauded or cheered while most of the other half carried on with "Mingulay." Tom stood up, smiling doggedly, and screamed,

"And now a local star, wee Willie Campbell!"

The endless choruses of "Mingulay" carried on while a ten-year-old boy in short trousers walked up to the platform, positioned himself in a classic pose, and launched into a high-pitched ballad in Gaelic. The rowdies fell instantly silent, and wee Willie Campbell, proud of his command over the audience, went into the entire forty-six verses. By the twentieth, the Big House party was chatting again, and the rowdies were passing bottles to one another to get strength for the rest of the song. This time Tom didn't risk another marathon. When wee Willie stopped, bowed formally, and took a deep breath for another long-distance run, Tom leaped up beside him, applauding, and took him as kindly as possible by the hand and dragged him off.

"A musical selection," he shouted. "By our one and only Geordie Mackay!"

Noise broke out as the Big House party, chattering gaily, got up and made for the door. The stragglers among them had some difficulty in leaving as Geordie was coming in from outside, red-faced and reckless as he flung elegant visitors to both sides and cantered for the platform. Among wild cheers, he made a preliminary examination of the piano keyboard and noticed that the black keys had been regrouped in threes and fours instead of twos and threes.

"Ach, to hell with them, I'll play blind," he said loudly to himself.

"Stone blind, Geordie! Puggled! Gutteracious!" the rowdies shouted happily. Geordie shot his cuffs, blinked a few times, struck a C chord one note too high, closed his eyes and let his hands play "Suvla Bay." Now the audience's feet were stamping in time and driving out of his mind the names of every other song he knew. He gave "Suvla Bay" nine choruses before he remembered "Whispering," and gradually his fingers recollected a few dozen dance tunes of the nineteen-thirties. Happily he switched off his brain and went on to automatic pilot. He was still in a trance, drowning in a flood of C major chords and riffs, when a mixed group near the front clattered outside with the macabre notion of organizing eightsome reels on the shore road.

The eightsomes, four sets of them, were well away when Tom Wishart managed to cut through Geordie's haze and ask him to play the accompaniment to "Only a Rose." With a shrinking heart, and an audience of fifteen, Tom heard the first bars of the introduction working themselves out in agony and then slipping noisily back into the key of C. But there was steel in the man's spirit. Against the screams of the dancers outside, and the clattering of two ancients in the audience who had got up and were doing a drunken dance in the aisle, Tom bulged the veins in his forehead and sang on through the entire corpus of Sigmund Romberg. Life, after all, was sweet, even in the key of C, because it had reached its lowest moment and everything that ever happened in the next forty years had to be an improvement.

Nat and Harry had built a fireplace on the beach with boulders to Mary's design so that she could conduct a sausage barbecue to fill in the long interval before the fireworks started and keep the kids occupied and out of each other's hair; and so that she could keep herself busy, because with the possibility of freedom and privacy only a day away, she found that she had started to erect unbearable erotic fancies. She couldn't bear to look at Nat, she almost hated him. She concentrated on organizing collections of driftwood and counting the sausages, with Sam hovering helpfully near her and possibly, she thought, as bad with erotic fancies as herself.

Harry and Dee and Sally and Timmy joined in a chaotic series of eightsome reels on the promenade. Nat and Hughie, both surprisingly sober and respectable, were loyally sticking Tom Wishart's concert out to the end. It was almost sinister to see Nat putting himself to so much suffering in the cause of civic duty.

The sight of the barbecue fire started an outbreak of imitations, and half-a-dozen bonfires smoked into life along the beach. She sternly turned her mind from her selfish visions so that she could enjoy the gala feeling of what was, after all, a beautiful night and worth remembering. In the confusion, it was possible that the barriers had partly broken down between the Big House guests and the human beings. Some of the guests, bored with their own conversation, were actually joining in the reels and tentatively throwing bits of wood on fires, although others were already being ferried out by motor launch to the Lady Joyce, for a grandstand view of the firework display.

Stacey Boag, energetically collecting tree trunks from the

tide line, felt herself responding vividly to the spirit of carnival. Absentmindedly she had surrendered her hope that the villagers held a Feast of Beltane, and wondered whether she should simply invent one, though this was rather against her principles as she wanted her book to remain absolutely true as an objective study of real life she had seen. Absentmindedly she was also regretting that she hadn't performed an act of genuine drama that afternoon; that she hadn't suddenly stopped during her walk with Martin Stoddart and commanded coldly *Kiss me*. Of *course* he would have done it — what man wouldn't in the circumstances? It really was a pity that she hadn't conducted that experiment in relationships, because the detailed consequences could be perfectly priceless as material.

Flushed with exertion and the glow of the barbecue fire, she resolved to seek out Martin and force a dramatic situation on him. She saw him, and saw with disgust that his wife was with him, clinging to his arm while he patted her hand with blatant uxoriousness. Looking at them, Stacey thought, The devils, they look as if they've had a quick tumble in bed before they came out.

For the first time, her artistic intuition had coincided with an objective fact. After years of boredom with Isa, Martin had gone home from his walk so stimulated nervously that he would have gone to bed with a wounded grizzly, and had astonished Linda by ordering her to get out and enjoy herself with the young people. Unable to recapture the tongue-tied wooing approach of his early marriage, Martin had then bluntly demanded of Isa that she should repair to bed with him at once. He was staggered by her instant, joyous submission. She had always been feeble and inhibited; but then, he forced himself to consider, he had always been furtive and matter-of-fact. Maybe he had been ignoring something good and wasted several years ignoring it when it was available for nothing.

He didn't actually want to get effusive afterward, and have Isa getting above herself, but he couldn't resist a feeling of benevolence, and the way she clung to his arm wasn't at all uppity, but proper and respectful and grateful. He was beginning to appreciate the hot weather at last.

Balked and irritated, Stacey remembered Hughie Mackay, and saw him nearly at once, spilling out of the village hall in a small knot of people.

"Hello there, Hughie!" she bellowed. He came over to her, rather furtively and quickly, and she took his arm.

"It's yourself, Stacey, and by Joves you're a sight for sore eyes after twenty-two yards of music from the polis — sharp as a . . . sharp all the bliddy way."

"What hard muscles you've got," Stacey said recklessly, crushing his arm. "I haven't seen enough of you lately, you beastly man."

"Ach, I'm snowed under, fair snowed under," Hughie said. "But we'll have a fine time tonight with the squibs and rockets after."

"Don't imagine for a moment I'm letting you out of my sight now I've caught you," she cooed, and he squeezed her arm in return. A tough hard man, hard calloused hands.

"Ach, there's a dampt beggar's carburettor choked and nothing will do but it's got to be got going this minute," he pleaded. "But I'll be straight back and no mistake, I might even ask you for a Strathspey or a reel if my boots can still remember the steps."

She let him go with real regret, wondering if it would seem normal and friendly if she kissed him in the flickering dark. Probably not.

"Don't you dare go back on that," she warned him. "Em,

if you don't see me here I may be up at the cottage. I don't
like fireworks all that much. Not the cottage," she added
quickly. "The studio." Nobody would be back in the studio
too early.

"Ach, you've got the good taste there, Stacey, what is fireworks but a lot of bangs anyway — I'll be looking for you."

He vanished very quickly into the darkness, and she muttered "Mhm" under her breath and began to stroll aimlessly
along the beach, carefully steering away from the barbecue
and drifting toward the cottage road.

Louise felt she ought to be having a wonderful time, es
pecially since the barbecue fire was *exactly* like one in *Good
Housekeeping*, in one of those marvelous two-page color
pictures you want to step right into. But there was always
something lacking in the attempts real life made to imitate
the super-reality of *Good Housekeeping*. The people were
wrong, primarily — Sam mooching about like a great oaf,
with no idea of the finer things; and Mary organizing everything with imitation efficiency, as if she too had read those
Good Housekeeping features. The idea of Mary presiding
over a barbecue was incongruous, really, when you thought
of her background, and it was absurd how the children and
even strangers rallied round and helped her as if she were
really a high-class hostess.

Most of all Louise felt cheated by the sight of the motor
launch, a beautiful thing of pale varnished pine, whirring
richly to and from the Lady Joyce with cargoes of *real* people, who would be lounging on the decks like Kodachrome
pictures holding drinks with ice in them and enjoying brittle talk, and probably feeling superior and tolerant of the
folk lighting fires on the beach and all those uncouth dancers.
The thought of the party on the Lady Joyce was more than
she could stand, and it was no use inviting Mary to join her

in wistful talk of how nice it would be out there, because Mary would say it was a bore out there. Mary was not only lacking in imagination, she could be downright coarse nowadays.

She regarded, with a fixed smile, the cowlike enjoyment Mary was getting out of the futile little barbecue and the inane enthusiasm of the Youth Hostelers who were humping great logs up from the beach, and irritation and frustration built up in her till she knew she would scream.

"I must go up for a scarf," she said. And all Mary said was, "Fine."

Nobody cared whether she went or stayed. She had a quick impulse to order Sam to go up for a scarf for her, because he was nearly enjoying the barbecue instead of moping after her as he should have been. But she stopped herself in time, because she wanted to get away even more than she wanted to punish Sam. She tried to keep smiling and walked away from the fire. When everybody else came back home, she could ask them about the fireworks and be sweet to them and make supper and make it plain she didn't at all mind missing all the fun.

The fireworks display was timed for 11:54, the minute at which Winston had entered the world. There was a long time to go before then, and there was a late license at the Tala, so Mary knew that Nat would have taken Hughie along for a drink. Fine. This was the last time she would have to organize entertainment for people outside the family, and the family could entertain themselves. In future, she would be in at the Tala with a roar. For tonight, she could occupy herself with Sally and Timmy and stomach it.

Winston and Tony Hammer were not among the Big House party who had left for the Lady Joyce. The reeling whirls of flesh on the promenade held them with the fascination of a slave market. Winston kept glancing sideways at Tony to see exactly how Tony went about surveying the goods, and how he would make his choice and claim it. Tony, he thought, was nervous, or perhaps jumpy with anticipation, and Winston prayed that he wouldn't catch sight of either of the Boag females and discover that they were impregnable and that he, Winston, had lied.

"That for an hors d'oeuvre," Tony suddenly said. He was looking at rather a nice-looking little thing in a blue dress, and before Winston had time to agree, Tony had advanced on her. The girl had dark hair and her face was flushed from being flung about in a dance, and Tony said loudly,

"All that frightful exertion does shocking things to the old metabolism, sweetie, and the only cure is a gentle stroll."

"No, really," the girl said. But Tony had her by the arm and was laughing jovially, perhaps a little too loudly, and the girl was allowing herself to be led along the coast road while Tony's voice prattled on.

It did work, then, and the infuriating thing was that Winston couldn't see what Tony had done or said that was so special. It simply worked with Tony, that was all. Winston took a flask from his pocket and shamelessly downed a long drink of ready-mixed gin and French, and put the flask away and pondered.

He couldn't, it was impossible, anyway, all the bints about the place were already hooked by a lot of louts. As the drink reached his stomach and met what had gone down before, he recovered some of his stout British pluck, and noticed at the same time that neither of the Boag females was visible.

His cheeks were beginning to glow, and in a mild way, so was his view of the world. What the devil had he been moping about? Even the most willing bit enjoyed a bit of horseplay, come-and-get-me nonsense. Could it be possible that he had been given the signal and failed to follow through with a second and a third swing? Dammit, whether it was possible or not, he would have a try. He straightened his shoulders in case anybody had been looking at him, and strode through the darkness, swaying slightly.

It was Sally who told Harry about the dark villain who had led Linda away, and for a moment Harry was inclined to shrug his shoulders and forget it. Linda was really very nice, but now that he had Magda back again, he didn't have to bother about her, and he had only been looking for her as a dancing partner, not for anything else.

"But he *dragged* her," Sally exaggerated, adding casually, "I expect he's a raper, he looked Latin."

"Rapist," Harry corrected automatically. "You should have your mouth washed out with soap and water. Which way did they go?"

"That way." Sally had lost interest. "But I expect she wanted to be ravished anyway. Do you want to dance?"

"You can dance with Timmy, he's a raper too," Harry told her cruelly, and as she yelled "Ha ha ha," he walked doubtfully along the shore road, feeling foolish.

It was by luck that he found them, and only because Tony Hammer had a carrying voice, which happened to be saying, "Not to worry, Lindy baby" as Harry was passing the derelict lifeboat house. They seemed to be inside the boathouse, and there was no way in through the nailed-up door on the shoreward side. Harry started to go round the building on tiptoe, miserably aware that he was behaving like a peeping tom. The boat gates on the seaward side were also nailed up, but an area of the wood had rotted and fallen away.

"*That's* better," Tony was saying, and there was the noise of little movements.

"Now don't be *silly*," Tony said, a little testily. It was odd that Linda was saying nothing at all. Perhaps she was unconscious, but no, of course she must be conscious or Tony wouldn't be talking either. Then Harry remembered how tongue-tied Linda always was. She might even be so shy that under assault from a beastly spoiler she would be too embarrassed to protest in words, and merely struggle . . . and perhaps even be too embarrassed to struggle vigorously. He paused for some seconds, holding his breath.

"Ah, would you!"

After all, what could he lose if he went in? The worst that could happen would be embarrassment. If he went away, the worst that could happen might be worse. He started breathing again, and stepped boldly through the gap in the gate.

"Oh!" he said. "Is there somebody there?"

"Go away," said the voice of Tony. "What do you want?"

"I'm looking for a lifeboat."

Now he heard Linda utter a muffled "oh!"

"Is that you, Linda?" he asked in surprise. "I thought you were dancing."

"No." Her voice was breathless and it was impossible to analyze any particular intention in it.

"Would you like to dance?" he demanded. "This is Harry."

"Yes."

There was no doubt now. She had recovered some of her breath, and the Yes was fervent. His pupils were now dilated, and he could vaguely see them, Linda held firmly against the dark-haired man.

"You're a nice little man," Tony said, struggling for icy composure, "but this is my dance, so toddle off back to your bagpipes, do."

Harry's embarrassment fell away from him.

"Let her go," he said civilly, "or I'll thump you."

"Ha! The dramatic touch!" Tony laughed, and Harry considered that he might be a champion boxer, or a karate expert. As Nat always said, there was a lot of it about. Rather than engage in a formal bout which might be humiliating, and since Tony was still holding Linda tightly against him, Harry drove his fist at the man's eye. Tony fell back, and Linda jumped into Harry's arms, which was awkward but quite pleasant. Tony was breathing hard, with one hand to his face.

"Really," he said, "the *fuss*. Everything they say about this crazy country is the gospel truth." He carried off his exit superbly, leaving them both embarrassed.

"Was he trying to rape you?" Harry asked, and Linda shrugged in the dark, probably blushing. They stood for a few seconds, and then she said,

"Oh, you know. The usual things boys do."

Harry sat down on a broken bench, and Linda sat beside him. At least she didn't think he was a nuisance.

"I suppose I would do the same things," he said guiltily. She didn't say anything.

"I suppose I wanted to kiss you too," he said. "It's very difficult."

"Yes." It was a bit like talking to a backward child, who couldn't contribute anything except agreement.

"Did he hurt you?"

". . . no."

He couldn't get through to her mind. He didn't even feel physically excited by her, but in a puzzled impulse to experiment, he put a hand on her shoulder and turned her slightly and kissed her on the lips, then let her go. She didn't say anything.

"Would you rather go back to the beach?" he asked desperately.

"If you like."

"Did you *enjoy* that?" He wasn't sure whether he had enjoyed it or not. She exhaled in helpless inability to supply an answer. But when he put his hand on her shoulder again and turned her, she came willingly enough, and put a hand on his shoulder as they kissed again. She felt nice. He let her go again.

"I'm engaged," he said. "No. I've got a steady girl friend."

"So have I."

This made the whole thing so silly that he kissed her again while he thought of something else to say. There was nothing electric about her response, as there had been with Ada, but she was placidly submissive and cooperative.

"You don't enjoy it much," he accused her, and she said, "Yes," in mild protest.

"It's not fair to your boy friend."

"No." She sounded unsure but willing to agree. He kissed her again, and again she responded with docile acceptance.

"If I raped you," he said impatiently, "you wouldn't even have the gumption to fight or scream."

"You wouldn't, would you?"

"I might, for all you know."

She didn't answer this.

"Maybe we'd better go back to the beach."

"If you like." She sounded regretful, but not bitterly regretful. He took her hand and led her out through the broken gate, and then tucked her arm in his and walked slowly toward the bonfires. After a few steps he stopped, and without prompting she turned toward him and they kissed long and gently. This happened three times.

"I don't understand you at all, Linda."

"I'm not very bright."

"You are."

"You're only saying that. I'm dim."

"Do you never talk even with your girl friends?"

"Oh yes, a lot, I chatter a lot."

"Okay, chatter."

She laughed, nervously, and then laughed again in amusement. He squeezed her arm.

"Do you think, ever?"

"Yes, all the time. But it's only silly thoughts."

"What are you going to be?"

"A children's nurse."

"What kind of silly thoughts?"

"Oh. You know. Thoughts."

"I don't. I *want* to know."

"I'm not telling you, then." It was the first positive tone he had heard, the first hint of jocularity.

"I wish I could get to know you better, Linda."

"So do I. You're intelligent."

"Havers."

"You know you are."

"Oh, well . . . I have a steady girl friend."

"Yes." This time there was a definite note of wistfulness.

"But she isn't here yet."

"No."

They stopped and kissed again.

"Gather ye rosebuds while ye may," he said.

" — Old time is still a-flying."

"Go to the top of the class."

She tucked her arm in his and they walked very slowly as she laughed.

Sam loved fireworks, but he knew he wouldn't enjoy them. Louise had gone up to the cottage, and that meant an aftermath of martyrdom, because she hadn't come back with her scarf. Anyway, apart from his knowledge that she was making him feel guilty, he knew she must be making herself feel miserable, and after a brief review of the situation, he decided that it was better to offer his sympathy and his presence now, and be snubbed, than not offer it and be worse snubbed later.

Even so, he hesitated as he approached the cottage door. He wasn't going to enjoy the first minute very much. On a craven inspiration, he remembered that he and Nat had stocked the studio not only with whisky and beer, but with gin, which Louise wouldn't detect on his breath. He moved silently to the studio and went in.

"Is that you?" It was a whisper from the direction of his own bed, and his mind whirled.

"Yes," he whispered. He moved gingerly through the darkness.

"Good," said the voice. Could it be Louise? He had a joyful surge of gratitude. He reached down and a hand fumbled with his, closed on it and squeezed. Sam knelt on the floor, and she whispered, "Well!" and he knew it wasn't Louise. He couldn't remember seeing Mary during the few minutes before he had left the beach, and his heart thumped painfully at this thought. He reached out his other hand, and it touched what felt like a silk robe, which moved under his touch. He was touching skin, soft and resilient. He bent forward and kissed her, letting her hand go, and her arms came round him with almost masculine force as his own hand slid downward and encountered nothing but skin. It wasn't Mary.

"It's Stacey!"

"It's Sam!"

The whispers were synchronized, and then Stacey uttered an impish little giggle. Why complicate life by suggesting that it was supposed to be somebody else? Hughie might not even come, and whether he did or not, she was in Sam's power . . . both ways.

"Well?" she whispered against his face. His free hand grabbed all over her and she took his head in both hands and kissed him so that her hands wouldn't get in his way in whatever he had to do.

Louise couldn't even concentrate on the new copy of *The Queen* in her lap. She was too infuriated, and most of all at her own mistake in leaving the beach and staying so long that she couldn't think of how to explain it if she did go back with a scarf. But she had come to a decision, and she was throwing the magazine down when the door opened and a slim young man with golden hair poked his face into the kitchen and eyed her muzzily.

"Who are you?" She jumped in fright.

"Winston Harper," he muttered, "and I'm twenty-one today."

"Mr. Harper!" Louise's depression whisked away. "How nice, er, charmed, I mean, how do you do?"

"I am in need," he said, with cold dignity, "I am in need of a good woman."

"You have been drinking, young man." Louise was delighted to have a laird's son at a disadvantage, to be able to chide his shortcomings. "Come and sit on the sofa and I'll make you some *very* strong *very* black coffee."

"Sofa's a good idea," he agreed, and came in and sat himself on it without lurching too much. "Who the hell wants coffee? You're much more nourishing than coffee. You're very calorific," he assured Louise, and detained her with a hand on the arm as she made to rise.

"Thank you, I'm sure." Louise was now happily in command of the situation. He was a very sweet boy, and who could blame him for having a teeny bit too much on his birthday? "I'm just a teeny bit old for you, though, do you not think?"

"No." He stared to bring her face into precise focus. "You're fine. Do I kiss you first?"

"Now Winston!" But the hand with which she slapped his was gentle and indulgent. "You're a naughty boy, and you shouldn't give an old lady like me ideas."

"Very well, kiss first." He had to reach awkwardly to grasp the woman and pull her toward him, but it was true, these things were easier after a few drinks.

"Really, you mustn't, you silly boy!" She turned her head so that he kissed her cheek.

"Not fair," he said.

"Well, just a teeny kiss, you silly boy." She turned toward him and he kissed her. He put his arms round her and held on till his breath gave out. Then she got up very firmly and prised his hands away.

Winston was momentarily balked.

"Have a drink," he whispered. "I like a girl tha' can hold her liquor. Come on, if you don't have a drink I'll be offended."

For no reason Louise found herself whispering too. "Coffee is much better, young man." But to humor him she took the flask he was holding out, a perfectly beautiful gold flask, terribly heavy, and poured some of its contents into a tumbler. He put his hand over hers and held the flask till the tumbler was nearly half full.

"Bottoms up," he whispered, and put the flask to his mouth. Louise smiled tolerantly and sipped the tumbler. It was bitter, but quite nice; not hot and acrid like whisky.

"Every drop," he whispered, and actually put a hand to

the base of the tumbler. She gulped frantically rather than
have it spill down her chin.

"Now kiss," he whispered. " 'S my birthday."

"Oh, all right! What it is to be young."

She let him clasp her and kiss her, rather wetly, and when
she paused and she couldn't escape from his arms, she stayed
still to conserve her strength. She was only half conscious of
his moist lips and half conscious of a warm glow spreading
inside her chest.

"Never mind bed," he whispered. "Sofa'll do." And he
actually began to drag her to the sofa and force her down on
to it.

"Now, Winston." She was quite sharp and firm this time.
"You're overstepping the mark. Get up at once. That will
do."

His weight was holding her down in an undignified
sprawl.

"Please," he whispered brokenly. "Be nice. Please? Never
done it. Twenty-one years old, and never been kissed."

His weight slumped to one side and relieved the pressure
on her, but his face was so stricken that she patted it impul-
sively.

"You poor silly boy," she said, hearing her voice as she
spoke and approving of it. "But I'm a married woman."

"You don't like me," he said bleakly.

"Now you mussenoo that," she said. "You must not do
that, that is naughty."

"It's beautiful. Soft!"

"Stop it at once."

"For a minute."

He took his hand from her breast, to her relief, but she
realized with dim alarm that he was disarranging his clothing. This would positively not do.

"That's better," he grinned, and kissed her. She tried to wriggle her head, but her neck was heavy, and in any case, it wasn't the kissing she minded, and she was feeling rather silly. When his hand came down on her again and gently massaged her, she decided that there was no harm in that, as long as it went no further. But it would, it would, and although she was feeling hazy and light-headed and not caring as much as she should, she would not, she could not, permit the awfulness of having her clothes pulled about, and besides, it was dangerous.

"S'lovely," he whispered, and seemed in no hurry to make any further progress.

"Yes, it is nice," she said thickly, and holding onto the remains of her steel sense of right and wrong, she said quickly, "But there are limits, Winston, you naughty naughty boy . . ." He shook his head doggedly at this, and in a kind of terror, her mind groped dizzily for a way of escape that wouldn't annoy the poor boy. " — but there are things a nice girl cannazoo, cannot do . . ." he kissed her, and when he stopped his mouth was trembling.

"You poor boy, I know, man is always the hunter, but no, please no, Winston, not yet, jussa moment, no I insist, you're going too quigly . . . I'll do something for you," she added with what was becoming drunken cunning. "I can help you, now juss don' do anything, there there, Louise will take care of you."

In the outhouse studio, Stacey had long since zipped herself into sensible slacks and a sweater, and Sam was standing numbly in the dark trying to apologize.

"Don't be a goof, Sam, you're a sweet man and you haven't deprived anybody of anything." Stacey whispered firmly. "Damn!"

"What's wrong?"

"Oh hell, nothing. I don't *remember* what happened between! I don't remember you taking off your damned trousers."

"I did it quietly." Sam was deeply shocked. "I didn't want to embarrass you."

"Oh, hell." There was a touch of resigned gaiety in her voice. "That's real life for you, it's worse than novels. And don't worry, I'll never tell Louise."

"Oh my God," Sam whispered, "Louise is in the cottage all this time!"

"Courage, brother!" Stacey whispered. "Let me out first and I'll slip down the bramble path. Then you can go in and no harm done."

Sam didn't believe it, but he stood, sagging, as Stacey slipped out of the studio and vanished round the side. Then he braced himself, decided against another gin, and walked firmly to the cottage door and opened it.

Louise looked up with a blazing face. Winston, his face slack and flushed, lurched round to stare at Sam. His shirt was hanging out of the front of his trousers.

"Where have you been?" Louise responded automatically to the arrival of Sam, but her voice didn't have the authority it needed, and even as she was speaking, she knew she sounded silly. Sam tried to think quickly, and failed. He had an idea that he ought to punch somebody, or thrash somebody, but he couldn't think of how one started to thrash people. He advanced a step into the kitchen and glared at Winston and said, "Get out!"

"Delighted." Winston was fully as confused and unsettled as Sam, and only his years of training prevented him from grabbing at the flapping end of shirt and stuffing it back into place, which would have been an undignified admission of guilt. "Jolly nice evening," he said, and lurched past Sam and into the darkness. Sam stood aside to let him pass, and clenched his fists in order to look aggressive and purposeful. When Winston was safely away, he stood, gazing fixedly at Louise, and decided that silence was not only convenient, but brilliant. She stared back at him, and tried to recover her lifelong posture of superior morality.

Sam went on staring at her.

"Well, what have you got to say?" she demanded. "Stop standing there looking like a fool."

"Go to your room." Sam wasn't sure what made him say this. A whole list of possible phrases had run through his mind, and most of them sounded insane, but he couldn't be silent any longer, and this was less insane than most of the things that occurred to him.

"You've got some silly idea in your head," Louise said, rather high-pitched, and Sam interrupted her with a violent movement of the hand, and said,

"Go to your room!"

"Don't you dare talk to me like that!"

"For the third time — " Sam moved a step toward her, and his mind was a glorious confusion of relief and righteousness. There was something else too, a horrified thrill at the knowledge of betrayal, of his cold unwilling wife's having engaged in an orgy of passion that he had never enjoyed. This feeling came uppermost, and he was filled with anger.

"Get upstairs!"

"It's not what you think! I might have known you would think the worst. I should never have married you!" Louise almost managed to work herself into an attitude of moral superiority again, but before she could get it properly organized, Sam swung his hand and slapped her on the cheek.

Even as he swung, a lifetime of inhibition slowed the stroke and it landed with a pat rather than a wallop. But it was enough. In an instant, Louise wanted to murder him, and particularly she wanted to murder him because she knew he was twice her weight and she was helpless. He glared at her with her head swaying, and stuck to the only line he could remember.

"Go to your room."

"I'll never speak to you again," Louise cried shrilly, and Sam came out of his trance.

"You'll do as you're told," he said slowly. "Trollop," he added, with a surge of satisfaction because fluency had come to him.

"It was nothing like that!" Louise was quite frightened and mixed up as he advanced on her again. "That's all you would think about—" Sam lifted his hand again, and she backed away, petrified with surprise and fear. Sam felt the explosive growth of confidence and virility. He was a man. He was almost inclined to grab her by the hair, drag her upstairs and work his will on her, but some remnant of caution warned him not to push his luck and fail in what would have to be a dramatic and successful operation.

"Don't say anything," he gritted. "Go upstairs and get to bed or I'll . . . I'll spank you," he ended lamely.

"If you so much as—" Louise tailed into silence as he flexed his long arms and leaned toward her. She burst into tears and scrambled up the steep staircase, tripping and destroying her dignity and hating everything in the world. There would never on earth be a way of telling anybody what had happened, the recital of the events itself would be more squalid than actual guilt because she had no words for it. Sam, staring stolidly at her as she ascended, had a final inspiration.

"I'll talk to you about this tomorrow night," he said. "Shurrup!"

Life had actually come to its end. She wanted to throw herself on her bed, but the bunk was too narrow for that. She leaned on it, weeping with anger and shock, and since it was dark, she started to unfasten her dress at the side. As she did so, one of her fingernails scratched her skin at the waist, and she cringed, and then dug the fingernail in quite hard again. She couldn't believe that she was thinking what she thought she was thinking. She tore the dress off over her head and stood in the dark, panting, and wondered what had become of her.

EIGHTEEN

TOM WISHART was back on duty, whether he liked it or not, and after his debut as a concert artist, he quite liked it. In fact, some of his passionate belief in the policeman as public servant and confessor had dropped from him, and he was enjoying the savagery of authority as he pushed people back brutally from the immediate area of the fireworks display. For the first time in his life, he found people obeying his brusque commands, even though he wasn't in uniform. They knew that he meant it. They backed away and left a safe circle inside which the two expert Englishmen could begin their operations, and contented themselves with shouting, "Fire! Fire! Fire!" in a threatening monotone. Then they fell silent, there was a mass holding of breath, and then a civic exhalation as a rocket fizzed, hovered and shot splendidly into the moonless sky. It seemed to rise for half a mile before it burst into three separate bangs and three separate clouds of red and white and blue stars. Instantly, three more rockets followed it, fanning out and heading for the far shore. The murmur of approval from five hundred people was like a roar, bang bang bang, roar.

"Can I have another sausage?" Timmy shrieked. Mary held out a stick to him, and he picked a sausage off the end of it and screamed with pain. Sally yelled at him to shut up.

"It looks better from the edge of the water," Nat said. He had appeared from nowhere, and Mary gave him a cold look and said, "Thanks very much."

"I've been looking all over for you," he said blandly, his face lit up by a gigantic catherine wheel and so innocent that she wanted to slap it. As another rocket went off, there was a sputter out at sea and the rocket's path was crossed by a rocket from nowhere.

"He's sinking," Nat said amiably. "That's a distress signal." The second rocket was from one of the cabin cruisers, which had moved and insolently anchored near the Lady Joyce to enjoy the fun. From another of them, a Very pistol banged and a red flare shot almost horizontally toward the shore. Five hundred people ducked in automatic terror.

"I'll take your name!" Tom Wishart shrieked at the half-visible cabin cruiser. A set piece in the official fireworks display had started to flare and crackle and bang, and his voice was lost. Somebody on board the Lady Joyce was calling angrily through a loud-hailer. Another Very light hurtled recklessly towards the village, with a higher trajectory this time, and the crowd cheered it.

"We'll have the place overrun with lifeboats in a minute," Nat said happily, and put his arm round Mary's waist. "I can feel your hot flesh through that sweater, it's disgraceful." She caught one of his fingers and scratched it with clinical cruelty.

The professional fireworks men, nettled and challenged by the outbreak of unofficial competition, switched their program and brought in a massive rocket that left the beach with a dense cloud of cordite smoke and soared steeply inland. The population wheeled to watch it as it followed the line of the string road and made for the dip in the skyline. It was already falling out of sight when it loosed its cargo of stars and explosions and screaming devils, and they echoed back and forth against the hills. The last bang came when it had entirely disappeared, a tremendous distant roar that reverberated for over a minute. The populace kept staring at the hills, and then yelled in approval.

"By Joves, it's started another landslide," Hughie Mackay said in awe, appearing from the direction of the beach. "Either that or there's another of these bliddy Japanese submarines at us."

"It *sounded* like an explosion," Mary said. "A real explosion, I mean."

"It's the eccentric harmonic effects you get near the North Pole," Nat remarked chattily. "The aurora borealis is doing it all the time."

"Oh my God," she muttered, and he patted her soothingly. The crowd had lapsed into hysterical laughter here and there, and noisy speculation. Looking stern and dutiful, Tom Wishart was picking up his bike from the side of the hall and throwing himself in the saddle for the climb up the string road. Sally broke away from the fireworks and started to run in his wake, and Timmy followed her, shouting resentfully, and in a wave of hysteria, the Youth Hostel crowd leapt up from the heath and pounded in pursuit.

The fireworks experts set off a huge frame of bangers and catherine wheels spelling out the name Winston, but the cheer was thin and scattered as half of the audience had melted away. The angry voice on the loud-hailer was booming again from the Lady Joyce, but the words were indistinguishable. Even the older generation was deciding that it couldn't miss the excitement of the torpedo over the hill, or the land mine, or the old wartime shell, or the underground ammunition dump, all of which people were suddenly reminding one another had been a menace since 1945 when the Army should have been cleaning the place up and not leaving their rubbish about to destroy the entire Highlands without a four-minute warning.

Rather reluctantly, Nat let Mary persuade him that they too should follow the crowd.

"Nat wants to see wovely wockets," he complained.

"I'll strangle you," she muttered. "You've done it this time. What have you done? I might have known there was something on when you didn't even get drunk. What in God's name did you do?"

"It's the heat, my God, and the country, and the flies," he said airily, "Gad, I knew I shouldn't have exposed my womenfolk to this accursed climate, they go mad, I tell you, mad."

She couldn't bring herself to speak to him, she was trembling with anger and fear. She hurried and left him behind, and he loped along behind her humming under his breath. She ran, but he kept up with her easily. As they went over the crest, she saw scores of people standing along the edge and staring down into the gulley. Down below, the younger people were scrambling about on the rocks, some with flaring torches. The fat young man from the Youth Hostel appeared just below the road, panting as he heaved himself upward and brandishing a lump of rusty metal.

"It's a shell," he shouted. "I've found a piece of shell!"

Nat reached out a hand to help the boy up, and examined the find with bland interest.

"The boy's right," he said. "By Gad, I'll instruct my lawyer to write a stiff note to the War Office as soon as he gets out of jail."

"Is it a shell?" Mary was confused.

"Och, it's a bit of a shell and that's the truth," Hughie Mackay said happily. "There's a fine thing for you, an armed invasion by the English Government on an innocent village, it's the United Nations we should send for, and the Declaration of Human Rights."

"Gad, that could have been a nasty show," Nat said in his Colonial Governor character. "Demn good thing the natives were in the paddy fields at the time."

"Man, you wouldn't believe a wee thing like a shell could fill the Devil's Drap as neat as a whistle," Hughie said. "You would nearly think it was a new road down there if you covered it with a bag or two of secondhand tar and put up traffic lights."

Tom Wishart had hauled himself up on to the road, clutching another piece of metal, and he was sternly ordering the fat Youth Hosteler to lay his trophy down at once, carefully.

"This will have to be reported to Oban," he said solemnly.

"Aye, you're right, man," Hughie agreed. "They'll send a Royal Commission down and we'll have the full explanation in three or four years, I wouldn't be surprised."

"It's a shell all right," Tom said, quite compensated by the gravity of the situation for his disastrous concert appearance. "The rocket explosion could have set it off."

"Just so, sympathetic sound waves," Hughie agreed, "Man, you've hit it there, you've got the scientific deduction off pat, Tom, I would promote a man like that straight off if I was the Home Office."

"I'll have to cordon the area off."

"You'll be needing a big ball of string for that, I'm thinking," said Hughie, "but you're the expert in public administration, but myself, I think a wee word to the villagers not to go about banging things with hammers would do the trick fine. Shells is tricky things if you bang them with hammers."

"Come up out of there!" Tom called to the people below,

hardly hoping that anybody would obey but enjoying the authoritative sound of his voice. "Don't touch anything!"

Mary was holding Nat's arm and praying that he wouldn't say anything. He didn't. He stared cheerfully down toward the sea, where a great fall of broken rock had crashed into the Drap and filled the place where the old bridge had been blown up.

"You could nearly drive a truck across that," Tom Wishart said solemnly.

"Ach, I wouldn't chance a thing like that, man," Hughie said, "the place is likely bristling all over with live mortar bombs and grenades, would you not think so with your experience?"

"I doubt it," Tom was solemn and meditative and important. "If anything was live down there it would have exploded by now."

Farther along the road, Dee's head appeared from below as she was hoisted up on Archie McBain's shoulders, and he vaulted showily up after her.

"I can't stand a show-off," she was saying. "There's too much of it about, do you know that?"

"I never did a thing," Archie complained.

"That's the worst stage, when you don't even notice you're showing off," she said firmly. She walked up toward the crest, and Archie humbly strode beside her with his hands pushed into his pockets. Tom Wishart walked along the road calling peremptory orders with his chest stuck out, and Hughie strolled in his wake, telling him how scientifically he was handling the crisis. Mary caught sight of Sally and Timmy, and ordered them back to the cottage with unusual sharpness. Sally ran and Timmy panted along behind.

She didn't look at Nat, and didn't move to take his arm as they walked back.

"These tropical nights are very tropical," he said.

"I don't want to speak to you again as long as I live," she said. "I hate this place."

"It gets people like that when the home leave is overdue," he said easily. "I'll dig you a swimming pool to take your mind off it."

"Dig? With dynamite?"

"Gad no, the rippling muscles and the swing of the mattock," he said. "Dammit, we're too soft nowadays, a man needs to get to grips with reality."

"Shut up."

"Curious incident, that, this was a Restricted Area during the war, Hughie Mackay says, commandos and sabotage exercises and everything — the beach used to be plastered with old bombs. And dynamite, of course, they went in a lot for dynamite. Nobody'll ever know who left it lying about, thank Christ."

"I want to go home," she said. "I'm sick of Ochie."

He had her by the arm and was forcing her gently but insistently on to the wrong fork and down the other narrow road to the beach.

"There *is* one other method of sickening the landlord," he said, and she pulled her arm away impatiently.

"I can't stand it!" She looked round quickly to make sure nobody was near to hear. "Landlords, and Louise and her awful brat, and you acting like a delinquent — you don't need to sicken the landlord, you've sickened me."

"I have done my duty by queen and country," he piped. "Honest, Mary, you can stop worrying, I've called off the war, it was midsummer madness, I tell you, madness. How would you like to be a lady?"

"Nat, just shut up, I've had enough." She hated him for his cunning and his invulnerability as he talked on musingly. Her system, she thought, had been subjected to too many shocks. Weeks of Louise, and the heat, and frustration, and irritations, and terrors, had taken away her taste for anything in life.

"Nice poetic note, really," Nat was saying, "I wish I had thought of it myself as a fiendish masterstroke. Arnold will spew, he'll openly spew. Sir Nathaniel Boag, I would have to buy a coat of arms, of course, and a horse or two, consonant with my elevated status."

"Oh, stop gibbering, Nat," she said wearily, "I'm not amused."

"It would be a betrayal of my humble origins and my stern egalitarian principles, mind you, and that would be absolutely dandy for a start, I've always fancied doing a picture of myself as Judas. Sir Judas? By God, that wax-faced Yankee Muzak machine would howl. Lady Boag. That should get you quick service at the secondhand clothes shops."

"Don't go on and on, Nat, I'm tired of you. What if you had killed somebody?"

"Ach, I'm away on to the new exciting chapter in the life of Fearless Nat, the scourge of the Highlands. Well, do you or don't you fancy being a lady?"

"Eh?"

Nat sniggered.

"Some cretinous hoor's got the names mixed up in the Carlton Club — I think they meant old Charlie Gloag the tree-painter, you know old Charlie, the camera eye of 1912. Ach, no, it would be pandering to the accursed Establishment. I'll tell them to stuff it."

"What about Charlie Gloag?" It was no use, he had trapped her again into listening.

"It isn't official, of course," he said in his Head-of-the-Secret-Service character. "Eat this message as soon as you've memorized it. That's how they do it, did you know that? In fact, what the silly cows do is buy you a brandy and then ask how you fancy it, and if you say Nothing under a peerage, they make you pay for the brandy and deny they ever saw you. It's so that nobody can get the offer and then turn it down publicly."

"The offer of what? You're not — " in spite of her disgust and weariness, a hysterical giggle burst up from somewhere, " — they're not offering you a title!"

"Ssh!" He grabbed her arm and looked round furtively in the darkness. "Follow me." He half-dragged her up a steep bank and on to a grassy plateau above the road. They could hear voices on the road behind them. Nat lay elegantly face down on the grass and peered over the edge.

Tony Hammer and Winston Harper were walking down toward the shore.

"Rather a novel hazard," Winston was saying, in an off-hand way that sickened Tony. "I was surprised by an outraged husband. I tossed off a few words of airy badinage and left him reaching for his axe, actually."

"I don't believe you."

Their voices began to recede down the road.

"The crucial point, I find," Winston was going on happily, "is to direct the whole operation psychologically. Some bits like the brutal approach, some like the rather shy youth style — aim at the mother instinct and so on. Who gave you the black eye?"

Tony cursed himself for not having thought of an outraged husband before Winston did.

"That," he said, "is a rather lengthy tale."

"These Scotch girls pack a decent old wallop, don't they?" Winston laughed callously. "I shouldn't feel too badly about it," he added, with a generosity that infuriated Tony. "I was gilding the lily a bit when I told you about the Boag women. They both worked the old judo on me too, I should have warned you."

"I would like to meet the wench who could work the judo on me," Tony said sullenly, but Winston merely laughed gaily and patted him on the arm.

Nat and Mary had heard little of this exchange, but Nat let the boys vanish completely before he rolled over on his back.

"I reckon I've got the right hawk-like features for a Sir," he said. "I would have to behave with nauseous decorum all the time, naturally, and side with the laird against these dispossessed pigs in the village. A riding crop, I fancy, to wallop my leg with while I was striding through the canaille. Don't be mad, Mary, there wasn't any risk, honest."

"Oh, Nat," she said, "you are a rotten bastard." She knelt beside him and scowled at him. "You're no damned use to me, did you know that? No good."

"I'm immature," he said, with spurious melancholy. "But Egad, a man has to do something with his vital forces when your bedroom is full of frozen-tailed hoors."

"You could have forced your way in," she said, still resentful. "A woman isn't supposed to have to pursue people."

"I like this place," he said, ignoring her. "I found it one night when I was out robbing a train. It's the biggest nuptial couch in Argyllshire."

"Stop talking like that," she said. "I still detest you, you've put ten years on me, and every time you start off your filthy talk we end up doing nothing. Was that what the letter was about? If you joke about it I'll punch you, Nat, I swear it. You're not going to be a sir, I couldn't stand it."

"You do flit from tree to tree," he complained, and put his fingers round her wrist. "It's a hundred percent guaranteed all-wool — us prospective knights aren't supposed to blab it even to the wives of our bosoms, but the hell with it, it's too good to keep. They don't do anything official unless they're sure you're on. The letter was one of these cryptic notes from old Masterton, all in code, in Braille so that they can back out if they come to their senses."

"Tell them to back out," she said. "Lady Boag! It sounds like an insect."

"Naw, come on, honest, Mary, don't take my toy train away before I get a look at it. What do you say we kid ourselves on for a week that we're taking it, and *then* I'll tell them to take a flying leap."

"What's the sense in that?"

"Stop being mean," he whined. "It's my only chance to enjoy the secret dream of my childhood."

"Stop talking nonsense, you don't want it either."

"I didn't refer to my own ennoblement," he said superciliously, "I referred to my long-standing lust to knock it off with a titled lady." She could feel his hand trembling where it held her wrist, and she knew he wasn't being funny; or at least, that if he was being funny, he was being desperately earnest too.

"In the long grass?" Her voice broke on the last word. "We're insane." He pulled her across him and over on to the grass, very slowly.

"I'm sick of Ochie too," he muttered. "Sick sick sick. But I'm getting better. Slow?"

"Yes, slow, slow. You should have brought me here before."

He was touching her with an old familiarity that was as new as the first time. "Bunk beds," he muttered beneath his breath. "They can be glued together, did you know that?"

"Tell me tomorrow." She had no energy to spare for talk. "You're a good kid, a good kid. Everywhere, Lady Boag."

"Sir."

"Lady."

"Sir."

It was almost worthwhile . . . no, she corrected herself, it was completely worthwhile, to have waited and fretted. He raised himself on his hands and looked at her and winked. She laughed out loud, and stopped suddenly. It would be exactly like Sally and Timmy to come back looking for them.

"It's better than booze," Nat remarked. "It seems damned absurd that untitled people should get it."

"I wouldn't mind a swimming pool," Mary said. "A fish pond, anyway. If you have any strength to dig."

"Gad, woman, I'm still fit for a day's work."

"You're going to save your strength during the day for the next month, Nat Boag. Sirs don't labor in the fields. Anyway, it's too hot for *day* work."

"Ochie's not bad, actually, kid." He rolled over on his back. "This hot weather's good for the back."

"It's been driving me loony."

"What we want," he said suddenly, "is more of the gemutlichkeit routine, picnics and swimming and long walks with the ickle chillun — that's what holidays are for, Daddy teaching junior to play cricket and catching crabs."

"Sure."

"Are you taking me seriously, woman? Kid ol the kids, that's what we want. We can bring a tent up here and go into recluse."

"We'll go for picnics and you'll teach junior to play cricket, you slavering ape, now that you've sorted out *my* problems."

"Temporarily."

"I *might* admit you to my presence again, now and then, if you're damned respectful and plead and whine." She punched him lightly in the solar plexus. "The rest of the time, we'll have a nice family holiday, all sweet and icky and respectable. You can have too much of the torrid passion, you know."

"You'll take what you get, girl, and for a start, you can spend tonight in my sleeping bag, and boo and fiddle-sticks to middle-class morality. Well, isn't that a ——'s ——! It's flaming raining!"

He leaped to his feet as a big drop splatted on to his forehead, and pulled her up. They scrambled down the bank on the road, and the rain came down in a dense warm sheet that soaked them completely inside a minute. They ran hand in hand, Mary laughing and Nat swearing. It was a nice place for a family holiday, it really was. They might hire a boat, she thought, and picnic on one of the islands; and the next day she would mark out the place for the fish pond and do something positive about cleaning up the old varnish in the kitchen; or maybe paint the outside woodwork white. Or pale blue? And there were three trees that would have to go, and some old roots to be dug up.

It was frightening how time slipped past in Ochie and nothing got done. Everybody would have to be energetic and organized and make the most of the place before the summer ended.

Nat gave up swearing and resigned himself to being soaked, licking the rain as it dripped from his nose.

"You know what we need, kid?" he said. "We need a holiday."

"I've been thinking the same thing myself," she said. "Somewhere at the coast where you can relax."

"Ah, you would ruin a man with your evil wiles and your spine and that damned scratchy fingernail. The flaming rain's getting worse, a pox on it." He put his arm round her waist, an awkward pose for running, and they ran like whippets.